WHEN EVERYONE'S A VIRT
WHO CAN FREE THE HUMAN SOUL?

THE CLOUD

A SPECULATIVE FICTION NOVEL

ROBERT RIVENBARK

STORY MERCHANT BOOKS
LOS ANGELES
2022

ISBN: 978-1-970157-34-5

Story Merchant Books
400 S. Burnside Avenue #11B
Los Angeles, CA 90036

www.storymerchantbooks.com

Interior format & cover design by IndieDesignz.com

*HISTORY IS A NIGHTMARE FROM WHICH
I AM TRYING TO AWAKE.*
—JAMES JOYCE, *ULYSSES*

*GO, GO, GO, SAID THE BIRD:
HUMANKIND
CANNOT BEAR VERY MUCH REALITY.*

—T.S. ELIOT, *FOUR QUARTETS*

ACKNOWLEDGEMENTS

I could not have written this book without the encouragement, guidance, and wisdom of those who believed in me and this project. I dedicate this book to my mother Janie Jenkins Johnson, who gave me life and unconditional love. I thank Elizabeth Lyon for her invaluable guidance in editing the initial draft. I am deeply indebted to Dr. Kenneth Atchity for his brilliant creative direction and editing as I hammered out subsequent drafts. Special thanks also to Kathleen Freels Rivenbark for encouraging me to pursue this project and for her tireless proofreading and suggestions throughout, and to Kate Danaher for proofing the novel and offering many helpful suggestions. I also thank Anthony Moschetto for his expert copy editing on the final draft. Finally, I wish to honor the memory of my father-in-law Paul Kwilecki, Sr., one of America's great documentary photographers, who told me decades ago, "If you would but persist in your folly, eventually Nature will yield up her secrets to you." She has.

Quotations from the poetry of T.S. Eliot are from *T.S. Eliot: Collected Poems 1909-1962*. New York: Harcourt, Brace & Company, 1991. Print.

1

As the 7:00 a.m. bullet rounded a curve in the elevated track, Blaise glimpsed the Santa Monica coastline, where a two hundred meter dyke barely held back the Pacific. Everything he'd worked for was here. He was the best virtual reality programmer at Mythoplex. He had a brilliant future ahead of him. But despite these reassurances, the urge to see his city drowned lingered at the edge of his mind like the laughter of a lunatic god.

The bullet jetted over a sleek, hatchet-shaped bridge. He glimpsed the abandoned I-405 freeway, long given up to tumbleweed, then a blur of blonde foothills where the towering Mythoplex logo, which had long since replaced the Hollywood sign, glittered against a pristine sky. Then came Mulholland Drive's ridges and North Hollywood's terraced canyons, crammed with live/work/play pods offering upscale condos at staggering prices. He'd never want one of those bloated monuments to vanity. Even if Cherry and his daughter Mei had survived, Blaise aspired to the simple life of a workaholic VR storyteller. Surely his grief over their deaths would dissipate with time.

His mind drifted back to the possibility of a flood. Although the Cloud Monitor never mentioned it, he knew from covert server searches that the Pacific sea wall, which stretched from Tijuana to Vancouver, had failed at its extremities. The Baja peninsula, much of Mexico and southern Arizona, British Columbia, and Alaska had long since vanished beneath the insistence of engulfing tides that made the antediluvian age a distant rumor. But he wasn't supposed to remember that. So he raised the volume of his neurofeed to distract himself.

Neurofeed played relentlessly in his head like a schizophrenic monologue. You could try to ignore it; you could lower the volume or even switch it off for short periods. But it was life's inescapable soundtrack and sightscape, and the Cloud Monitor considered any lapse of attention outside working hours unpatriotic and punishable by death. From a bank of Hong Kong AI servers, a female voice with the reassuring cadences of the North Am Midwest delivered propaganda and holographic imagery to all Class II through IV professionals 24/7. "Cloud life is full life, Cloud life is full light," was her signature sign-on for exuberant reports about the ever-rising standard of living, the latest victories against the Caliphate, and sultry intros to titillating VR series. Blaise ground his teeth at the Monitor's saccharine cadences. He had written her monologues before his promotion to Class II games planner, and he knew she was bleating pure fiction. But he had to listen and pretend to believe just the same.

The Monitor couldn't read thoughts, per se, but its AI servers had encoded a vast library of traitorous brainwave patterns. Any departure from a quietly optimistic state of mind could bring instant termination. Like everyone else, Blaise had learned how to control his emotions, thoughts, and physiology to keep his EEGs within acceptable ranges as the Monitor crowed about how the Cloud oligarchy had created a corporate utopia, free from the corrupt national governments that had plagued the past. The relentless repetition worked so well it placed people in cities as diverse as Shanghai, Sydney, and San Francisco on an identical footing of mental compliance.

Sitting across from Blaise, a couple of commuters in maroon jackets chatted. The man wore a silver bracelet that projected holographic images at eye level. It was obvious from his furtive glances and over-confident tone that he was trying to impress the woman.

"Nothing can touch *Viral Empire*," he declared.

"No way. *Glider Kill* rocked my world."

"Not even in the same class. *Viral Empire*'s sex-slaughter index is off the charts." He spoke into his silver bracelet. "Episode seven, jungle scene."

A naked man and woman in coitus appeared and floated before the couple at eye level. The young woman shrugged, unimpressed.

"I'm into girl-on-girl vids."

The man looked distressed, then grinned.

"Here's something you've never seen." He spoke into the bracelet again. "Mantis release 4.0, test footage."

That attracted Blaise's attention. He scrutinized the couple as they watched another holographic display and glimpsed a pair of round, red, faceted eyes on stalks. He focused instead on the look of abject terror spreading over the woman's face.

"Where'd you get that?" she gasped.

The man apparently didn't realize what he was risking. "We're re-coding it," he answered with pride. "Enhancements."

"It's horrible! What if the Cloud Monitor caught you? Or SWAT?"

How'd this idiot get access to—that? Blaise wondered, his heart pounding with fear for this couple, who could be terminated for sharing forbidden images. Anyone riding the bullet might report them.

The young man blanched as he noticed Blaise's burning glance. He spoke hastily into his bracelet. "End display."

The images vanished. Blaise felt some relief, followed by a yearning to escape before he got ensnared in the couple's predicament. He repeated his mantra internally to calm himself.

At Wilshire Station, Blaise's car disgorged a horde of lean, fit Class II and III VR men and women wearing varying grades of silk or spandex cutaway jackets, shrink slacks, shrink-skirts, and diaphanous blouses with colorful Chinese patterns. Everyone's foreheads were stamped with K-Spot neurofeed implants over their third eyes, and each of their faces was set with square-jawed determination.

A woman in the crowd shrilled with laughter at a colleague's remark. That brought back the shriek of a lasered female commando under Blaise's command that he had been forced to leave behind in a firefight eight years ago.

Don't leave me out here, lieutenant!

He tried to outrun that scream by shouldering through the crowd, reassuring himself that eventually, he could somehow forget his hallucinatory stint as a Cloud army lieutenant fighting the Caliphate in Nigeria, where blood lust had pulsed in his temples and balls on mosquito-infested nights before firefights; and the stench of lasered flesh and screams of villagers his platoon slaughtered had magnified his urge to kill. He ached to forget that period of his life, but the images were cauterized in his memory like a frozen bolt of lightning.

He passed under the red and yellow Chinese arch into the blazing heat of a July morning. Average temperatures had risen appallingly over the past decade. The commuters yearned to escape the merciless glare, which would superheat L.A. by noon. They surged into a long, air-conditioned plexiglass tunnel that climbed up a low incline. Ahead lay pseudo-green space running up to the Vessel, a knock-off of an identical structure that once stood in Hudson Yards, destroyed in the Caliphate dirty bomb obliteration of New York City: a six hundred ton beehive-shaped tower with over a hundred and fifty flights of stairs and twenty-four hundred steps, built to encourage controlled interactions between citizens, with intricate bronze-colored stairs climbing and descending to nowhere and no purpose. Behind the Vessel loomed Mythoplex tower, a glittering needle in a spiny landscape of polycarbonate, glass, and steel. Over its entrance doors, the name and logo appeared:

MYTHOPLEX
PERFECTING THE METAVERSE

Anxious to begin his day in the only place where he could push the world's confusion and chaos from his mind, Blaise hastened into the cavernous lobby. There a holographic mural loomed, showing against the backdrop of Shanghai's Yuyuan Gardens the historic handshake between Chairman Mao Zedong II and U.S. President Brent Cadwallader III, the last independent politicos to join the Cloud board in Hong Kong. Beneath the mural a legend read:

OUR CLOUD FOUNDING FATHERS

It's a man's world again, echoed a sad voice from his childhood: his mother's. She'd been a published novelist before VR entertainment replaced books. After Blaise's father had abandoned them, her career had collapsed. Her only relief were childcare payments, cheap wine, and memories of a misty golden time that had been totally eclipsed after the Caliphate had dirty bombed Western capitals and the Cloud corporate patriarchy seized power.

"The Cloud calls it progress, but it's devolution," she had cried bitterly when she was drunk, and he had pretended to grasp her meaning to please her. She was a slender brunette with limpid eyes and beautiful pale skin. He had loved her scent of cinnamon and cardamom, the way she had caressed his hair and spoken to him in a maternal voice saddened by sorrows inexplicable to his eight-year-old mind.

Saddened by his memory, Blaise hustled with other VR professionals toward a translucent elevator car. He noticed, in a seating enclave with maroon couches, a girl around eight or nine, who cried softly, thumb stuck in her mouth. The sight of her pierced Blaise's heart, as always happened when he saw a girl around his dead daughter Mei's age.

He approached, knelt, and took the girl's hand.

"Hey, hey. Easy now. Where's your mommy? She work here?"

The girl nodded and sniffled. Blaise shook out a pocket handkerchief, dried her tears, and wiped the snot from her nose.

"Where'd she get off to?"

The girl pointed to an alcove at the lobby's edge.

"The ladies room? Why'd she leave you out here?"

The girl shrugged and sobbed loudly.

"OK, OK. Shh. Shh. We'll find her."

He walked hand in hand with the child to a female receptionist in a pale linen jacket, blouse, and skirt, who studied a holographic screen behind a counter below the enormous patriotic mural.

"Didn't you see her?" Blaise demanded.

The receptionist barely glanced at the child. "I have no authority to intervene."

Blaise rapped the counter hard enough to startle the receptionist. He pointed to his cutaway blazer lapel, studded with a gold sun disk containing a blue K-Spot.

The receptionist turned pale. "Sorry, sir," she replied in a quaking voice.

"Your name?"

"Anne Boleyn IX, sir. Really, I'm so sorry."

"Not half as sorry as you'll be if you don't take her to the ladies room and find her mom."

The receptionist hustled around the desk to the girl, who eyed her with suspicion and refused to let go of Blaise's hand. The receptionist knelt and gently dislodged her, whispering shaky reassurances as the girl eyed Blaise with hope and fear in her eyes.

Satisfied when the receptionist led the girl away, Blaise pressed into one of the crowded lifts, where an inner floodgate burst. Memories of happy moments with his dead wife Cherry and Mei flooded his mind. His heart churned with longing for those early days, when he had hoped with all the yearning his heart could muster that the sanity and security of a wife and family would make him forget his violent past. But the wartime memories were coiled in his gut like a colony of tapeworms. The sweating nightmares had returned night after night; the flashbacks had haunted his days like furies tormenting him for unforgivable acts. Cherry had struggled courageously to help him for as long as her hope and love had endured. But his PTSD was like a storm tide repeatedly crashing against a coastal column of rock. Eventually, his long silences, his refusal to discuss the war, and his sudden violent tirades over trifles had worn away her capacity to care. Mei, for her part, had come to look upon her father with fear and hatred. Blaise responded by burying himself in his work. Awards and recognition had followed, and coding new VR series became his oxygen in an arid, airless world drained of all meaning.

Blaise tried to imagine meeting another woman like Cherry—or his mother, for that matter. Not likely. The Class II women he worked with were as hard, relentless, and ruthless as the Pacific that surged against the L.A. sea wall.

In the lift he tried not to inhale his colleagues' personal pheromone scents or notice how many had paid for prosthetic surgery to make themselves look like VR stars. He was particularly careful to avoid locking eyes with female colleagues. Mythoplex management forbade flirtations or romantic relationships between employees; everyone was expected to have VR lovers through their entertainment subscriptions.

At floor 103, Blaise hastened past a security checkpoint with SWAT cops in black uniforms. In his lofty office, he slid the door closed so he could code beyond the reach of jealous eyes and acidic gossip. He reduced his neurofeed to the soft murmur permitted during working hours. His wall of holographic awards testified to his prestige as the creator of *Viral Empire*, the most popular VR series three years running. On one wall, the recursion formula expressing the fractal process identified by his namesake, the first Blaise Pascal, pulsed with electrical surges. Blaise loved fractals, those infinitely complex patterns repeating over and over in a feedback loop driven by recursion. For him, the equation didn't express chaos theory, as mathematicians claimed; it symbolized the worlds within worlds springing from his imagination.

He booted up his holographic deck and voice-coded part of a new module for *Gilgamesh V*, his new series set in ancient Babylon. This thundering epic featured hordes of gods, goddesses, kings, queens, soldiers, blood-drenched battles, and a bastard pretender who, with his high priestess, angled for a tottering city-state's throne. It was the perfect subject matter to support the historical inevitability of patriarchal rule.

He had dictated several hundred lines of code when Mitsuko breezed into his office—a familiar and unwelcome presence signified by an effluvium of jasmine-scented disapproval. A Class I executive games supervisor, she wore a blue silk cutaway jacket and blouse, her long, flawless legs wrapped in a navy-blue kimono skirt accented by black high heels. Regal and erect, she never tired of reminding colleagues that despite her father's lackluster status as a Beijing business magnate, her mother was a direct descendant of the twenty-second Japanese emperor.

Technically, Blaise reported to Mitsuko; and he despised her because she had sent the Mantis to murder two of her predecessors—both friends of his and fellow veterans—and he was certain she planned to terminate him at the first opportunity. But Director Minsheng Lu had entrusted Blaise with many special projects, and had given him his own team of assistant programmers. For now at least, Blaise was free to vent his spleen on her for her constant attempts to undermine him.

"The first quadrant?"

Blaise refused to glance away from his wall-sized holographic screen, which featured an ancient Babylonian throne room with frescos depicting rows of golden lions, running below tessellated slabs of black obsidian, bordered by blue and gold arabesques encircling stylized stands of date palms. Male courtiers in sumptuous robes, spear-bearing guards, and noble ladies with black-braided hair and colorful gowns watched a Babylonian king with a beard and gold conical crown orate from his throne. A tall, muscular, naked warrior with flowing black locks, Gilgamesh V, crowned by a lion's head and pelt, rushed in with a band of warriors. Gilgamesh hacked his way through the courtiers, mounted the dais, and ran the king through with his sword.

"I asked you a question."

Mitsuko would go on breaking his concentration until he responded. He spun around toward her in his floating cockpit chair. "There's no need to repeat yourself. I ignored you precisely the first time."

"Answer me. Without sarcasm."

"I'm going to keep making you look brilliant. I'll have the first quadrant laid in by next Friday."

"Vidracom wants it to air in ninety days."

"Oh, darling, go buy yourself a personality, won't you?"

"How dare you call me. . ."

"Sorry. Thought you'd prefer that to fuck you, bitch. As for *Gilgamesh V*, they'll have it in sixty days with a little luck."

"I'm not interested in luck. Only results. Is that clear?"

"Last time I checked, I haven't missed a deadline in seven years."

"Rising so recently from the barbaric North Am military class, you lack perspective. That makes you over-confident."

"Whereas you, Mitsuko, are descended on your mother's side from Japanese Emperor Seinei, who was born wise, with white hair. I understand he had only adopted sons, which makes your claim to be his descendant a bit bogus, no?"

"How dare you!"

"Sorry for the mean, awful, accurate things I say."

Mitsuko approached Blaise until she was so close her belly nearly touched him. He pushed away in his cockpit chair to avoid the heat and scent of her.

"A Class III junior games planner will help you meet that deadline."

Rage surged up in Blaise's face and lips like lava that threatened to erupt with lethal force. He repeated his mantra internally to keep himself from attacking her physically, which would mean his immediate termination.

"Minsheng gave me full authority to finish this series without interference," he replied, measuring his words carefully.

Mitsuko's lips curled into a grimace. She was probably monitoring his EEG and knew she had gotten to him.

"Your character arcs are slipping."

"This from a woman who hasn't coded even a porn vid in four years."

"Your protagonist's crises are not physical but emotional, and may The Cloud preserve us, psychological. Subscribers want action heroes and heroines, not advanced neurotics."

Her critique infuriated Blaise, but he tempered his rebuke. "We both know you're wrong. So why don't you go away?"

A dark flame of rage showed in the folds of her epicanthic eyes. She clenched her dainty fists, but managed to restrain her explosion.

"When your incompetence finally shows, remember I gave you this chance to hide it. Progress report at week's end."

"Don't hold your breath."

"You'd better meet that deadline. Or your honeymoon with the director will come to a fatal end."

"Do underestimate me, Mitsuko. That should be entertaining."

She issued a grunt and stormed out. He heard the clacking of her high heels diminish down the corridor like a bad memory as his door slid shut. He enjoyed insulting her, but every victory was short-lived. He kept his neurofeed at low volume rather than silence it because she might upgrade the Cloud Monitor's EEG surveillance on him from random to focused and perpetual. Dread prickled his spine like tiny electric shocks. Perhaps soon, very soon, the Mantis would materialize to fry his brain, despite his relationship with the director.

But wasn't he safe from the Mantis, after all? His coding impressed Class I executives, who relished the profits from VR subscribers addicted to his cunning plot nuances and character subtleties. He was a Shakespeare among games planners; his groundlings wanted blood and lust, and he gave them plenty. Still, it wasn't enough to guarantee his safety. Not with Mitsuko hovering.

Blaise distracted himself from such thoughts by coding intently all morning, relishing his escape into a world built from his blackest obsessions, sublimating his angst in his characters. Twice, as he coded dialog and played it back, a high-pitched woman's voice in the series reminded him of Aisha, the wounded female commando's plea from eight years back, so he pushed himself harder to finish the next block of coding.

His new series would cost Class I, II, and III subscribers a hefty percentage of their annual salaries, but everyone would eagerly pay it. *Gilgamesh V* was sure to have mass appeal thanks to Blaise's programming breakthrough: algorithms that radically intensified the experience of living inside a VR protagonist's body, to the point where pain was felt as sharply as pleasure. The fantasy deeply affected the body's physiology, so Blaise had to code special safeguards against actual organ failure.

Blaise had set his epic in the sixth century B.C., when the city of Babylon, with its hanging gardens, ziggurats, and friezes of winged lions and bearded kings, was fading under the sway of the Persian Achaemenid Empire. King Marduk-apla-iddina II had seized the Babylonian throne, but had ruled only nine months, giving Blaise's Gilgamesh V time to plot his own bloody coup with the high priestess at the annual Akitu Temple New Year festival. Blaise had spent days coding the festival's dazzling procession of gods and goddesses, their statues in sumptuous robes atop bejeweled chariots that processed through the Ishtar Gate, a forty-eight-meter passage inlaid with carvings of open-mouthed lions, bulls, and dragons. On their way to the royal palace, the soon-to-be-assassinated king, with his courtiers and priestesses of Ishtar, had navigated broad avenues and gardens shaded by tamarisk trees and date palms. The city was scented with aromatic plants and dominated for miles by the ziggurat of Etemenanki, dedicated to Marduk, which reached for the sky in eight recessed terraces. Street mobs, drunk on mead and wine in honor of Ishtar, gorged on ample fare in the street markets, while the men crowded the goddess's temples to visit Ishtar's holy prostitutes, who waited, almond-scented, with open legs for any who came to honor her.

At noon Blaise's door slid open. In walked Harper, a Class III assistant games planner in a yellow linen jacket. Harper was a lanky black Alabama girl who hadn't quite lost her drawl despite living in L.A. for years, though she had picked up the sunshine smile and depressed angst of the City of Angels. Harper had deluded herself into thinking that Blaise, a fellow Southerner, would advance her career. Like every other leech in the games planning department, Harper's only chance for advancement lay in sucking up to a master mythologizer like Blaise. But Blaise found her a painful reminder of a dim past and stagnant culture he longed to forget. Nothing existed for him now but L.A. and the virtual universes he coded.

"Hiya, Blaise. Circular sushi today in the commissary. Ya hungry?"

"I'm kind of in the zone with this."

"Yeah, know," Harper replied. "Hey, no problem. I'll just head on down, then."

Harper's hurt tone reminded Blaise that it wasn't wise to snub a subordinate; it might create the impression you were antisocial. With Mitsuko coiled to pounce on his first exploitable mistake, Blaise decided to take the higher ground.

"Know what, I could use a California roll right about now."

Harper studied his face. "Hey, you OK? You look kinda stressed."

"Her royal highness was just in here, spreading her slime."

"Bitch on wheels," Harper agreed. Then her face brightened. She reached into her jacket pocket and pulled out a credit chip. "Almost forgot. Kiley asked me to give you this. You won the soccer pool this week. Nice spread you gave for the L.A.-Sydney playoffs. Paid off big time." She pushed the chip into Blaise's hand. "Buy us all a couple rounds at the next game night out."

"Thanks, Harper," Blaise agreed, though he had missed the last two game nights, a risky strategy since failing to show team spirit could arouse the Cloud Monitor's attention. But Blaise couldn't bear hanging out with sycophants who dreamed of one day replacing him. He had told them he had to code late on a special project for the director, an excuse that brought awed respect.

Harper sauntered beside Blaise down the corridor past colleagues whose jealous glances relieved her, for a few minutes, from the twitchy fearscape of her thwarted ambition. She and Blaise took the lift down with other Class IIs and IIIs and caught bland scents from the commissary's healthy all-organic fare; their neurofeed announced the menu accompanied by circling holographic beauty shots. Beyond the floor-to-ceiling commissary windows, the aquamarine towers of the L.A. skyline stretched into the distance like the curvature of a dream. A few executive hovercars streaked between scrapers.

The board had long ago eliminated smog by moving manufacturing to unflooded areas in Mexico Quadrant and by restricting road traffic to rechargeable autobots. And autobots were rare now that Class IIs, IIIs, and IVs took the bullet train alongside Slags, who used it to get to their drudge work.

"Snagged the ultra-VR Gal Gadot package," Harper bragged over her sushi. "Classic early twenty-first century. Always did love Wonder Woman. Now I got ninety days of Gal sucking me senseless at a steal of a price."

"Great stuff, Harper," Blaise yawned, recalling that he himself had coded the CereFuck promos for the VR lover models so popular now that biopics set in the early twenty-first century were all the rage. Tom Hardy, Bradley Cooper, Ryan

Gosling, Cillian Murphy, Lady Gaga, Jennifer Lawrence, Emily Ratajkowski, Karlie Klause, Kylie Jenner. All hot sellers. Dead divas and hunks for deadheads like Harper.

Harper gave Blaise a swift sidelong glance. "Seen Tolsen's new series?"

"I don't follow Mitsuko's coders."

"VR effects were bland as dirt. The storyline? Pathetic. I can code circles around that Okie."

"Harper, you'll get your shot at a series. When you're ready."

"I'm gonna explode, Blaise. Second unit code-correcting Tolsen's fuck ups? That's rookie shit."

Blaise and Harper made a great show of enjoying their sushi, aware of the hundred or so colleagues pretending not to eye Blaise with envy. He picked up a few warning pings in the reactive beat of his heart. He sensed tension in the air, an effluvium of jealous anticipation, expressed in furtive glances as people whispered to companions, a few even daring to gesture at Blaise. Icy needles of fear pierced his heart. Was something afoot? A rumor making the rounds about him—perhaps concerning yet another hot project the director had in mind? Minsheng's special projects could bring unimagined rewards or abrupt termination if the results were unsatisfactory. This all-too-familiar angst precipitated one of Blaise's mood swings. *I can't bear much more of this shit* flashed through his mind: the jealousy, the relentless competition, the urgency to create VR series everyone would forget in a month or a year; the endless coding, the pseudo-life in a faux live/work/play pod with no one for company but VR lovers; and his relentless nightmares and flashbacks. Blaise suppressed these criminal thoughts beneath the iron discipline of his mantra. He repeated it until he was convinced his thoughts were pure alpha waves.

His conversation with Harper attracted a couple of Class IIIs, moths drawn to Blaise's flame. Tolsen was one of them; he pretended he hadn't heard Harper's insults earlier. He and the other Class III, Phuong, took two just-abandoned seats and congratulated Blaise on his new series. They asked for details, and had to settle for his reply that it was classified and none of their business in any case. Disappointed that they couldn't steal anything of value, they tried to impress Blaise with the latest Slag jokes.

"Hey Blaise, what do you call a Slag girl who can outrun her brothers?" Tolsen snickered. "A virgin."

Tolsen and Phuong howled with laughter.

Blaise rolled his eyes to feign boredom, though he resented this kind of humor. He had a soft spot for Slags, who reminded him of the poor blacks he had grown up with back in Atlanta.

"I got a better one," Phuong blurted. "What's the difference between a Slag baby and a pizza? A pizza doesn't scream when you put it in the microwave."

Blaise looked Tolsen and Phuong up and down.

"The first time I heard those, I found them mildly offensive," Blaise rejoined. "But hearing you repeat them, I realize that light travels faster than sound. That's why people like you appear bright until they speak."

Tolsen and Phuong, clearly embarrassed, excused themselves, saying they had to get back to work. As they were leaving, Phuong whispered some quip to a Class III assistant programmer, and she shrieked with laughter, prompting Blaise's nightmare from the night before to rush back with the force of a plunging sword. In it, he was belt-beamed to a seat in a bullet train that was clearly out of place in the arid Australian outback he glimpsed outside. The scene shifted, and he saw his daughter Mei tied to a bed, weeping, surrounded by thugs with blackened teeth, unkempt beards, and greasy hands as she whimpered like an animal with its leg caught in a trap.

The nightmare had had the sharpness and clarity of VR feed, and Blaise had suspected, when he woke from it, that perhaps it was something Mitsuko had cooked up. Remembering it now impressed on him that Cherry and Mei were dead, dead, dead, and he found himself aching to be with them. He applied his mantra to blank out his emotions, but Harper's clichés and suck-up stories, designed to impress, rushed to Blaise's brain like a drug and drove him over a precipice into the void. In the crystalline purity of his despair, he felt he was bursting from his body like a bug through a withered pod.

2

AS BLAISE AND HARPER HEADED TO THE LIFT AFTER LUNCH, they ran into a clot of sycophants trailing Director Minsheng Lu. A fit, athletic Class I Chinese executive in his sixties, his face refreshed by prosthetic skin-grafting, the director wore a silk cutaway jacket and trousers that displayed a gradient of metallic peach, red, yellow, green, and aquamarine, all blending into each other to create a disorienting effect.

Minsheng's hands were foreshortened, gnarled, and massive as mandrill's paws. His gait and gestures were precise, and his eyes impassive, like a shark's. He advanced in slow strides, like a stalking animal. Something wasn't quite right about his left eye, a feature that had disturbed Blaise the first time he and the director had spoken privately. The left eye was slightly larger than the right one, and it gave his face a menacing look. Long used to Minsheng's deformity, Blaise chuckled now at the way the director's lackeys tried to avoid glancing at the gouged-out eye until a sycophant on Minsheng's left stole a look and shuddered, almost imperceptibly, at the oval holographic lens with an eye image masking a red hole.

A gold sun disk with a blue K-Spot embedded in a white circle studded Minsheng's lapel, matching the smaller one imprinted in his forehead. Having survived many Cloud board wars while he clawed his way up Mythoplex, the board's entertainment division, Minsheng regarded the world through an impenetrable eye that terrified subordinates and executives alike. People whispered that the director was in line to join the board of directors in Hong Kong; as such, none of the restrictions they observed applied to him. Rumors flew that he had ordered eighty Mantis terminations over his career. He had seven mistresses on four continents. He had conquered numerous wounds and diseases—including laser blasts, poisonings, cancers, tropical fevers, and less exotic maladies such as hypertension, stroke, and other conditions related to his all-devouring drive for power—all without resorting to Medco tech. He had survived everything, including assassination attempts, through a force of will that made him soar above mortality with the effortlessness of levitation. Then there was his reputation as a former Special Forces colonel with genetically enhanced strength and lethal martial arts skills. He had applied these skills to Caliphate troops in personally executed atrocities, a tradition he continued by torturing Slags to death during orgies at his San Fernando Valley estate.

"Blaise, a word with you," the director intoned when he reached Blaise and Harper.

Blaise bowed from the waist. "Of course, Director Minsheng."

Harper and the sycophants peeled away from Blaise as he entered the charmed space around the director, a bubble of privilege only the most gifted, ruthless, or brazen could access. The director strolled ahead, leaving behind the others, who glared at Blaise with murder in their eyes.

The director had a private lift. He eye-scanned the door open and gestured for Blaise to follow. As the car shot up to floor 118, Blaise caught the scent of the director's underarm sweat, metallic with a tincture of gunpowder and oblivion. It made Blaise queasy, this smell of power and death. He suppressed his reaction with silent mantra chants. He glanced at his superior with a carefully controlled smile. Minsheng grinned but kept his good eye impassively focused on the elevator doors.

"Relax. I won't be grilling you about coding today, Blaise."

The lift doors opened into the director's suite, a museum of scented teakwood, bonsai, and a Zen fountain. Along the floor ran seven onyx sculptures of gradually increasing scale, organic ovals with holes in their centers, vibrating on a frequency Blaise found faintly hypnotic. Behind a black desk, a window gave on a vista that stretched beyond L.A.'s garnet and amethyst towers, across San Fernando Valley to the distant foothills. On two walls hung classical paintings of mountains floating in mist; a third featured a painting of the Seven Immortals gathered around the goddess Quan Yin.

The director showed Blaise to a maroon leather couch and sat across from him in a plush chair, his expression as opaque as the onyx sculptures on the floor.

"Would you care for tea?"

Blaise noticed a holographic clock on the director's desk that said 1:37. Blaise ached to get back to his coding, but there could only be one answer to the director. No sarcasm was possible here.

"I would be honored, sir."

A tinkle of glass.

Blaise glanced around at a Japanese girl with ivory skin and limpid eyes, draped in a red and gold kimono, hair accented by hairpins shaped like tiny red branches. She pushed a wheeled tea service. Her body emitted a mysterious scent that Blaise found irresistible. He wondered if she was the director's flesh-toy, but buried the thought beneath his mantra to avoid the Cloud Monitor's notice.

She served the director and then Blaise. Minsheng gazed through her as if she were glass. He made a tent of his fingertips and pressed them to his lips, his gaze focused on Blaise with disturbing intensity.

"This new series you're working on. Quite an accomplishment."

"I'm honored, sir."

"I've just returned from Hong Kong. I'm appointed to the board of directors."

"Congratulations, sir."

Minsheng nodded graciously. "The board spoke about your pilot episode. Did Mitsuko tell you?"

"Only about the deadline for final coding to Vidracom."

"What deadline?"

"Ninety days from now, sir."

"This project is far too important. I grant you four months."

"Mitsuko said we're under contract."

"I know the Vidracom CEO. He'll understand."

"Mitsuko won't be pleased."

Minsheng guffawed. "Nothing about you pleases her."

"Sorry to hear that, sir."

"She complains about your jibes at her. What of it? She's irrelevant. Replaceable in a heartbeat. Only you matter, ultimately. And we both know sarcasm is a good way to cope with the tension between neurofeed and one's actual thoughts."

"My thoughts are one hundred percent patriotic, sir."

"Relax, Blaise," Minsheng said. "Even I have the occasional errant thought."

Despite Minsheng's reassurance, Blaise's armpits bled cold sweat at the prospect of being caught in the crossfire between Mitsuko and the director. It was essential to walk the razor's edge with them, and he had no idea where the director was taking this interview. Was Mitsuko behind this, laying a trap? Was Minsheng testing him to expose actionable thoughts? If the Cloud Monitor picked up an errant brainwave, a subconscious hint of dissent . . .

The girl bowed to the director. Blaise watched with furtive lust as she wheeled away the tea service with mincing steps. When she was gone he turned to the director, whose good eye exposed a fierce, fleeting emotion Blaise had never seen before. It vanished in an instant as Minsheng cleared his throat.

"You have a level-three security clearance, correct?"

"Yes, sir."

"Excellent. Excellent."

He considered Blaise with what appeared to be calm regard and made a short, correct bow of the head. "We've watched your development with great interest."

"Thank you, sir."

"In seven years you've accomplished more than most game planners do in a lifetime. A bold achievement after two years of exemplary military service."

Blaise wasn't sure how to respond. Why was the director complimenting him? It didn't make sense, coming from a man whose aloofness was legendary.

"Oh, yes," Minsheng nodded. "I say this without hyperbole. No, no, we recognize superior talent and are inclined to reward it. Tell me, how would you feel about a promotion?"

Blaise pictured life as a senior executive like the director. A life without coding: a borderless tundra where nothing could free him from the cold, dead hand of grief and chaos. The prospect terrified him almost as much as the Mantis.

"A promotion, sir?" he gulped, the words catching in his throat.

The director smiled. "To Class I games supervisor, with a security clearance of five. Working in a private office with a security shield. No more prying eyes from inferiors. Oh, and a forty-percent salary bump. I'll make your raise retroactive to the beginning of the month."

Blaise felt a rush of vanity and delight followed by terror. The board never handed down a promotion without extracting a price.

"I'm honored," he managed, his voice husky with fear despite his attempt to sound blasé.

The director bowed his head again, something an executive never did except to acknowledge a colleague.

"If I may ask, sir, what will Mitsuko make of all this?"

"We're promoting her to senior vice-supervisor. That will allow her the blue silk jacket. And a director's pin. Something she's long coveted."

Blaise felt his angst ease its grip on his heart. So, he was to survive Mitsuko's jealousy and resentment after all.

"Will I still report to her?"

"She will continue to head up the games planning team, but with a separate staff. You will report directly to me. Tell me, are you familiar with the Lazarus-D initiative? Or *Homo Deus?*"

"I'm afraid not, sir."

"Our immortality program for Class Is. I'll arrange neural training and longevity injections."

So I'm going to live forever, Blaise thought, trying to process that. He wondered if a board-mandated eternity would include relief, perhaps after centuries of effort, from his near-debilitating regrets.

Minsheng considered Blaise through tented fingers. "Sudden change can be disorienting, even when it opens new worlds," he said, finally. "But you adapt well to abruptness. That's why I'm sure you'll agree with my next request. I'd like you to code a new sequence for *Gilgamesh V.*"

White-hot rage ran through Blaise's veins at the ease with which the director had robbed him of the creative freedom he had fought so hard against Mitsuko to win. He repeated his mantra to hide his anger.

"My request disturbs you?"

"Not in the least, sir."

"My executive neurofeed reports your brainwaves have lost their alpha curve, and your pulse is racing."

"Terribly sorry, sir."

"I'm only asking for a slight change in your storyline."

Blaise pushed back against his rage against Minsheng's intrusion into his holiest of holies. "What did you have in mind?" he managed.

The director signaled for Blaise to rise and then nudged him forward in a slow, counterclockwise circuit of the cavernous office. He stopped occasionally to let Blaise admire one of the sculptures, his good eye black and impenetrable as the abyss of deep space.

"Your hero is a pretender named Gilgamesh. The Babylonian epic has him seek immortality but fail to find it. Whereas your rebooted protagonist seeks an earthly immortality by seizing power in a decaying city-state."

Here it comes, Blaise thought. *He's going to gut my series—months of sweat, sleepless nights, migraines, all for nothing—because some bastard on the Cloud board ordered it.*

"That's correct, sir."

"I'd like you to code a new twist in the plot, in which the high priestess brings Gilgamesh a vision from the goddess Ishtar. The priestess will proclaim that immortality is attainable from a potion prepared by her temple prostitutes."

"Excuse me, sir, if I may, but that would . . ."

"This potion, let's call it Anima, is so powerful, so ecstatic in its effect, that everyone who uses it loses interest in everything else."

"But wouldn't that ruin my storyline?"

"I'm sure you can code your way around it."

Blaise repeated his mantra to calm himself. "And the purpose of this change, sir?"

"To allow Slags, who'll pirate your series—and Class IV subscribers—to addict themselves. And remain submissive."

Blaise found the director's notion absurd. Anima was a hopelessly antiquated approach to delivering pleasure, a prehistoric echo from ages when the pleasure center was only a knot of nerves, fist-smashed by ancient drugs, and not an infinitesimal speck in a vast programmable neuroscape. What could it mean? Had the board descended into madness with this abrupt change in creative direction?

"Aren't they submissive enough as it is?"

"You never know when a dog could turn rabid. The important thing is, *Gilgamesh V* will be massive. It'll sweep the awards. We'll rake in billions to fund the board's Caliphate war and replenish our own Mythoplex coffers."

The director rose and padded with quiet dignity to his desk. He passed his hand over a crystal. A wall mountainscape vanished, and a world map materialized. The Cloud Bloc—North America, Europe, Russia, South Africa, the Sudan, and Asia—lighted up. Holographic thumbnails in blue, red, green, and gold glittered, the green thumbnails marking L.A., San Francisco, Toronto, Atlanta, London, Moscow, Beijing, Teipei, Tokyo, Johannesburg, Sydney, and Hong Kong.

"As you know, the Caliphate dirty bombed the cities in red thirty years back. These others, in green, are remaining strongholds under Cloud rule. Power shared, of course, at least for the moment, with our dull-witted allies, the Russians. But how long can our empire last? The global Slag population has swelled to twenty billion. Did you know?"

"No, sir. I didn't."

"Imagine all of them—all those billions—as Anima addicts. Uprisings would be impossible. Caliphate legionaries will pirate Anima, too, by the way. Their regime must allow some respite from the squalid misery they subject their armies to." Minsheng gave Blaise a long appraising stare. "I share this classified information on the assumption that you've accepted your promotion."

A slouching stirred in the room. Blaise cut his eyes toward a huge jointed, greenish leg at it pressed heavily into the carpet.

Minsheng re-seated himself on the couch, where he crossed his legs and watched Blaise impassively. Blaise felt a surge of despair, followed by resignation. There was no escape. Mitsuko had obviously convinced Minsheng to terminate him. Nothing could be done except to steel himself for it. He glimpsed yellow, enormous fang-like mandibles as they issued a chirruping like millions of crickets.

"Quite an achievement, isn't it?" Minsheng observed.

The Mantis crawled on spiny legs, and it displaced the air like a fetid ingot with a burning carrion stench. Blaise gasped at the sight of the slimy, greenish thorax, disturbed by the ripple of unseen muscles, like an enormous snake with jointed appendages. The head had jeweled red eyes sprouting from stalks and a triangular snout with pink, wormlike mandibles and palps wriggling over a black maw.

"A team's been refining it since you left the project," Minsheng boasted. "It's the perfect VR assassin, summoned through your forehead K-spot by cloud-based electromagnetic pulse. To an outside observer, the Mantis is vaporware. To your body, however, it's utterly real."

Blaise heard its heavy tread approaching. *Let it end quickly*, he thought. *Better than another minute in this lunatic world.*

Minsheng couldn't help but brag about this loathsome creature, though he had contributed nothing to the Mantis's actual creation. "Even now your amygdala's shooting electrical signals to your hypothalamus, raising your blood pressure to lethal stroke threshold. Should its claws close on your leg, your flesh will part as if hacked by a machete. Oh, and how do you like the reptilian skin? A twist to increase the terror, the kind our ancestors felt hiding in trees from carnivorous reptiles."

Blaise's heart pounded as he felt the creature's rank breath touch his face. A horrible death was a shriek away. But then, abruptly, the Mantis vanished, which left Blaise panting, sweat-soaked, and shaken.

Minsheng rose from the couch, approached, and pressed a meaty paw on his shoulder.

"Relax, Blaise. I was only making a point. You've accepted your promotion. Your neural scan shows it. I'm deactivating your neurofeed permanently. A Class I doesn't need the conditioning reserved for lower classes." A pulsing light glittered in Minsheng's palm. "Your thumbprint on the contract, if you will. Then no more Cloud surveillance. Ever. Of course, you're free to surveil subordinates' EEGs."

With some trepidation and still uncertain whether the Mantis might reappear to finish him off, Blaise pressed his thumb into the tiny contract icon and heard a faint internal click, nothing more. Then, silence: the silence of the

Grand Canyon in a winter snowdrift. It was a stunning alteration, as if he had lost one of his senses, accompanied by deep relief from the burden of having to suppress his emotions.

"Amazing, isn't it?" Minsheng observed. "Absolute silence in your mind after a lifetime of neural chatter. Who needs it? You have creativity, passion, independence of thought."

Minsheng's toothy grin under his ruined eye made his face a grimace of madness. "You flatter me," Blaise managed as he had a momentary hallucination of the director biting into his face like a rabid dog.

"You and I live to create, build, innovate," the director breathed with evident self-satisfaction. "Slags live to breed. Breeding, reproduction. Disgusting! An evolutionary relic. We're immortal now. We don't need children. Only pleasure. For example, that girl who served us tea earlier? A new class of pleasure android. A breakthrough in synthetic real-flesh, much firmer than VR holographics. No sponginess."

"But isn't the whole concept behind VR to replace naked sensory experience something more vivid?" Blaise blurted, suddenly terrified that the new androids might replace VR and render him and his years of refining his coding talent obsolete.

Minsheng chuckled. "Yet even you have a taste for Slag girls. A harmless pastime. And a good release from VR sensory overload." He paused to give Blaise a long, appraising stare. "But Blaise, you haven't visited the Zone in months. And you've let your VR subscriptions lapse."

Minsheng's words stunned Blaise. Here was the man who had lashed Blaise on to ever greater achievement for the past seven years, the taskmaster who had championed Blaise's drive to create monster hit VR series that had raked in billions for Mythoplex and the Cloud. Why would he advise Blaise to ease back on the throttle when the Gilgamesh series would demand millions of lines of new code?

"My work is my only pleasure now, sir," was all he could think to say.

Minsheng led Blaise back to the couch and settled into the plush fabric next to him with a smug, satisfied expression that made Blaise want to smash him in the face.

"All work and no play, Blaise. It's not healthy."

"I'm so close with *Gilgamesh V*, sir. I don't want any distractions."

Minsheng considered him with a paternal smile.

"I believe you lost your wife, whom you called Cherry, two years back?"

Where the hell is he going with this? flashed through Blaise's mind.

"Yes, sir."

"Cherry took her own life after human traffickers kidnapped and murdered your daughter Mei. Your EEG scans suggest you feel a certain responsibility. Not so. Your behavior was impeccably correct."

Blaise glared at Minsheng, then averted his glance, thinking, *One roundhouse kick to the throat is all it would take for you, you son of a bitch.*

"Oh, and that business with Aisha, the corporal you left on the battlefield in Nigeria, eight years back. Yes, I know about that, too. Apparently you carry lingering guilt concerning the incident."

A voice echoed in Blaise's memory: a young woman screaming, *Don't leave me out here, lieutenant!*

"Nonsense. You sacrificed her to save your platoon. You were a superb officer. Your kill rate is legendary."

"I'm just a games planner now, sir," Blaise replied through clenched teeth.

Minsheng leaned close to him, and Blaise flinched involuntarily away from his fetid breath. "I want you to take the rest of the day off. A couple of days and the weekend. Make that Zone visit you've been putting off. It'll do you good. Then come back fresh Monday and attack that series with all your skill. A crew's moving your things into a new office as we speak."

Minsheng rose majestically and strolled to his desk. He picked up a flat box standing beside it. Inside was a navy-blue cutaway silk blazer with a Class I sunspot medallion pinned to the lapel. He presented the jacket to Blaise.

"Try it on. It's tailor made."

Minsheng took Blaise's old maroon jacket and dropped it in a waste bin. Blaise felt like a trained dog as Minsheng considered him in his new Class I attire.

The director nodded with satisfaction and clapped him on the shoulder. "Congratulations. You're one of us now."

3

BLAISE STOOD ON THE BULLET TRAIN PLATFORM WAITING FOR a car, oppressed by an overwhelming sense that Minsheng had highjacked his life. It was late, after working hours, and a crowd of Class II men and women in maroon jackets chatted with one another about the pleasures they anticipated in the Slag Zone, L.A.'s prime destination for professionals to do a little slumming to relieve the stress of Cloud duties. In addition to these pleasure seekers, a sizable group of Slags in dirty overalls and maintenance crew uniforms stood apart, speaking in whispers and eyeing the Class IIs mistrustfully. Holographic ads with attractive young men and women in the latest fashions leapt from the back wall whenever a Class II ventured close enough for an eye-scan capture. The ads irritated Blaise. They were like Halloween ghosts popping out to try to scare the well-dressed commuters.

Before the bullet train burst from the mouth of the tunnel, Blaise heard a high-pitched hum as it decelerated from a cruising speed of seven hundred kilometers per hour. It was the unmistakable whine from displacing air along the bullet's magnetic field, created by electrified coils in the guideway walls and track. That hum had always evoked a comforting delusion in Blaise, as if his world of PTSD flashbacks and workaholic stress had been opened by a tesseract that would admit him to a parallel dimension.

Passenger doors, aligned in pairs, whisked open in each car. As Blaise pressed forward with the Class IIs, a male android in a crisp gold uniform and bellboy hat touched him on the shoulder.

"Mr. Blaise Pascal? Where are you going, sir?"

For an instant, Blaise wondered if this might be a plainclothes SWAT cop here to arrest him. But no, the painted smile and depthless blue eyes marked this figure as an android.

"I'm boarding," he answered curtly.

"Oh, no, sir. Class Is ride up front."

The android gestured toward the bullet's needle nose. "Please, Mr. Pascal. This way."

Blaise spotted a couple of SWATs observing him. He decided to follow the android to the lead car, which gleamed like burnished silver. A sleek door slid open, and Blaise found himself in a posh suite with a long, plush green couch accented by gold and maroon cushions. Tropical potted plants, soft-glow wall lamps, and the strains of a string quartet sweetened the atmosphere. Through an alcove at the car's back end, he spotted a staircase and bannister under a lozenge-shaped ceiling lamp. In gaps between the picture windows, heavy gold and maroon curtains afforded a view of the tunnel wall.

"You will need a belt beam, sir," the android explained. "If I may offer you an apéritif?"

Blaise sank into the couch, wearied by the day's events. A translucent belt beam snapped into place around his waist. A tray of hors d'oeuvres, liqueur bottle and glass had been set out on a coffee table before him. The male android offered Blaise the glass.

"Patron Lalique Limited Edition. Your favorite liqueur."

"When I can't get sake. Sure. Why not? It's been a helluva day."

The bullet door slid closed, and the train bolted into the tunnel. After a few stops the car decelerated and pulled into the station Blaise wanted. As he stepped onto the platform, he noticed an old-fashioned ATM machine next to the bullet train ticket dispenser. It reminded him he needed cash, a lot of it, something he never would in his live/work/play pod, where monthly bills and other transactions debited and credited automatically when his paychecks hit. But here in the Zone, Slags paid for everything in cash. Glancing about to make sure no mugger lurked, Blaise approached and spoke his authorization code to the ATM. An eye scan touched his iris, and he was amazed to find that his bank balance had nearly tripled, a perk of his promotion to Class I, courtesy of Minsheng. A tray opened. He felt archaic pleasure from the feel of crisp green bills in his hands.

The train hummed and vibrated behind him. Then a tone sounded, and the train sped away, exposing a grimy mosaic spelling SEPULVEDA BOULEVARD, a musical name suggesting festivity and flowers, accompanied by the hum of unseen lighting over a tobacco-stained concrete floor. Rubbish and condoms were piled in corners. Graffiti splashed the walls: obscenities in English, Spanish, and some obscure Cyrillic script, beside vandalized holographic ads with flickering images of last year's fashions and models. Down from the escalator shaft came voices and an aroma of peppery street food. Blaise shoved past Slags headed uptown for their shifts, and glided up, up, up into the fetid fumes of South Central L.A. He hastened across the lobby with its reek of dried sweat. Red, yellow, and green posters promoted the latest wrestling matches and displayed men with ferocious masks and muscular bodies. Tunes blared from loudspeakers, Latino pop ditties singing about passion and heartbreak.

On the street, he sweated profusely. No temperature-controlled bubble shielded him from the sun or the stench of the crowds that milled about the sidewalks and tarmac. Blaise heard snatches of guttural English, Spanish, Haitian French, Vietnamese, Chinese, Arabic, Russian, and other tongues. All of L.A.'s defeated populations clawed for subsistence here. It was past 1800 hours, but the sun glared mercilessly even as it sank behind the rooftops. Slags of all races came in and out of peeling botanicas, restaurants, dollar-discount stores, and low-slung plaster apartment complexes with orange slate roofs. They gave Blaise's navy-blue jacket a wide berth, and many of their faces were creased with fear, deprivation, and hopelessness. Slags had no official K-Spot third-eye implants, only tiny black Hindu-style forehead dots with minimal functionality. Many of the men were rail-thin wrecks who stank of cheap wine and cigarettes, fallout from lives eked out scrubbing toilets, repairing sewers, or maintaining live/work/play pods as their fathers, grandfathers, and great-grandfathers had before them. Others carried their poverty with dignity, dressed in clean, well-starched overalls, and they shared defiant peals of laughter with one another about an absurd world. Blaise was drawn to this better class of laborers because they carried themselves with an air of humble triumph over circumstances. As for the women, aside from a few skinny street hookers in see-through blouses, many were overweight and worn out by childbearing and labor and trailed by filthy children thinned out by hunger and disease. Yet here, too, he glimpsed dignity, a capacity for compassionate endurance. In many cases, these impoverished mothers managed to dress their children in clean, well-pressed clothes. It was clear from their maternal voices, their loving phrases spoken in a dozen languages, that they believed in a future for their children.

It struck Blaise that despite the way he used their women for pleasure, he harbored a furtive affection for Slags. They were, despite their crudeness, human, and their suffering merely a blunter version of his own. They fascinated Blaise, too, because each face carried the stamp of individuality, of variegated journeys through life, something that people in the professional classes had long since given up in exchange for VR addiction and submission to neurofeed propaganda. Hatred for the ruling order choked Blaise's heart. Minsheng's image rose in his mind, monolithic and implacable. But what was the use of hating Minsheng? Or The Cloud? Blaise was one of them now; Minsheng had said so himself. Best to accept the inevitable and plunge into the forgetfulness the Zone offered.

Passing a shit-smelling alley, Blaise saw two SWATs torturing a Latino workman with vintage cattle prods. The Slag, curled up in a fetal position, twitched like an epileptic in his overalls and boots. Blaise averted his eyes and saw before him a dripping wall stained with pigeon shit and grime. On its bleeding surface, someone had spray-painted ROBOT CELLS FOR STOICS. For some reason that line made him stop to witness the torture. A Class I executive could, of course, never dream of interfering with SWAT. This was their domain. Blaise couldn't afford to draw suspicion to himself. But he couldn't resist an urge to turn into the alley and approach a scene good sense told him he should run from as fast as his feet could carry him. The Latino man's wretched cries touched something within him deeper than caution. He couldn't bear to see anyone enslaved, particularly given how Minsheng had just placed him in that category.

The Latino man screamed "Dios ayúdame!" in a cry ripped from exhausted lungs.

One of the SWATs, a well-muscled thug, looked up from his victim to Blaise as he approached. "Restricted area. You'll have to leave."

Blaise flashed the optimistic smile he'd trained himself to display to the world. "Got a bit turned around. My favorite strip club's around here. Can't seem to find the street."

The other SWAT, a slender, wiry man, grinned at Blaise, obviously impressed by the Class I blazer. "That would be the Odradek Theater, sir. Four blocks from here. We'll be glad to direct you."

"Thank you." He glanced down at the Latino Slag. "Manuel?"

The Slag glanced up with terror in his eyes, but he clearly recognized Blaise.

"You know this turd?" the muscular SWAT asked.

"I think he's with the maintenance crew at my condo pod," Blaise replied, thinking, *Careful, this bastard's a killer.* "One of the others called him Manuel," he added pleasantly. "What's he done?"

"Leave, now, if you know what's good for you."

Blaise pointed to the sunburst medallion pinned to his lapel. "I don't take orders. I barely take suggestions."

"Show me some ID, asshole, or submit to a neural scan."

"You're the one who'll submit to the neural scan. Then you get a visit from the Mantis."

The muscular SWAT brandished his cattle prod, but the wiry SWAT looked frightened and grabbed his partner's arm. "I got a wife, kids," he pleaded.

Blaise sensed hesitation in the muscular SWAT and switched tactics. "Chill, buddy," he laughed. "I got no quarrel with you boys. Just doing a little location scouting. For Mythoplex."

The thin SWAT's jaw dropped open. "You work at Mythoplex, sir?"

"Guilty as charged. I'm a games planner."

"Would we know your stuff?"

"Watch *Viral Empire*?"

"You coded that?"

Got him now, Blaise thought. *Must be an aspiring actor.* "Pretty much."

"Best VR series ever! How do you think that shit up?"

"Can't shut it off."

"Hey, if you don't mind me asking, they ever hire new actors for those series?"

"Let me guess. You're an actor."

The thin SWAT blushed. "Took a few lessons. I was an extra in this commercial vid."

"Know Vidracom Studios?" Blaise answered confidentially. "Saturday mornings they have an open casting call."

"No shit?"

The Latino Slag had managed to take advantage of the SWATs' preoccupation and had crawled away, then had staggered to his feet and limped down a side alley.

The muscular SWAT noticed. "Our fish slipped off the hook."

"Let him go," the thin SWAT retorted. "I'm gonna make one of them tryouts. Get me an acting gig. Sir, we'll show you to Calle Ocho."

"No need," Blaise answered with a dismissive gesture. "Been there a hundred times."

The muscular SWAT's face colored. "Thought you said you were lost."

"Got my bearings now."

"You let that Slag piece of shit get away. Now you suddenly get your bearings? Let's see some ID."

Blaise felt an old but still familiar adrenalin rush. Blood pounded in his temples and tightened his scrotum, signaling rising blood lust. He calculated distances between him and the tall, muscular SWAT and the short, lanky one.

"I never argue with an idiot like you," Blaise replied firmly.

The muscular SWAT lunged at him with the cattle prod. Blaise ducked and rolled clear in a clean martial art move he had used in firefights back in the day.

Then he bounded up and delivered a roundhouse kick to the muscular SWAT's groin. The SWAT screamed and dropped his prod, clutching his balls as Blaise grabbed the rod and hurled it at the lanky SWAT, who was drawing his laser burner. The prod caught him across the face, breaking his nose. He crumpled to the ground, clutching it with hands that couldn't stop the spurting blood. Blaise rushed him, kicked him in the balls and scooped up his laser burner from the street. He pictured both SWATs smoldering in a stench of charred flesh and blood reek. Then horror overwhelmed him. This was precisely the kind of violence he had fled from to become Mythoplex's top games planner. So he set the laser burner on stun and sent both SWATs into temporary blackness they'd wake from in a few hours. He glanced about, giddy and sweating from the unexpected exertion, senses sharpened to a soldier's hypervigilance as he checked to see if surveillance drones might be cruising overhead—but nothing and no one were in sight.

He knew he had to clear the area before other SWAT patrols showed. But what had happened to the Slag? Against his better judgement, he made his way to the garbage-strewn alley and stepped into it. Fifteen paces down he found the stricken Slag, who knelt beside a girl of four or five. The girl, weeping, in rags, and stinking of piss, was thin as a sheet of smudged paper.

"Está bien, cariña. Está bien," the Slag kept reassuring her.

At the sound of Blaise's step the Slag clutched the girl.

"I won't hurt you," Blaise reassured him.

The girl pressed herself against the Slag, as if trying to burrow into him. Her eyes were wild as a bobcat's, and though the Slag stroked her ratty hair, and shushed her over and over, he couldn't silence her whimpers, which erupted into screams when Blaise took a couple more steps her way. Whatever had brought her to this moment had obviously driven her insane.

"Where will you stay tonight?" Blaise shouted to the Slag, so he could be heard.

"Aqui. We stay here."

Blaise approached the pair. The girl burrowed herself into the Latino Slag and wailed even more loudly. Blaise reached into his pocket and took out the $1,000 credit chip Harper had given him. He knelt before the girl and smiled.

"Cómo se llama, cariño? Solía tener una niña como tú."

The girl looked nothing like Mei; she had stringy hair and was pale as death. But she trilled in his heart, as if he were connected to her by an invisible wire. He flashed her a disarming smile, and stretched out his hand with the credit chip. Its metallic surface caught the glow from a streetlight. The girl noticed and looked at him curiously. Blaise gently opened her tightly closed fist and slipped the credit chip into it.

"There's a hotel a couple blocks from here," he told the Latino Man. "Get her there and buy her some decent food."

Moments later he sprinted past the two unconscious SWATs and reached the avenue. He was still carrying their laser burner. He wiped it down with a pocket handkerchief and hurled it down an alley. He passed odorous throngs of Slags when he reached Calle Ocho and made straight for the Odradek Theater. In a maw-like entryway, he pushed bills into the hand of a bearded gorilla in denim behind a barred window grill. Soon he was inside the forgetfulness of the black-lighted club, with its lavender colorscape and pornographic holograms. The barmaid who served him was a neo-emo Minnesota Swede in a black micro-skirt and transparent top. She sported self-mutilation scars on her arms, which were all the rage in her crowd, an emotional release from lives without future prospects. She recognized him as a regular and brought a bottle of black market sake. He handed her a hundred-dollar bill. A Guatemalan girl worked the stage pole with flaccid disinterest. The Class IIs who lounged about the railing yawned at her gyrations and refused to push any more notes into her garter.

"Any new talent?" Blaise asked the barmaid.

"A Brasilera and a China doll. You might like the China doll."

"Oh, yeah?" Blaise pushed another hundred into her hands. "If she's a looker, send her over after her set."

The sake was hot, the bottle large, the rush to his pleasure center immediate. The stringy-haired DJ in his booth at the back spun sultry neo-grunge rock and hip-hop from many generations back. Blaise's mind softened, released from the inner turmoil his recent violence had stirred up, and he melted into the pleasure of the archaic chords, the jangling guitar riffs and crass lyrics. Four bottles of sake later, inebriation and the glow of undulating flesh made him forget anything existed beyond this lavender club, with its reek of marijuana smoke and cheap cologne, coned-shaped black lights pointing at the serrated ceiling, and tangy, twenty-something talent gyrating, stripping, and scooping up tips.

Blaise was deep into his fifth round of sake when the new China doll stepped up on the runway, balancing on spiked heels. Her creamy skin, long, shapely legs, ample breasts, and waist-length hair mesmerized him. She danced with conviction and worked the pole with the skill of a Cirque du Soleil acrobat. She shed her bikini top and G-string in languid moves that brought a confetti burst of cash from the audience ogling her stage-side.

The barmaid approached to see if Blaise needed another round. He tugged her close. "Who is she?"

"Scarlett Johansson."

Blaise pressed another bill into the barmaid's hand.

"Bullshit. What's her real name?"

"Jin. From Shanghai, I think."

"Tell her to come see me after her set. Not these other assholes. Me. Tell her I want a VIP room."

His heart raced like a testosterone-bloated schoolboy's, and sweat dripped from his armpits, when Jin, the Chinese beauty, sashayed up in a blue silk kimono with a smile like iridescent pearls. She slipped into a chair beside him and crossed her legs in a way that wafted her perfume straight to his pleasure center.

"What are you drinking?" he managed in a husky tone.

"They got nothing worth shit here," she laughed. "Anything wet'll do."

"Sake? And a vitamin water so you can rehydrate?"

"Sure thing."

The waitress passed by after serving another customer. Blaise signaled her.

"Vitamin water. Two fresh glasses. Another four sakes."

The waitress nodded and left.

"Haven't seen you here before," Jin said. "'Course, haven't been here long."

"What paradise did you descend from?"

"Paradise? Yeah, right."

The waitress brought their sake and a bottle of water. Jin sipped the water and joined Blaise in drinking the sake. They watched another dancer stripping.

"You're a much better dancer than her," Blaise said. "You glide like a gazelle."

Jin gave him a wry grin. "Good line, there."

She toasted him, and they drank sake in earnest. Blaise, flushed and tipsy, ran his finger along her calf and thigh. Jin playfully nudged his hand away.

"Whoa there. Can you even walk to the VIP room? 'Cause you got sake bleeding outa your eyes."

"You really from Shanghai?"

"No way. I'm a Frisco gal. But Shanghai's got cache, y'know?"

"Yeah, know. So, what do you do when you're not driving men crazy with lust?"

"Grad student. USC."

"USC's still around?"

"Sure, babe. The derelict University of Southern California. They turned it into a vocational school staffed by cockroaches and rats. They let me take robo-classes from wheezing old profs, cuz no Class I or II bitch comes near the place anymore, y'know?"

"What do you study?"

"Philosophy and business administration."

"Philosophy?"

"Sure. No money in it, but beats the hell outa business classes. Nothing there but money-making scams I'm never gonna tap."

"Don't you like money?"

"'Course I do, babe. I'm gonna take a buncha yours in a few."

He brushed her hair back from her cheek with his fingertip. "I want twenty dances."

"Good God Almighty. Got myself a live wire here. What do you do?"

"Code VR series. I'm a mythologizer. A games planner."

"Wish to God I could afford VR. But it's cool, cuz I know this hacker dude? Lets me jack in through my K-spot."

"No shit?"

"I go crazy for historical series: ancient Rome, China, Persia, Egypt. Read novels, too. You know, the old-fashioned printed kind?"

"Used to read 'em back in the day. My mom encouraged me."

"It was my dad with me."

Desire washed over Blaise in a warm tidal surge. "I want you."

"You got me, babe. Twenty dances worth. Let's go."

"Look, nothing personal, but I gotta eye scan you first, make sure you're not an android. They creep me out."

She laughed, brought her nose to his and rubbed it. "My real name's Kristina Sun."

She took his hand and led him past the pee-reeking men's room, down the bar to a loutish Slag in ripped denim, who scrawled twenty dances on a tobacco-stained pad. Then Blaise and Kristina slipped into a room with a ratty couch, side table, and black light. She drew the curtain, hung up her robe and slipped out of her bikini. He slammed her against the wall and devoured her mouth with deep, sucking kisses, lost in the jungle of her hair and breasts, the silkiness of her belly and thighs. Her body burned new electrical circuits in his brain as it evoked the hallucinated apotheosis of a goddess. Kristina guided his middle finger down to the sticky miracle of her shaved pussy, gifted him with its carnal tang, its scent of generation, seed, and birth. Now was the time for one-liners and repartee to win her over and make her his sugar baby on a monthly allowance, but his sang-froid had fled. He of many elegant words and lines of code had been rendered speechless. He pushed her down on the couch, sucked and licked his way up her back, starting with her toes, and relished the salty perfume of her calves and thighs and the pertness of her savory ass.

"I gotta have you tonight," he moaned.

"Honey, we can't. It's the rules."

"Fuck the rules. I'll give you a thousand bucks extra."

"You'll get me fired."

"Two thousand."

"You're making my head spin, honey. I can't date customers."

"I'll sponsor you, baby," he promised when he came up for air. "I'll give you an allowance, just name it, I swear to God."

She peered into his eyes. "You're so full of shit. Promise a girl big bucks, get her hooked, then run out on her."

He tried to hold back the feelings beating in his fevered brain, but he was too drunk. "You're the most beautiful thing I've ever seen. My wife died two years back. I need . . . I need . . . baby, please, God, please."

"You're serious about the allowance?" she probed. She stroked his face, touching a glistening tear in the corner of his eye.

"Five thousand a month if you want."

"I do need the money. I got family."

"Kids?"

"No. My mom. She lives in a roach hotel out in the valley. Dead broke in her sixties."

"Where do you stay?"

"Apartment three blocks from here. Notice that Italian dive up the street?"

"Scalopini's?"

She nodded and grinned. "Open all night for folks coming off shift from the upscale zones. Wait for me there."

His heart swelled with drunken hope. "OK."

"Get a booth in the back so you can feel me up under the table," she giggled.

"When?"

"Midnight. I'm starved. We'll order antipasto, pasta and Italian sausage, garlic bread with extra virgin olive oil, a gallon of Chianti to wash it down. Then we're gonna fuck all night."

4

KRISTINA'S TINY STUDIO SMELLED OF STALE SWEAT AND INCENSE. A stench of rotting garbage wafted up from the alley below. But she kept the place spotless, had colorful art prints on the walls, and her bed was big enough for four. She was a ferocious lover and rode him with the passion and the fire of a dragon. When he was deep inside her, they came together, and it melted his mind, his sperm jetting into her womb like an electric umbilical that merged his soul and body with hers. From the tunnels of memory came a snatch of poetry his mother had read to him as a child: *Whispers and small laughter between leaves and hurrying feet, under sleep, where all the waters meet.*

Once, during the night, he blinked awake from a soggy dream to find Kristina beaming at him, her face illuminated by moonlight. Her lips brushed his as if she were kissing him in an unknown tongue, her body wrapped around him, scented with musk and woman-sweat and a tang of baked apple. Then he fell into a blue dreamscape, lulled by the sound of breakers foaming on a beach.

Hours later, when he dragged himself up from the swamp of a sake hangover, the sun blinded him from behind a rooftop outside the window. It was morning and stifling. He sweated in a tangle of bedsheets. His jacket and slacks were flung across the back of a chair in a corner next to a vanity table with mirror. He heard clattering from the kitchen, caught the smell of coffee, and something baking. He dragged himself up and dressed, found his shoes and socks and pulled them on. Through a pounding head he realized that his neurofeed was silent. He remembered the director had deactivated it. Then all the details of his meeting with Minsheng struck his mind like a natural catastrophe.

He blundered into the tiny living room and was shocked to find a rail-thin Caucasian woman in her sixties with graying, shoulder-length hair, sitting cross-legged on the couch in jeans and a denim shirt. The woman smoked an old-fashioned tobacco cigarette, which she stubbed out in a brass ashtray. She had a full-function K-Spot over her third eye. Certain he was about to be shaken down, Blaise ducked for the door.

Kristina came in from the kitchen in her blue silk kimono. "Wait. It's OK. It's my mom, Amelia."

Blaise gave the woman a sharp look. "It was consensual. And I've given her all my cash."

The woman flashed a wry smile. "Take a seat. We just want to talk."

"Really, it's OK," Kristina seconded her. "Please sit down. I'll bring coffee and biscuits."

"You look like you could use an aspirin," the woman observed. She reached in her shirt pocket and shook two tablets from a bottle. "Yep, still got aspirin here. No Medco dispensers in this rathole of a building. Take 'em. They're extra strength."

The woman extended her palm.

Blaise's headache pounded too hard to refuse. He settled down in the chair and popped the tablets.

"You'll be amazed how fast those work," Kristina encouraged. "A little trick an exiled biochemist pulled off. She altered the formula."

In fact, Blaise's headache was beginning to ebb.

"Must feel strange to wake up and find me here," Amelia observed. "Actually, it's not. We know about your situation with the director."

Blaise tried to neutralize the shock showing in his face. "How . . . could you possibly . . . know about that?"

"Relax, you're among friends," Amelia said.

"How do you take your coffee?" Kristina put in.

"Huh? Black."

Kristina vanished into the kitchen. Blaise glared at Amelia.

"You're supposed to be Kristina's mother? She's Chinese."

"Her father was Chinese. And back in the day, I was a games planner like you."

"For Mythoplex?"

"One of the first women allowed in the ranks."

"How do you know about me and the director?"

"We've got our own neuro-surveillance network, like the Cloud Monitor, only better."

"So you're a hacker."

"Every games planner's a hacker. We know the neural network cold. Some of the old-timers here helped design it. Not that tough to jack in."

"Jack in for what?"

"Once we tapped your EEG, we knew we had our man. The Cloud's AI firewalls stymied us at first. Luckily, we're perfecting a new psychic ability. We call it curseil. It gave us neural access."

Blaise struggled to process what was happening to him, but it was impossible. "So what is this curseil?" he demanded.

The question seemed to please Amelia. "We can't match the neural network's sophistication, so we researched ancient texts about meditative techniques that can link minds psychically. We're in the first grade with this stuff, but we've made some headway. With the full concentration of our curseil meditators, we can read thoughts."

"How is that possible?" Blaise asked, incredulous.

"It's based on Einstein's universal field theory and Heisenberg's uncertainty principle: the idea that sub-atomic waves and particles affect each other from great distances. Turns out people's minds are connected through a psychic substratum. We tap into that substratum—like cavers shining flashlights into the collective unconscious. With focus and discipline, we can zero in on a person's thoughts and read them for limited periods."

Blaise considered what Amelia had revealed. If she was telling the truth, if this wasn't a VR projection Minsheng had dreamed up to test his loyalty, the implications were staggering. If The Cloud ever co-opted curseil, the regime could achieve a level of mind control lightyears beyond neurofeed and the Cloud Monitor.

"OK, let's say you can read minds. Why would you want to spy on me?"

"You'll understand soon enough."

"Don't play games with me, lady. Explain yourself!"

"Relax. I told you, you're among friends."

"I don't need any friends."

"We think you do. How long do you think Minsheng will let you live after *Gilgamesh V* wraps?"

Blaise had always considered Mitsuko his most dangerous enemy. Minsheng, he had assumed, relied on his talent too much to vaporize him.

"There's no reason to terminate me," he blurted. "I've won all the awards."

"Your VR advances make you a huge security risk."

"Lady, you can't throw a scare into somebody who's already terrified. I don't buy your story."

"No story. A lethal reality. One you're creating for a madman who'll happily exterminate billions with it."

"What are you talking about?"

"You do realize this drug you're to code is fatal?"

"He just wants to keep the Slags submissive and, and make a mint for Mythoplex and the Cloud."

"You don't really believe he'd expend all that time and expense, not to mention his star programmer's blood and sweat, just to introduce a new sedative. Wake up, Blaise. This is his ticket to the chairmanship of the Cloud board. He'll take all the credit for this. And you'll be expendable. He knows you might use Anima to take him out."

"How can you know all this?"

"We've got him under surveillance, too. He's going to exterminate the entire Slag population. Plus as many of those poor Caliphate army bastards who sample it through black market K-spots."

Against his better judgment, Blaise considered the possibility that she might be right. How stupid he had been to let vanity and ambition keep him from considering that his promotion, his new office, and status, all of it, was bait to ensure compliance until Minsheng no longer needed him.

"OK. OK. So let's say there's a slim chance you're right about Minsheng. What do you and your daughter want from me?"

"You think Kristina seduced you for some sinister purpose?"

"Yeah, that occurred to me."

"We knew you frequented that club. Kristina's worked as a stripper before. Easy to get her hired. And she's your type."

Kristina brought in a mug of coffee and a plate of biscuits, took them to a side table near Blaise, and curled up beside Amelia on the couch.

"Dig in, Blaise," Kristina urged. "You can trust us. We've got nothing to do with that lunatic you work for."

Blaise's better judgment told him to run, and fast, back to what he knew, horrifying as it was. But something about Kristina and Amelia intrigued him. They had presence, solidity, a scent of real, un-virtual flesh that attracted him. He noticed Kristina's epicanthic eyes were the same blue as Amelia's. Her face had the same oval structure, her lips the same shapeliness. She was petite and fine-boned, like Amelia. Definitely her daughter. But that was hardly enough to justify trusting them. How in fact could he know this was reality? Maybe it wasn't. He traced his movements since his meeting with the director the day before and searched for an ellipsis in time, an entry point into a virtual world.

But everything that had happened to him struck him as real; his years of experience with VR confirmed it. Maybe these two hackers were telling the truth. On the other hand, if this were a loyalty test, and he failed it, he'd know Minsheng's claim that he disconnected his neural monitoring was a bluff, and the Mantis would come. Perhaps, after all, he was already doomed.

"This could all be a VR projection," he blurted. "Some fucked up loyalty test. Minsheng doesn't trust anybody."

"He trusts your vanity, your greed, your need to overcome a violent past," Kristina countered. "Come on. Drink your coffee. It'll clear your head."

Blaise bit into a biscuit, slurped the coffee to wake himself up, and watched the two women cautiously.

"OK. Let's say there's a slim chance you're telling the truth," he countered. "What do you want from me? To help you jack back into the Cloud? So you can hack Anima, take it offline?"

"We don't want to jack back in," Amelia said. "We wanna destroy the Cloud."

Blaise set down his plate and coffee and glared at them in disbelief. "Are you out of your mind?"

Kristina and Amelia studied Blaise intently, then exchanged glances. Kristina smiled.

"You know we're telling the truth," she said. "I sense it. So we're going to tell you our plan. But after we do, you're locked in. You'll have to see it through."

"Whoa, now. I'm not agreeing to anything here."

Kristina leaned toward him. "We've coded a killer worm, called Polyphemus, after the cyclops in *The Odyssey*. After it's uploaded, it'll go viral and take down the global neural network."

"That's impossible!"

"People with nothing to lose specialize in the impossible. We've beta tested Polyphemus. It's coded in micro-modules with cumulative impact. It will work. And you've got a level five security clearance."

"Nobody can hack past Cloud AI defenses."

"There's a coding threshold, a limit to detectable file size. It makes our worm undetectable."

"Their quantum servers can reconfigure firewalls at light speed. You plan is insane."

"No, Blaise. The Cloud board is insane. We want to restore sanity."

"OK, Ok, let's dial this back to reality. Say in some parallel universe I managed to get your worm past the firewalls and fried the servers. Then what? Everything would collapse."

"We're talking rebirth here, Blaise," Amelia put in. "Returning to the days when your mother was one of us."

"What do you mean?"

"What do you remember about her?"

"Very little. I was eight when she died."

"Please try," Amelia urged. "The more you remember, the freer you'll feel."

The two women fixed Blaise with focused expressions. His body tensed in the grip of some unseen force.

"What are you doing?" he gasped. "What's happening to me?"

"It's curseil. Trust me, you'll feel better after you tell us."

"I—can't."

"Yes, you can. Please. What do you remember?"

Memories he had long repressed surged up in Blaise's mind, and he felt an overwhelming urge to confess everything.

"The Cloud had seized power," he began. "Neurofeed and the metaverse were in their infancy. The United States had collapsed. Hong Kong had taken over."

"Good, good," Amelia encouraged. "What else?"

"Cloud propaganda made my mom furious. Must have depressed her, too. She drank like a fish."

"And your father?"

"He divorced her about a year before . . . before her stroke."

Blaise whistled to himself and wiped tears from his eyes.

"It's OK, Blaise, take your time," Kristina soothed.

"He'd moved to Hong Kong to help refine the neural network. How I wanted to be with him! But my mom kept me in a shithole Atlanta apartment after we lose our house. Called him a fascist pig."

"She lost a world, Blaise," Kristina rejoined. "One she helped to build. Your father was instrumental in destroying it. But he did take you back after she passed."

"No. He sent me to prep school. Later he bought me a lieutenant's commission in the army. Then he got me into UCLA. I never saw him after that. He was terminated in one of the purges."

"And your mother was erased from history," Amelia put in.

"Erased?"

"She was more than a novelist, Blaise," Kristina said. "In her twenties she helped women like my mom establish the matriarchy. They eliminated racism, crushed corporate conglomerates, created a compassionate society."

"Yes! I remember now. She talked about El Dorado. That's what she called it. When she was drunk."

"If she had lived, she'd probably have become a hacker, like us," Kristina answered.

"How? She wasn't a programmer."

"Women like her who survived the matriarchy's fall started the hacker movement. She'd have joined us. Anyone that brilliant with words could learn how to code."

Blaise, seized by sudden emotion, choked back tears. He flashed on a memory of when he was seven or eight. He had lain on a blanket with his head in the lap of his attractive but sad-looking mother, a youngish-looking woman in her late forties. She had worn a white cotton dress, its color stark against fiery pink azalea bushes behind them. Above, in oak branches, squirrels had skittered about, and the calls of many birds had given the afternoon a special ambiance.

"Blaise, honey," she had told him in a voice like a song, "it's been devolution since the first Pharaoh gazed out over the first causeway in the first city he ruled. That cold, masculine eye that built empires, designed bridges, split atoms and enslaved the souls and bodies of women. That's the cost of civilization, darling. Perhaps our matriarchy was an aberration. We lost it all, Blaise. But not our souls. Whatever happens to us, whatever the world is becoming, remember always, in your heart:

'Blessed are those who hunger and thirst for righteousness, for they shall be satisfied.

Blessed are the merciful, for they shall receive mercy.

Blessed are the pure in heart, for they shall see God.' "

Blaise found himself back in the tiny living room with the two women. "Wish to God she had lived," he declared. "I do. When she wasn't drunk, she was wonderful. She read to me. Books. Poetry. Taught me how to be a storyteller. Rocked me back to sleep after my nightmares. The scent of her hair—was like cinnamon and cardamon. Like the whole of creation growing inside her. I loved her so."

"We know, Blaise," Kristina said. "We think you inherited her rebel spirit, too. You've got the chops to hack Cloud servers—and the balls, the killer instinct."

"You're wrong," Blaise groaned. "All the courage drained out of me after I left the army."

"Yet you kicked the shit out of those SWATs last night," Amelia put in. "To save a helpless Slag and his daughter."

"How do you know about that?"

"One of our people trailed you from the bullet station," Amelia answered.

"OK, you've done your homework on me. So what happens after, assuming your worm works? A new stone age?"

Kristina rose from the couch, approached Blaise, knelt, and took his hand. "We'll rebuild the world, Blaise. There are hacker cells like ours in every major city. Here. In Canada. Europe. Africa. Asia." She took a tiny box from the sleeve of her kimono and handed it to him. "The microchip. I'll show you how to upload it to your holodeck. It has a signal code that activates to let us know when it's online. You upload one module per week, so the servers won't detect them."

Blaise hesitated and then took the chip, thinking, *What have I got to lose? Only everything.*

Kristina looked pleased. "When you get your next weekend off, we'll rendezvous in Reseda, an abandoned town out in the valley. SWAT rarely patrols there. Reseda. Remember the name. We built a community in the ruins. I'll introduce you to the others. And show you something amazing."

Blaise trembled at the magnitude of what she was asking of him. Kristina glanced at Amelia.

"Mom, could you?"

Amelia nodded, heaved up, slipped out the door and shut it behind her. Kristina took Blaise's face in her hands and caressed his hair.

"You haven't known what's real for so long. It's hard to trust it when it comes. But trust this, Blaise. This moment is real. I'm real. You're real. And your soul is real. More real than you can imagine."

She slipped his hand inside her kimono and pressed it to her heart.

"You think your heart died? It didn't."

She slipped out of her kimono and joined her scented flesh to his, until her caresses relaxed his body. She helped him undress, and coaxed him gently, coyly, back into the primeval pleasures they had shared the night before.

5

IN HIS RUMPLED NAVY-BLUE JACKET AND PANTS, BLAISE WAITED
in a train car with several Slag laborers for the bullet to streak out of the station.
He had passed up the Class I car to be close to the Slags. These were the people
he planned to risk his life to save if he found the courage to upload Polyphemus.
Were they worth it? He studied his fellow passengers, the common clay who
labored and stank and died by the hundreds of millions.

Outside the open doors, a male android in a gold uniform and cap was
hunting for him on the platform.

"Mr. Pascal, really," the android pleaded. "You belong in the lead car, with
the other Class Is."

Blaise ducked in his seat, so the android missed him as it passed the train
window. The doors closed, and the train hurled itself ahead.

When they were underway, Blaise noticed two male Slags who were
commiserating in a seat nearby.

"Can't take it much longer," one said. "My back's killing me. I can't sleep."

"You got no choice. Work or starve."

"Easy for you to say."

"Think repairing cesspools is easy? I come home every night with the smell
of piss and shit in my nose."

The train slowed to stop at a station, and the Slags trudged off the car. Blaise
noticed two SWATS on the platform and averted his eyes. The SWATs didn't
even glance his way.

The doors slid shut. The train hummed then sped out of the station. Blaise
trembled and wiped the sweat from his brow and face. He watched the dark

tunnel rush by the train window. The bullet train braked for another station. As the doors slid open, he saw, out on the platform, a lofty green, spiny horror backing a Class II man into a corner. The Mantis's mandibles issued a dissonant chirring as it stretched a green claw down to the man's K-Spot. The man collapsed as if the Mantis had sucked the marrow from his bones. Then the Mantis swung its prayerful claws toward Blaise, and approached, mandibles working. The train hummed, but the door wouldn't close.

Minsheng knows everything!—flashed through Blaise's mind. *He sent it for me! Or that bitch Mitsuko!*

The Mantis hesitated. Its eyes glittered like molten jewels, its head swayed back and forth, its antennae whipped the air. It raised a claw on the fulcrum of a spiny joint and extended it. Toward Blaise? Or was it reaching for another terrified passenger in the next car? The pod-shaped body shuddered, dipped on spiny legs, described a half-circle, and swung round in the opposite direction. When it had turned completely away from Blaise, its head sprang back toward him. Then it turned, crawled toward his car, and made a sudden leap. Mercifully, the train doors slid shut just as the extended claw reached them. It took a few moments for Blaise's stomach to catch up as the city transport hurtled from the station.

Blaise had never seen anyone die from a Mantis strike before. The shock of the real thing struck him square in the face like pressurized ice water. His heart palpitated. His underarms bled cold sweat. He experienced the dimensional fracturing of a dreamer startled from a nightmare. After a blur of brilliant tunnel, Blaise welcomed the drag of deceleration as the car glided into his station. The doors hummed open. He released the belt-beam and fled, terrified that the Mantis would materialize there.

As he mounted the escalator, holographic ads with siren voices tempted him with "Blaise, Blaise, this style's for you," from adolescent citizen-models in pastel yellow, blue and mauve shrink-suits, blouses, skirts, and translucent shoes. Holographic arms caressed his face and body; spectral lips and pheromone-scented hair brushed his face. These ads were meant to titillate and arouse, but in his panic, he felt he was in one of those nightmares trying to run from a pursuing horror. His legs seemed to churn in place, while it loomed closer and closer to crush the dead weight of his thirty-eight years.

When he reached the upper bullet train lobby with its AI-generated neo-hip-hop tunes, the banality of this familiar setting helped to dispel his panic. No Mantis had pursued him here. He was home, safe. He stepped into the cool, dry, temperature-regulated moonlight of his pod, Shanghai Estates, a Class II live/work/play townlet with faux grass, tropical flower beds, and brick, chrome, and neon restaurants fronted by softly gliding sidewalks that unfurled like an endless flag. The walks contained a smattering of citizens; it was after two in the morning. A crescent moon blinked through a cloud bank far above the horizon. In the horseshoe bend of the avenue, an autobot car rolled driverless into a side street. Along the broad green space, California palms soughed in cinnamon-scented breeze laced with pheromones to put him in the mood for his CereFuck.

Just past The Baying Wolf pub's faux Irish facade, he eye-scanned his way into his condo tower. Already the horror of his encounter with the Mantis was fading from memory, at least for now.

Freddy, the lobby android, with his impeccable silicone skin and gray Class V linen jacket, grinned as Blaise passed him under acrylic chandeliers.

"Welcome home, Mr. Pascal," Freddy chirped in a voice programmed for empathy. "New VR series re-running in five. You won't want to miss it: sex-slaughter index of nine." He chuckled to establish complicity in the pleasures to come, but it was a kind of laughter that had no lungs behind it.

Blaise tossed him a withering glance. He despised flesh-bots like Freddy, so crudely designed in comparison to his own sleek VR creations. He boarded the lift, shot up to thirty-six, and hustled down the brilliant corridor, hoping to avoid neighbors returning from their own carousing. To his bitter disappointment, he ran into Hu Long, a tall, lanky Chinese Class II, who muttered " 'H'lo" and hastened past, frowning, to the lift, as anxious to avoid Blaise as Blaise was to duck him. This revulsion was, Blaise suspected, an inevitable consequence of VR addiction. It made flesh-and-blood people, with their blemishes, odors, and nervous ticks, an unbearable offense to the senses. Aside from the Slag Zone, where unimproved flesh satisfied an exquisite hunger, like devouring a rare steak after a diet of tofu and salad, it was disgusting to meet another Class I or II. At work, you could compress them into the undifferentiated category of colleague, interchangeable binary units processing Cloud tasks, of no more impact than pulsing holodeck images. But here on the outside, a close encounter with another actual colleague was like blundering into a zoo: a malodorous reminder of the primeval animal beneath the prosthetic surgical enhancements and cosmetic body-scent that were de rigueur in the professional classes. He was relieved after he eye-scanned his door open.

The condo was as silent and empty as his hope for the covert mission Kristina had convinced him to undertake.

6

A WALL-SIZED HOLODECK SCREEN CRACKLED WITH CYBERNETIC
pseudo-life as Blaise coded the Anima drug into his *Gilgamesh V* storyline with
mounting dread and disgust for what he was doing. He had a small screen for
monitoring his code and a 3D one that previewed emerging scenes before they
appeared on the wall screen. He burned his way by slow degrees through code
until his voice grew so hoarse from verbal commands he resorted to a vintage
ergonomic keyboard to keep the rhythm going.

Behind his focused expression and artful commands lay stunned disbelief at
how he had managed to smuggle in the Polyphemus virus. Kristina had sewn the
microchip into his jacket lining and had explained it was coated with a cloaking
chemical that would get it through SWAT security checks. He had promised he
would upload a module each week, four modules in all, through the secure
Gilgamesh V server. But after his mind-rattling encounter with the Mantis in the
bullet station, he couldn't bring himself to risk even the first module. He
lacerated himself for his cowardice, but self-loathing was poor competition for
his terror of being vaporized. Even with his EEG monitoring deactivated,
something might give him away. He was walled off from colleagues in his
luminescent new office. But there were other forms of surveillance: spy drones
that flitted through office corridors like bats and old-school eye-scan cameras.
And despite Kristina's assurances to the contrary, Blaise knew there was every
chance that the Cloud AI-based firewalls would detect the upload attempt. Every
creak of his cockpit chair mimicked, in his mind, Mantis chirruping and
generated images of the appalling creature performing its spidery dance on the

bullet platform, as if to taunt—or perhaps warn him he was next if he didn't perform as expected. Who, he wondered, had sent the Mantis rushing for his bullet train car? And who had prevented it from terminating him?

Mitsuko startled him from his thoughts as she glided into his office pod in her new blue silk Class I supervisor's jacket with the sun disk director's pin.

"Sorry to interrupt your daydreaming," she lisped with oily aplomb. "Maybe we should do some coding this morning. Or are you too busy?"

Blaise rolled his eyes. "I'm always too busy for you."

"Keep rolling your eyes; maybe you'll find a brain back there."

"You know, Mitsuko, some people are like clouds. When they disappear, it's a beautiful day."

"Awww, you don't like me?" she mocked as she settled into a cockpit chair next to him and wafted her fetching perfume his way. "What a shame. I'll need a few instants to recover from the tragedy. So let's recap. Where's the biggest coding logjam in your view?"

"You really think I care what you think about coding logjams? How cute."

Mitsuko was the one who rolled her eyes now. "I look at you sometimes and wonder, 'Really? That's the sperm that won?' "

They kept up this acidic banter until daunting coding challenges absorbed them. Mitsuko considered herself a player now and brilliant enough to steal Blaise's thunder. Blaise blamed himself for this dispiriting development. His turmoil over colluding in genocide and his guilt over failing to upload the modules had slowed his creative momentum. Mitsuko had taken advantage of this to convince Minsheng to let her help Blaise through some of the toughest patches of *Gilgamesh V*—agonizing stretches of coding that would have broken a less gifted programmer, and which Blaise found even more excruciating given his horror about what he was creating. Besides, he had always prided himself as a rebel who coded alone, except for the boring, repetitive work he delegated to assistant games planners. It was infuriating to have Mitsuko insinuate herself into his daily round.

By this point, Mitsuko had made enough headway as his Gilgamesh co-creator to force Blaise's grudging concession that she possessed serious coding talent—a strength she hadn't demonstrated since taking on her administrative role several years back. Her collaboration with Blaise also impressed Minsheng. He ordered them to continue it, saying he couldn't afford to let the timeline slip. The board in Hong Kong had forced his hand, he claimed, and made him commit to delivering *Gilgamesh V* to Vidracom for global distribution in ninety days or less. Blaise suspected Mitsuko was behind this shift in policy. She had probably spoken to influential colleagues she knew in Hong Kong, and had promised to repay them with promotions after she scored her victory as co-creator of *Gilgamesh V*, which would propel her up the management food chain. So the board had ordered Minsheng to grant her a chance to shine, and Blaise had to resign himself to slogging through coding with her as many as sixteen hours a day. Often during these sessions he longed for Kristina, who lingered in his heart with salvific intensity, and he burned with the urge to upload the Polyphemus modules and rid the world of The Cloud; but Mitsuko, who watched his every move, would certainly see and send the Mantis for him. He had to find the right moment to make his move. But would the courage to risk that ever come?

When he couldn't bear Mitsuko's presence anymore, he complained to Minsheng, and told him she was hampering his progress.

"You have your orders," Minsheng countered with an opaque expression in his one good eye.

Seeing there was no way to get rid of her, Blaise suggested a middle path. "If she's got to be part of this, let her code from her own holodeck."

"Not possible," Minsheng retorted. "She doesn't have level-five security clearance. Only the global security director in Hong Kong can authorize that, and he moves like a glacier. Learn to tolerate her."

Blaise bit off his resentment and reflected, not without guilty relief, that even if he could summon the nerve to upload the Polyphemus worm, Mitsuko's intrusion made it impossible.

"By the way, the director has invited us to his estate this weekend," she mentioned to Blaise after they finished a particularly grueling coding session. "Some board members from Hong Kong will be there. They want to meet us."

Blaise realized with a sinking heart that Minsheng would expect him to escort Mitsuko to this posh event in an autobot. That meant making small talk with her all the way out to Minsheng's spread in San Fernando Valley. Mitsuko was the last person on earth he wanted to socialize with. She would report everything back to Minsheng, so Blaise would have to guard every word, each glance, and convince her his only concern was career advancement. But she was only the first hurdle in the minefield he would cross during a weekend spent rubbing shoulders with ego-bloated executives who had the power of life and death.

"Is the director sending autobots for us?" Blaise demanded to irritate Mitsuko; he already knew the answer.

Bitterness slipped through a crack in her elegant façade. "Class Is are expected to provide their own transportation. And the director would like us to attend together."

That meant Blaise and Mitsuko would have to split a two-day autobot rental, which would set them each back half a month's salary. Even with his hefty pay raise, Blaise could scarcely afford that, and it would be a hardship for Mitsuko, too, since she was widowed and supported a daughter attending a boarding school back east.

Why did the director want to throw them together outside the office? Romantic intrigue between them could put him at serious risk; they might conspire against him. Minsheng had used similar tactics himself during his climb up the Mythoplex ladder. But he wasn't a fool; the possibility of their collusion had undoubtedly occurred to him, and he was prepared. He obviously saw everyone, including them, as bacterial infections to amuse himself with until he chose to eradicate them. If he wanted Blaise and Mitsuko together, it could only be to make them more fully his slaves by addicting them to each other.

Blaise suddenly wanted to murder Minsheng and Mitsuko and escape their infernal stratagems, but that would be suicide and eliminate his ghost of a chance to upload Polyphemus. His head spun at the hallucinatory turn his life had taken.

Mitsuko cleared her throat. "I suggest we . . . share the expense."

"Yeah, know," Blaise sighed. "I'll reserve an autobot. I'll just need your credit chip." Then he couldn't resist a gibe at her. "You got one of those, don't you?"

She turned from the holoscreen to glare at him. "I don't like the idea of traveling with you any more than you do. But alpha females like me don't run in packs. So you'll have to leave your Slag whores at home and your sarcastic mouth, too."

She dug in her blood-colored purse and then shoved a wafer-thin credit chip into the holodeck payment slot next to his. He made the reservation with a few curt commands.

———◆———

The next morning Blaise pushed his heavy luggage on a hover cart down the hall to the lift. He assumed he would have to be well-dressed, with a change of clothes for each event, considering the Cloud luminaries attending.

Freddy, the lobby bot, lugged the bags outside and stowed them in the trunk of a thrumming autobot, which opened its door in a clean vertical arc. As the door swung closed, a Beethoven piano sonata Blaise had pre-requested flooded the compartment.

"Destination?" a female voice soothed.

"Ultimate destination 800 Carrer de Minerva, San Fernando Valley. But first, we have a pickup in the Clint Eastwood Condoplex. A Ms. Mitsuko Brown."

Later, when Mitsuko had settled into the compartment, and they hummed along the empty sunbaked freeway that knifed into the Valley, Blaise's eyes traveled her shapely legs. He admired the cut of her maroon mini-kimono accented by white cherry blossoms, despite the fact that he despised her. Yet here she was, in collusion with him, his new coding partner in the Cloud's Final Solution for Slags. And as much as he hated to admit it, Mitsuko symbolized power and prestige won against incredible odds, and it made her damnably attractive. Suddenly, he wished with mortal longing he could forget Kristina and Amelia and their futile plan. Maybe, after all, they were a VR projection the director had engineered to let Blaise toy with betrayal before committing himself to the *Homo Deus* age. Perhaps Kristina's prediction that the director would eventually terminate him was wrong, and Blaise would become immortal.

Mitsuko met his glance with a guarded expression as they bantered about office trivia and assassinated colleagues' characters. The wine dispenser replenished their glasses with good, sturdy Pinot Noir. Blaise wanted sake, but there was none to be had except in the Zone. He reflected bitterly about how the board had outlawed high-grade sake in North Am to support Asia's dominance in the rice wine market, leaving only the middling-quality black market swill Blaise favored.

They had a long drive ahead. Silence between them wouldn't play well with Minsheng when Mitsuko reported it. Blaise knew vanity ruled Mitsuko's heart, so he had little choice but to feign interest in her background.

"So, you grew up in Beijing? Amazing city, from what I hear."

Mitsuko glanced at him and, obviously drunk enough to take the bait, replied, "Yes. It's quite beautiful. My father was born there."

"No shit? So when'd you move to L.A.?"

"Ten years ago," she replied. "The director brought me over. We were both at Mythoplex in Hong Kong."

"You worked in the capital? Impressive."

Something in his tone obviously rubbed her the wrong way. "Why the sudden interest in my background?"

He tried to laugh off her objection with a shrug. "Long drive, and nobody else to talk to."

She studied his face for signs of trouble. "Why should I tell you anything you might use against me later?"

Blaise let out a chuckle. "What are you worried about? You're Minsheng's golden girl."

"Hardly. But even if I were, you'd have nothing but contempt for it, like you do for everything else."

He shrugged. "So I'm an asshole. But we're stuck with each other this weekend, right? So, let's try to keep it friendly. Who knows what kind of games Minsheng's crowd may get up to? Right now, they see us as two patriotic techies helping them rid the world of the underclass. Wouldn't be smart to show them we actually despise each other."

She thought that over for a bit, studying the desert as it rushed by outside.

"Come on, loosen up," he urged. "It'll look better to them if we know a little bit about each other. What was it like growing up in Beijing? You were a little princess, right? Must have been pretty sweet for you."

She considered her answer before she replied. "We were very comfortable. The director knew my father. They served together in the Caliphate wars. Then they made a fortune in weapons manufacture."

"And you wind up in Hong Kong. Amazing. Never been there except in VR feeds. Must be stupendous. Who'd have thought the Hong Kong global banking conglomerate could seize power from that tottering Beijing communist regime? Nobody talks about it much—too scared of the Cloud Monitor picking up errant EEGs—but I heard Beijing bankrupted itself by spending too much on foreign wars. That and over-producing consumer goods to keep the population quiescent after communism had become intolerable. Only Hong Kong realized a corporate oligarchy armed with Beijing's surveillance tech could produce the global empire those communist dinosaurs lusted for."

She gave him a long, hard glance. "Are you jealous of my time in the capital?"

"Can't I admire the capital? Everything's not all about you."

"I didn't say it was."

Mitsuko noticed how his eyes traced the line of her skirt up her back and around to the silken opening of her blouse. That seemed to reassure her. She smiled the smile of vanity and spoke words oiled by wine.

"Hong Kong's nice to look at, but unbearably old," she admitted. "Everything there stinks of tradition. I was glad to get out. Life's looser in North Am. L.A., particularly."

"Yeah, know," he agreed—though he wasn't sure what she was implying. He dispensed another glass of Pinot Noir.

"And you?" she inquired. "Where'd you grow up, Mr. Number One VR Series?"

Blaise grinned at her implied jealousy. "Atlanta, on the east coast. My family's old American Southern. A bit petrified, like Hong Kong from the sound of it. My mother was a novelist."

"A novelist?"

"Oh, yeah. She actually wrote printed books, back when people read them. Made decent money at it, too."

"And your father?"

"Mythoplex computer engineer. I barely knew him. He sent me to good schools. Bought my army lieutenant's commission. Pulled some strings to snag me a scholarship to UCLA. But my creativity, my love of art—that's my mom's doing."

Mitsuko pursed her lips in a frown. She never liked to hear any praise for another woman.

"I had a minor in art," she revealed. "I've always had a sense of design and color."

Her cologne, hair oil, and Japanese skin lotion intoxicated Blaise despite his better judgment. He wondered what she might do if he slid over and nuzzled her neck. But he sniffed something wrong: the faintest hint of musk. That didn't fit Mitsuko's natural or enhanced fragrances, so where was it coming from? Then it struck him: pheromone scent! Someone—probably at Minsheng's bidding—must have planted it in the autobot's air-conditioning system to waft Blaise and Mitsuko into each other's arms. That's what had loosened their tongues and softened their patter to the pleasantries they had just exchanged.

"To hell with this," Blaise muttered. "Coffee, black," he ordered the beverage dispenser and slid as far away from Mitsuko as his seat allowed.

Mitsuko, displeased, or perhaps bored by his silence, drifted into her own thoughts. Half an hour later, the autobot turned off the freeway into a side road. Cactus, tumbleweeds, and arroyos encircled them. It was early afternoon. Outside, the sun had baked the landscape in shades of brown, gold, and chalk. Blaise recalled that North American Indian tribes once lived here, hunter-gatherers who knew how to get water from cactus and roots, or so legend had it. He traced the irregular declivities, the immeasurable tracts of white and yellow sand, rocky outcroppings and gullies where flash floods had washed away soil and rearranged the colorscape. Why had Minsheng chosen such a desolate place for his palace? Perhaps to ensure his victims had nowhere to run when the torture and slaughter began.

"How did the director manage to build an estate way out here?" Blaise asked in a tone of feigned wonder, as if he admired Minsheng's extravagance.

Mitsuko peered out at the unfathomable desert. "It was here long before the board promoted him to director. It belonged to a movie producer back when they still called it Hollywood."

"Impressive. Have you been here before?"

Mitsuko shot him a dark look. "Never. He was close to my father, not me. He's treated me like just another employee from the start. I've clawed my way up . . . despite him."

This boast was meant to impress Blaise, but instead, it wrenched his heart to think that his own trepidations might tempt him to betray Kristina and the other hackers for Mitsuko, Minsheng, and the other sociopathic corporate types he would soon meet.

"Quite an achievement for you," he lied.

After what felt to Blaise like an eternity, they reached the estate compound, which spread to the horizon behind a shimmering security shield. They passed from desert to grassland watered by sprinklers that described arcs thousands of meters wide. The autobot slowed while something scanned its CPU; then, the car accelerated. The translucent security shield curved above them into the far reaches of the sky, where a Cloud air force hover-gunship streaked by. What was it patrolling for? Interlopers? No one could sneak in through the security shield they had just passed through. The gunship was probably hunting victims trying to escape the director's hospitality. Dread gripped Blaise's heart. He had entered Minsheng's lair, and he had no idea what might be coming or whether he would leave here alive.

They reached irrigated fields with palms, desert flora, and a vineyard with grape clusters spreading away in clean, robotically-manicured rows. Blaise couldn't imagine what it cost to water such a spread: a sum far beyond the director's salary and Mythoplex stock options. Clearly, Minsheng had raked in billions from armament conglomerates that fed the endless Caliphate wars.

A whitish shape loomed at the horizon. As they approached it, Blaise noticed how Minsheng's mansion adhered to the style and grace of a Roman villa, surrounded by cypress and Italian stone pines. Here, under the security dome, semi-tropical conditions prevailed. A lake sheltered swans, whether products of nature or cybernetic engineering, Blaise couldn't tell. It was a vista meant to inspire wonder, but to Blaise, it looked like a foreboding tableau hiding lethal traps.

Beyond the lake, rosebushes fronted a columned terrace. A four-level fountain gushed into a marble basin supported by stone dryads. Behind the fountain, stairs climbed to a broad façade, built around a reproduction of the Arch of Constantine in Rome. From this focal point, the mansion spread away in wings under a higher, recessed story inset with temples supported by Doric columns. A driveway curved around the lake in an ascending arc of dressed stone blocks that issued onto a plateau where dozens of other autobots had parked. Their car glided up to an entrance flanked by Corinthian columns and a ceiling with Roman mosaics depicting family life. Armed SWATs in black uniforms patrolled the perimeter. Four slender, handsome Slag men in pale blue cloaks approached.

As the autobot door glided up, one cried, "Welcome to Villa Minsheng Lu!" He extended a hand to help Mitsuko from the back seat. "We'll carry in your luggage, ma'am. May we ask your names?"

Blaise climbed out after Mitsuko, scoping out his surroundings, his heart pounding with trepidation about what might be waiting in this bloated palladium.

Mitsuko smiled at the attendant's comely face and biceps. "Ms. Mitsuko Brown, Class I. And this is Mr. Blaise Pascal VII, also Class I."

"The director is expecting you. Your suites are just this way."

Blaise glanced nervously back at the SWATs as their entourage passed under a curved ceiling with erotic frescos. Beyond lay an atrium with a vaulted ceiling, corridors punctuated by gardens, pools with giant koi, and more corridors and gardens. Finally, they reached an atrium in the center of which stood the statue of a boy with bronze arms raised toward a skylight. Beyond a portico with fretted borders lay a columned garden open to the sky, and beyond that another atrium and garden, and another and another, as if to infinity.

Blaise scanned the walls for surveillance cameras. None were visible. Then, beyond an adjoining garden, he saw something airborne glide past in a corridor—a surveillance drone. Minsheng was watching them. And to what purpose? Had they reached the center of the director's labyrinth? Or was this only the periphery of a fractal maze reflecting the dark intricacies of Minsheng's mind? Had the director seen through Blaise's pretense of loyalty? Did he know Blaise had nearly killed the two SWATs back in the Zone? Did he know about the Polyphemus worm? Had he decided to let Mitsuko complete the series and murder Blaise by Mantis claw, or in some even more horrible and protracted fashion?

Blaise wondered how many guests before him had pondered such possibilities. He mentally retraced the corridors he and Mitsuko had just passed through, the bends and turns, the foliage, flowers, and fountains they had seen, the pale, freckled and dark-skinned attendants in blue tunics, whose smiles promised pleasure and indulgence.

Could he find his way back to the entrance and make a run for it if he had to? Or had Minsheng designed this maze to encourage—and then frustrate—escape once his victims realized what was in store for them? Even if Blaise could dodge the attendants and find his way back to the parking area, could he get past the SWATs guarding it? If he did manage to slip away in his autobot, the chances were slim that he could dodge the aerial gunship he had seen circling the sky like a vulture.

He repeated his mantra to calm himself down. Perhaps, after all, his fear was unfounded. Maybe Minsheng was going to let him finish *Gilgamesh V*. If that was the case, Blaise's best chance of survival lay in giving an award-winning performance to convince the director of his loyalty. Then, back in L.A., he could take his shot at uploading Polyphemus.

"Ms. Mitsuko," one of the attendants lisped.

His voice startled Blaise from his reverie.

"This is your suite," the attendant continued. "Inside, you'll find gowns, headdresses, sandals, cosmetics and perfumes from the first century BCE. Dress in your selection and issue a voice summons to the holoscreen. One of us will escort you to Director Minsheng's banquet."

Another attendant approached Blaise. "Your suite, Mr. Pascal," he beamed and gestured with a freckled arm.

The door swung open with a robotic click. The attendant showed Blaise inside and fetched his luggage from the hover cart thrumming outside in the atrium. Blaise found himself in a room with cream-colored walls divided by maroon-striped borders, hung with paintings of climbing vines and Cupids bearing lyres. There was a klinai covered in striped cloth with tasseled pillows, a circular table with fruit bowl, two wicker chairs, and an oak cabinet. In one wall, a holodeck stared blank and black. The attendant showed Blaise to a bathroom with a Japanese-style suction toilet, a mirror and sink, and a shower with erotic frescos. It all looked inviting, but this could be nothing more than an elegant prison cell, meant to give Blaise a false sense of security, just before the attendants dragged him before Minsheng and his guests to entertain them with his death agony.

"Class I males wear senatorial togas and sandals to the banquet," the attendant lisped. "You'll find everything in the bathroom, including nard-based hair pomade and sheep intestine prophylactics—though of course the sheep guts are props, for those who prefer historical authenticity. Usually after sex, Class I ladies take a morning-after pill. You won't gain half a kilo of weight this weekend, thanks to the vomitorium, or be troubled by any unwanted pregnancies, Mr. Pascal."

So apparently, Blaise was expected at the orgy. His termination would come later in the weekend, if it came at all. But why obligate Blaise to consort with the global players Minsheng had invited here if he didn't plan to keep him alive? Blaise sighed at the futility of trying to attribute rational motives to a madman who planned to annihilate billions.

"I'm curious," he commented in a blasé tone meant to hide his anxiety. "How many board members are attending?"

The attendant bowed and spoke to the holoscreen. "Guest list, please."

A video collage displayed footage of luminaries from Hong Kong, Toronto, Johannesburg, Tokyo, and Sydney, executives of frightening and legendary power whom Blaise recognized from neurofeeds.

"The director expects you and Ms. Mitsuko in an hour," the attendant informed him with a smile that deepened the dimples in his freckled cheeks. "Please issue a voice command when you're dressed."

He bowed and left. Blaise pondered what it was going to be like to mix with Minsheng's crowd. What if he disappointed or angered some Olympian executive who could summon the Mantis?

Later, dressed in a toga praetexta, Blaise considered himself in the bathroom mirror. He had to admit, he liked the robe's sweeping folds and scarlet border, but the sandals pinched. In the bedroom, he issued a summons to the holoscreen. Moments later a knock came. When he opened the door, he found Mitsuko in a blue silk gown with her hair piled up Roman style, accented by a tiara. As much as he disliked her, Blaise had to admit she was ravishing.

"We're expected to go in as a couple," she mentioned in a hesitant tone. Undoubtedly, she disliked him as much as he did her, but they both had to make the best of it.

They followed two attendants who waited outside. After many porticos and gardens, they reached their destination. Exotic aromas and fluted and stringed instruments greeted them as they passed through bronze doors into a hall with a floor of green-striped marble squares bordered by maroon tiles. Triclinia abutted the walls before tables laden with food. At the back, a fresco depicted temple colonnades and misty mountains. Slags in brown robes served delicacies to some two hundred mostly male Class Is in togas and gowns. The executives reclined on sides and bellies, a mix of Asians, Caucasians, Indians, and Africans.

A horn brayed. Six slender, naked Slag boys pulled in a gold and alabaster chariot. They circled the floor before coming to rest before an elevated couch. Minsheng stepped out in imperial purple and laurel crown. He dismissed the chariot and reclined with aplomb, attended by serving girls in pink gowns. He surveyed his guests and raised a silver goblet when he spotted Blaise and Mitsuko.

Their escorts showed them to adjoining triclinia. Servers arrived to fill wine goblets and serve platters of pheasant, thrush, wild boar, oysters, lobster, venison, and a sweet-sour gelatinous delicacy Blaise had never seen before. He and Mitsuko set to with Roman spoons and found everything delicious. Along one wall, boilers, similar to samovars, emptied hot water into tureens. Slags ladled wine mixed with water into flagons from which others filled goblets to slake serious executive thirsts. On the floor, teenaged girls and boys in translucent robes whirled about in balletic arcs. As dancer after dancer stripped naked, others carried them to stages formed by human trellises that lifted them like sacrifices to some priapic god. Periodically, a dancer pirouetted over, fragrant and sweating, and crawled into an executive lap like a spider.

"All a bit Felliniesque, no?" a male voice whispered to Blaise.

Blaise turned to the wry grin of a square-jawed sub-Saharan of noble bearing in a Roman general's uniform.

"I mean seriously, how gauche can Minsheng be?" the man guffawed in a rich baritone.

Blaise gave him a blank stare. How could anyone dare speak of the director this way?

"Why would anyone set himself up in a renovated villa straight out of a VR series? A Roman orgy? Please! It's too vulgar."

"I see," Blaise responded, not sure what else to say to this imposing figure.

"In Tokyo, these events feature cosplay stars, creamy-skinned Japanese sluts stripping out of intricate kimonos, and super-heroine costumes. Much more stimulating and artful."

Blaise feigned a smile and nodded.

"Ah, but how rude of me." The man extended a hand that gripped Blaise's with near-crushing strength. "Jacob Zuma IV, Johannesburg." And then, as if that weren't impressive enough, he added, "Deputy Chairman of the Board."

"Pleasure to meet you, Deputy Chairman," Blaise replied with his heart in his mouth. "I'm—"

"Blaise Pascal VII, the genius behind *Gilgamesh V*. And your charming companion?"

Mitsuko had taken a male dancer across her lap and stroked him like a Persian cat.

"Mitsuko Brown."

"A brilliant mythologizer in her own right, but not in your league, of course," Zuma affirmed. "Tell me, how on earth do you manage to come up with such exotic storylines? Your creative range is phenomenal."

Blaise shrugged off the compliment. It was best not to appear too vain in a powerful executive's eyes. "My mother taught me the classics."

Zuma let out a hearty laugh. "Such modesty. It's charming, really. And here you are, named after the inventor of one of the first computers."

"That was my father's idea."

"But really, Blaise Pascal. Stunning! Back in the seventeenth century, your namesake said we're all betting our lives on whether or not God exists. Think he was onto something with Pascal's wager?"

"I couldn't say."

"Does the question interest you?"

"Not really.

"No?

"No, sir. I did a survey course in ancient religious mythologies at UCLA, but the so-called sacred texts those myths are based on have been deleted from databases. There's no point in speculating about them. Why do you ask?"

"Simple curiosity. Director Minsheng says you have a brilliant, probing mind."

Was Zuma trying to lure Blaise into disparaging remarks about Minsheng? Or did he want an ally against the director?

"Tell me, given Minsheng's plan to annihilate all Slags with Anima, what's your opinion about his notion for tidy disposal of Slag bodies?"

"He hasn't discussed that with me," Blaise answered carefully. Zuma could be probing to determine Blaise's loyalty and report his findings back to Minsheng. Or perhaps he wanted Blaise to engage in a plot against Minsheng, who was now Zuma's competitor on the Cloud board.

"Really?" Zuma smiled. "Well, perhaps you've noticed the new geodesic incinerator going up in L.A. They had to roll aside two treaded robotic skyscrapers to make room for it. Similar incinerators are going up in every major city. Minsheng plans to divert regiments from our military to dispose of Slag bodies. I wonder how wise that is, now that the Caliphate's launched this new war."

A thought struck Blaise. Might the C-suite oligarchs like Zuma be considering Blaise for a board slot? Improbable as it was, other top games planners had ascended to that rank. Blaise's ego swelled into immensity. At the same time he felt a guilty pang for mentally betraying his promise to Kristina and Amelia. But wasn't it lunacy to think the Polyphemus worm could work? The Cloud Monitor would detect the attempt, and he would be dead and all hope for Polyphemus lost. Suddenly, he hated Kristina for convincing him to risk it. At the same time, the memory of her brought a pang of longing and desire.

Blaise signaled a serving boy for more wine. It had a salutary effect. That, and also the pheromone scent Minsheng had undoubtedly released in the hall. Blaise glanced at Mitsuko, who had lost track of her serving boy and eyed Blaise with relish, her lashes half-closed, strands of her hair loose about her slender face. The wine and pheromones had apparently changed her loathing for Blaise into lust. Perhaps she had always harbored some nascent desire for him, despite her hatred for everything he represented.

She brought her lips close and whispered, "Make love to me."

Succumbing to an attraction he had long suppressed, he gave her a deep kiss and slipped his hand under her gown to her swelling breasts.

Many around the hall were kissing and humping. Then came a new and unexpected delight: from ceiling fissures, rose petals fluttered down in delicate, tumbling masses, collected on the floor, and came to rest on food dishes, drinking cups, and bodies greased with food, sweat, and sexual juices.

As he caressed Mitsuko, Blaise heard Zuma's baritone in his ear. "'Everything is impossible until it's done.' A great man from my country, Nelson Mandela, uttered that. In my experience, however, the impossible stays impossible. Unless you have the will to transcend it."

Blaise broke from Mitsuko long enough to smile at this enigmatic remark. He studied Zuma's beaming face to see if he meant it as a compliment to Minsheng or an insult.

Zuma gestured Blaise closer and breathed in his ear. "Would you care to indulge in a special little entertainment? Nothing like Director Minsheng's vulgar spectacle. It's, how shall I put it, a special prerogative. An amusement for the discerning."

Mitsuko nuzzled his neck. Blaise wanted her, but something in Zuma's voice intrigued him enough to push her away.

"What did you have in mind, sir?"

Zuma gestured to a Slag, who approached with a frightened smile. His expression softened after Zuma whispered to him.

The Slag rushed away to one of his pals, then returned. "In the senate chamber, sir."

"Shall we?" Zuma inquired. He rose in his gold breastplate and scarlet cloak. His gladius clinked in its sheath.

Blaise couldn't refuse an invitation from the deputy director of the board. He heaved up unsteadily but managed a polite bow to Zuma. Mitsuko glared at him, then pulled a new serving boy into her lap.

The Slag guided Blaise and Zuma through a rain of rose petals that gathered in greater and greater masses on the floor. Blaise felt grateful to escape the orgy.

It stank too much of Minsheng and his baroque decadence. After a corridor with colorful frescos, Blaise and Zume came to a fragrant garden and approached a bronze door that swung open of its own accord. Encircling a tiled floor emblazoned with the imperial Roman eagle, two dozen executives in togas reclined and chatted. After Zuma showed Blaise to a marble bench, an anticipatory vibration hummed through the chamber. Conversations died as the executives turned their attention to the pit.

"I think you're going to enjoy this," Zuma whispered, his breath oiled with wine.

Electronic whirring echoed, and the pit turned in graceful arcs as it gathered momentum and descended into black, which closed over it like a great eyelid. Then came cries, harsh commands, and more whirring. The eyelid opened, and the floor ascended, no longer turning and no longer empty. A dozen Class III and IV sub-executives in linen jackets huddled in the pit, pale and trembling. They glanced about like startled birds. Harper, Blaise's subordinate, was one of them.

"In Johannesburg we have the Diepsloot township," Zuma whispered. "Have you heard of it?"

"I'm afraid not."

"Just north of the suburbs. A relic from the days of apartheid. A place where the desperate poor eke out short, brutal lives. More than a century after Mandela became President, Diepsloot is alive and festering with the puss of a million wounded souls. I was among the one-hundredth-of-one percent who escaped by winning a scholarship to a Mythoplex university. Spent years clawing my way up. Now, here I am on the board of directors. I assure you, Blaise, the elite rise to the top because they are born to rise. The rest get what they deserve."

On all sides executives leaned toward the pit while the sub-executives blinked back at them with bovine eyes. The executives raised their arms, palms down, as if to bestow a blessing. Zuma gestured for Blaise to raise his arms, too. Blaise did, though he had no idea what he was doing or why.

In the pit, a nimbus of firefly lights coalesced. A towering green-clawed apparition materialized with a scraping like crickets, magnified by many orders of magnitude. The sub-executives fled like lemmings, but a force field stopped them cold at the pit's perimeter. Their screams pierced the chamber like pigs in a slaughterhouse as the Mantis crawled after them on spiked legs. They darted and ducked its claw, screamed for mercy, or protested their innocence. Blaise struggled to keep his eyes off Harper, his gaze blurred by watery eyes. The Mantis cornered and finished them one by one. When the last victim collapsed, the Mantis turned translucent and vanished into the electric mist from which it had emerged.

Blaise heard Zuma's oily whisper in his ear. "How does it feel to be a god?"

7

BLAISE SAT BOLT UPRIGHT FROM A NIGHTMARE FILLED WITH the screams of pigs and the brassy tang of spilled blood. Two Slag attendants in blue tunics smiled at his bedside. For what? For the pleasure of murdering him? His heart beat a tattoo against his ribs. His nightmare was far from over.

"The director would like to invite you to breakfast," one of the Slags informed him. "We'll show you to his suite."

The hallucinatory events of the previous night rushed back to Blaise in all their horror. The orgy, the encounter with Zuma, the slaughter in the senate chamber. Was the director going to congratulate him this morning for his performance at the mass execution or vaporize him for failing to show sufficient enthusiasm? Or did Minsheng have other tortures in mind?

"Wait in the corridor while I clean up," was all Blaise could think to say to the attendants.

They bowed and pulled the heavy door to his suite shut behind them.

Blaise washed up and pulled on his toga and sandals. He chanted his mantra and tried, unsuccessfully, to silence the wires of terror pulsing in his veins. What was about to happen? What did Minsheng have up his sleeve? Was there any escape from him, other than groveling?

The attendants guided Blaise through corridor after corridor. In his panicked state, the marble floors echoed his footsteps with reports as fatalistic as the blows of a judge's gavel. Should he run? Run where? Run how? He felt as trapped in Minsheng's labyrinth as those sub-executives trying to flee the Mantis in the senatorial pit. In a burst of nostalgia, Blaise recalled the sights, sounds, and smells of the Slag Zone back in L.A. He longed for that squalid district as if it were a lost paradise, infinitely preferable to the opulent hell he was trapped in now.

They reached a bronze door which swung inward. The attendants showed him through an enormous bedroom suite with wall mosaics depicting orgies. They led him onto a balcony overlooking a stunning vista of vineyards, watered by giant sprinklers spewing far across the hermetically-sealed desert. The temperature was pleasantly warm and humid, unlike L.A.'s blistering heat.

Minsheng, in his imperial robe, reclined on a triclinium, while a naked Slag girl gave him a foot massage and another fed him an omelet with a side of the gelatinous delicacy Blaise had sampled at the banquet. A breeze carried from the vineyards, but in Blaise's state, the whisper of soft winds struck his fractured nerves like the report of gunshots. Minsheng gestured him to a place beside him.

"Please help yourself. Ostrich omelet and pickled jellyfish."

As another Slag girl dished up, Blaise's stomach heaved. "I'll pass on the jellyfish, thank you," he croaked.

Disgusted and frightened as he was to share breakfast with the madman who had orchestrated last night's slaughter, Blaise set to with the omelet, but he managed only a few bites; his queasy stomach nearly made him gag. He graced the director with a trembling smile while the serving girl poured mulled wine with water for him. Minsheng signaled the naked girl to remove Blaise's sandals and massage his feet. Blaise's nerves were so on edge her touch sent electric jolts of pain through his body.

Blaise wondered if he could make a dash across the vineyard if things went south. Scanning the horizon, he noticed what looked like silver towers rising up from behind a distant hillcrest: new construction, perhaps for another, even grander villa to stroke Minsheng's bloated ego. Then he saw an air force gunship streak far overhead. No use trying to run, not from a heat-signature-targeting laser cannon.

The director beckoned for the naked girl to return to him. He fondled her pear-shaped breasts like a shopper squeezing oranges at the supermarket.

"Blaise," he mused, "when I was a boy, my honored father told me life's value is measured by scale. Do you follow me?"

"I'm . . . not sure, sir."

Minsheng smiled indulgently. "Most of the so-called human race, have, at most, a postage stamp of scale. They orbit their days like flies circling a turd. The sum total of what they think, feel, and do is squalid, brief, and insignificant. Whereas those of us who follow our deepest urges to the limits—well, we attain scale. Do you take my meaning?"

"I . . . think so, sir," Blaise returned, trying to figure out where the director was headed with this.

Minsheng gestured for the naked girl to go to Blaise. She sat and pressed his hand to her breast. Blaise snatched his hand free as if she might be a poisonous plant. She looked sheepishly to the director and saw that he dismissed the refusal with a smile.

"Sorry, sir, I have a bit of a hangover this morning," Blaise fumbled.

"Perfectly understandable. And how are you getting on with Mitsuko? She told me she mentioned my connection to her family to you."

Had Blaise let something incriminating slip to that bitch? Was Minsheng about to pronounce sentence before summoning the Mantis?

"Yes, she did, director."

"What did she say exactly?"

He's toying with me.

"She said you and her father were in the armament business."

The director let out a rich guffaw. "True enough. What else did she tell you?"

He knows everything. He's going to vaporize me.

"Not much, Director. Only that she grew up in Beijing. And worked in Hong Kong."

It's coming. Now.

Minsheng issued an indulgent laugh. "Tell me, Blaise, what would you guess her age to be?"

What the fuck is this? More games? A last playful swipe of the cat's paw before shredding me?

"I'd guess her to be around my age, sir," Blaise rasped, his throat as dry and cracked as the desert. "She's remarkably youthful-looking," he replied, unsure how he was supposed to take Minsheng's remark. Was it a dig at Mitsuko or at him? Or just the loose association of a psychotic mind?

"Yes, she is thirty-eight. And will remain so forever. And what about me? How many years has Father Time tolled against me, do you think?"

"I wouldn't know, sir."

"I am one hundred and eight," the director announced with evident satisfaction. He gave Blaise a moment to absorb that. "Mitsuko and I are beneficiaries of Lazarus-D. I mentioned Lazarus-D to you when I gave you your promotion. And you'll soon receive your medical evaluation, so you can begin receiving injections. Barring a lightning strike or earthquake, Class Is live forever. We refer to ourselves as *Homo Deus*. A new, immortal race."

Blaise had to admit it was a tempting prospect. Who wouldn't want eternal life? But wouldn't it be unendurable knowing billions died to give him immortality?

"The board is pleased to grant you this gift. What's more, if you continue to progress in your career, you'll someday own a spread as grand as this." He gestured toward his vineyards and then spoke in a more intimate tone. "Truth be told, Blaise, most of the board members began as VR mythologizers, same as you. Finesse in mass propaganda ranks higher in our economy than military expertise or managerial skill. You'll see. You're going to travel with me to Hong Kong four times a year. The pleasures and privileges there will stagger your imagination. That, Blaise, is scale."

So I'm going to survive this weekend? But how can I endure another minute of this lunatic's company, much less an eternity with him and his kind?

"I'm honored, sir," Blaise gushed as if overwhelmed by the director's generosity, while his mind groped like a blind beggar at possible escapes from a situation that seemed like a psychotic episode. Revulsion at himself was followed by a deeper revulsion for Minsheng, who was tempting him, corrupting him, by offering him the one thing that everyone longed for: an escape from death.

I've got to get out of here now, or I'll never turn back.

"Sir, you know the Anima coding's been a nightmare," he managed, trying to steady his voice as a sudden thought struck him.

"Yes, I'm aware of that," Minsheng rejoined, studying his face with interest.

This won't work. But it has to. I can't bear this anymore!

"Well, you see, sir, something came to me this morning," Blaise continued, struggling to keep panic out of his tone. "I just may have hit on the way to bypass that snag with the bitrate transfer." Minsheng leaned closer, and Blaise saw something, hope or greed, possibly both, glint in the director's good eye. Good. He was buying it. And shifting the topic to a technical glitch helped steady Blaise's nerves. "It's such an honor to be here this weekend, sir," he stressed. "But honestly, an insight like I've had doesn't come along often. I'd like to get back to my office holodeck to test it before I lose it. Mitsuko can stay. I don't need her to solve this."

Minsheng pursed his lips. What was running through that twisted mind?

"If this works, sir, I might be able to finish coding the series a month sooner than our deadline," Blaise added.

"Perhaps you're on to something there," Minsheng affirmed.

Blaise's heart leapt with hope. He had found a way out of the labyrinth!

"If you think it's this important, I could order an autobot to take you back to L.A.," Minsheng added in a reasonable tone. "I keep a couple of autobots here that can do twice the speed of the standard model. And don't worry about Mitsuko. I'll explain why you had to leave early."

Relief flooded Blaise's mind like a spring of fresh water.

Escape! Out of this madhouse, so I can think again!

The director dismissed the Slag girls and placed an arm on Blaise's shoulder.

"There's one little matter we should clear up before you leave," he confided. "We were a bit concerned about your reaction to the Mantis terminations last night. Perhaps it was unfamiliarity with the proceedings or your association with Harper. But surely, you've grasped by now your Class I status gives you the power to summon the Mantis. You can terminate anyone you like. Slags, Hadjis, if you catch one, even SWATs. They're Slags, after all, promoted beyond their competence."

Blaise felt all hope drain out of him.

"Let's give you a chance to redeem yourself, shall we?"

The director spoke into a small holodeck on a side table. "Send him in."

The two attendants in blue tunics who had brought Blaise to breakfast dragged in a gaunt Slag man in overalls, shoved him forward and backed away.

"Please, boss, you got the wrong guy," the Slag pleaded. "I ain't done nothing wrong."

"So," the director concluded. "A small demonstration of your new status."

Blaise glared at the director. "I beg your pardon?"

"It takes only an effort of will. He's just a Slag. What is he to the billions you'll help us obliterate?"

"I don't feel well, sir. I think I'm going to be sick."

"Too much wine and rich food. By all means, visit the vomitorium. But first, this little favor."

Blaise knew if he hesitated to terminate the Slag, he would be next. If he was, no one else would have a ghost of a chance of uploading the Polyphemus worm—which he saw in a flash as an absolute necessity, his only chance to restore sanity to the world.

"Please, boss, let me go," the Slag pleaded. "I got a wife and six kids. They got no chance if anything happens to me. I'll do anything you want, your honor. I'll suck your dick."

Blaise couldn't bear the man's whines any more than he could the thought of his own termination. Minsheng scrutinized him, and Blaise knew it was now or never. So he concentrated on the Slag and willed the Mantis to come.

Nothing happened.

"Just relax," the director soothed. "Clear your mind. Repeat a single utterance: 'Come, death.' I've uttered it hundreds of times. It's hard in the beginning. But consider: you're only squashing an insect."

"Please, boss, let me off the hook," the Slag pleaded. "Oh Jesus, please. I don't wanna die."

The director's good black eye—a grotesque counterpoint to the left one with its holographic lens—scrutinized Blaise with cruel precision, and it increased Blaise's terror. He couldn't commit the murder Minsheng had ordered; he wouldn't, and yet he felt something slip down inside him like a tribal mask. Behind it lurked acquiescence and a burning urge to survive at any cost. A swirling, firefly-speckled cloud coalesced before the Slag as the huge Mantis, with its whirling, faceted eyes, solidified. The Slag tried to shield the ink spot on his forehead from the claw.

How does it feel to be a god?

"Get down on your knees and don't speak," Minsheng ordered the Slag, who complied, trembling and weeping. Then Minsheng scrutinized Blaise. "Your psych profile says your suffer from PTSD. A legacy from your military service in Nigeria. You and I have discussed that. But you're demonstrating right now that creativity is a wondrous way to defeat it. The Mantis is the highest order of artistic achievement."

"I . . . became a games planner to . . . to . . ."

Minsheng nodded. "To erase the horrors of war from your mind. To free you from your nightmares. Sublimation. A strategy that released your brilliance. A talent you might never have tapped into had you not endured two years in Nigeria."

Blaise glanced up at the director, trembling with rage. One well-placed palm blow to Minsheng's chin would throw his head back just enough for Blaise to deliver a death kick to the base of the director's fatty throat. Minsheng would be erased from the world. But then, so would Blaise. And there would be no one to upload Polyphemus.

Minsheng gestured toward the trembling Slag.

"One act of will, and you'll prove that your life truly has scale. You'll free yourself forever. Gods have no use for guilt, Blaise."

Blaise couldn't resist the director's iron logic any longer. So he focused his mind on the cowering Slag, and willed the Mantis to crawl to him and touch his forehead with its claw. The Slag collapsed like a bag of bones. Blaise slumped to his own knees and stained the balcony with vomit as he churned up all the rich food, mulled wine, and pheromone scent he had absorbed since arriving at the estate.

8

BLAISE WOKE FROM A SWEATY NIGHTMARE. MITSUKO GAZED down at him with an expression one part maternal solicitude and two parts angst, the same angst that had plagued him his entire adult life.

"You fainted," she soothed, dabbing his forehead with a moistened towel.

"Where am I?"

"At Minsheng's estate."

"How long have I been out?"

"About three hours. How are you feeling?"

"Like I've had my stomach pumped."

"You left a pool of vomit on Minsheng's balcony," she observed, lips pursed in a wry smile.

The moment when he had terminated the Slag rushed back to Blaise like a hammer blow. He propped himself up on his elbow. It set his head spinning.

"Just rest," she cooed, and nudged him back down. "It's a terrible experience, I know. But you've proven yourself. You have the director's full trust now."

"You sure about that?"

She dismissed his concern with a shrug. "I fainted myself the first time. We all have to sacrifice a Slag. It's a rite of passage for everyone promoted to Class I."

Remembering that Mitsuko had also murdered many times, including two colleagues, army veterans he had been close to, gave Blaise no comfort. He started to speak but bit off his words.

"You can speak freely," she reassured him. "We're in Minsheng's wing, not the one they first put us in. There's no surveillance here."

Blaisé glanced around the room. He saw no holoscreen and couldn't spot any surveillance cameras.

"You're sure?" he asked uncertainly. "I could swear I saw a drone cruising a hallway when we first arrived."

"To keep an eye on the servants. They're Slags. Here in his wing, surveillance isn't needed. Board members often stay in these rooms."

He didn't fully trust her confidential tone, but the trauma from what he had done forced him to speak. "How do you live with yourself, knowing you've terminated people?"

He regretted the question immediately because she'd almost certainly report him to the director for asking it, surveillance or no surveillance. He was disturbed to see her expression harden into that opaqueness he had seen many times. Had he given away his life with his idiotic question?

"It was me or him, just like with you. Besides, you're a soldier, remember?"

He breathed relief. Her tone carried the barest hint of vulnerability, which gave him the courage to risk another question.

"How many have you terminated? How many Slags?"

Mitsuko studied one of the gilded Cupids adorning the wall. "What's the difference?" she shrugged. "We're about to annihilate all of them."

"And you're OK with that?"

She peered at him as if he were speaking gibberish.

"They're only Slags."

"So tell me. How many terminations?"

She considered it for a moment, then shrugged. "If you must know, twelve Slags, seven Class IIIs, and..."

"Yes?"

"My husband," she replied in an uninflected tone, like someone under anesthesia. "He was plotting with some of the board to assassinate Minsheng and the chairman, who've been friends for decades." The words came harder now; emotion quavered under them. "The chairman ordered the conspirators' spouses, all Class Is, to terminate them."

Blaise heard anguish in her words. Was there the smallest chance that she felt as isolated and lonely as Blaise did? And if so, could he exploit it? Was she asking herself similar questions about him?

"Did you love your husband?"

She nodded.

"Then how——?"

Her stony expression dissolved, by degrees, into tears, which she tried to hide before she buried her face in the towel and sobbed. Hope flooded Blaise's heart. He wondered if he had misjudged her. Maybe she wasn't the monster he imagined her to be but rather an angst-ridden pawn like him. On the other hand, she had received *Homo Deus* treatments. She was going to live forever. Who in her right mind would risk losing that?

She wiped away tears and straightened herself up to her full dignity. He considered her movements with a trembling heart, afraid to risk any more questions. But he knew he had to if he was going to get anything of value from her. Minsheng had probably sent her to spy on him, and her romantic advances at the orgy were most likely Minsheng's idea. But something flitted across her face that gave Blaise the impression something else might be happening: a furtiveness, a hint of naked need, that prompted Blaise to caress her fine-boned chin. Perhaps, after all, she was as human as he was and equally miserable. She reached a trembling hand to his lips, as if to reassure herself he was real.

"Do you despise them?" he asked. "The board? The director?"

She studied him with an unreadable expression.

"They keep you tied up in a thousand knots, don't they?" he pressed. "Fear, angst. Eating you up inside. Am I right?"

Her lips trembled. She nodded and fought back more tears. He knew then he had struck a chord. Here was his chance to press his advantage, and he dug in hard.

"They call us the privileged class, but we're just carp swimming in a fish bowl," he asserted. "We manipulate the masses for them. But the director, the board, are manipulating us. And always will, neurofeed or no neurofeed. They talk about Lazarus-D technology. *Homo Deus*. Eternal life. But what kind of life is that, really?"

"The only life that gives my daughter a chance."

"Is this the life you want for her?"

Her tone hardened. "What else is there? I have to get her hired on at Mythoplex. They don't hire many women, but I can pull strings. And I have to be here, to watch over her. Without Lazarus-D tech, my years would catch up with me eventually. All my diseases and genetic defects."

He considered her answer before he risked an even more dangerous question. "But this isn't the paradise they promised, is it? Think about it. Your daughter is how old?"

"She'll be twenty-one next month."

"And you're thirty-seven, right? So when you're 150, she'll be, what, over a hundred? You'll both have love affairs, marriages, careers, travel, pleasures beyond counting——"

"What's your point?"

"Eventually, you'll be crones who look a century younger. Sleek bodies with great-great-grandmother's minds. What will an eternity built from organ upgrades, disease reversal, and cybernetic devices really feel like?"

"Wonderful, I'm sure."

"What will it be like to know your daughter as a friend, then a rival, then a hateful memory you can never lose? Yesterday's darling girl will be tomorrow's bitch. Think of all the mother-daughter resentments, rages, and wounds piled up over decades and centuries. You'll both be crushed by the weight of them, like grapes flattened by stones. Even if you move to opposite sides of the planet, you'll know she's there, and she'll know you're there, too."

Mitsuko considered that and shuddered. "Maybe it won't be like that."

"Of course it will. After you've both run through the CereFuck library, slept with every flesh-bot android, pursued every profession, enjoyed every achievement, what will you talk about? What will you share on your two hundredth reunion cruise? The stale stories you've repeated since she was a girl?"

He could see his words had hit the mark. She had to wipe away tears again.

"I wake up mornings feeling like Sisyphus pushing his boulder up the hill," she confessed. "But I do what I have to do."

"But what I'm asking is whether that's enough. Repetition. Century after century. How can we bear ourselves after we've exhausted every human experience and can only repeat them *ad nauseum*? That, Mitsuko, will be hell."

She considered him for some time before she replied. A sly smile touched her face. "I see you're a philosopher."

"Is that bad?"

She let out a giggle. Her mirth struck him as so inappropriate he grimaced.

"Don't look at me like that," she chided. "Philosophizing is attractive. No wonder you code so brilliantly."

"So what's so funny? I just gave you a description of hell."

"It's given me something to consider," she answered, and shook out her hair in a fetching manner. "I've had thirty-seven VR lovers since I lost—terminated—my husband. And coded seventeen VR series. And I wake up every morning knowing it all means nothing. But my feelings are bound to change. Don't you see? I'm going to live forever. Just like you. Our feelings will change, Blaise. Because what's our alternative? Eternal blackness. Death."

She gave Blaise a tender, indulgent look and brushed his cheek with her fingertips. Was this simple seductiveness, prompted by Minsheng? Or was something else happening? Some covert message carried to him through her perfume?

"You're a romantic," she teased. "A romantic about death. You talk as if plunging into infinite black could actually be something to wish for. Know what I think? I think on some level, you *want* to die. You're, what did they used to call it? A depressive. You hate the idea of eternal life because you hate yourself."

That hit home deeply enough to silence him for a bit. But he sensed something else was lurking behind her mockery.

"You've got something else on your mind, don't you, Mitsuko?" he probed. "Something that's eating you up. Why not get it off your chest? Who else have you got to confide in? No one else gives a shit."

She glanced at the door as if expecting a platoon of SWATs to rush in. Then she took several deep breaths. "He ordered me to come with you this weekend. But I came on my own this afternoon. He doesn't know I'm here."

He traced a lock of her hair with his fingertip. "Then tell me the truth. What do you think about him, really?"

That gave her pause. "I despise him," she admitted, finally.

"So do I. So why would he throw us together? Why risk creating conspirators?"

She glanced again at the door, as if to reassure herself that no one was there. "He wants to be chairman of the board."

"What's that got to do with us?"

She studied him with a panicked look in her eyes.

"Come on, God dammit," he urged. "We've got to trust each other if we're going to survive this."

He heard relief in her voice when she final spoke. "He thinks we can help him. He's got some scheme, an offshoot of *Gilgamesh V.* Some kind of covert coding."

"What kind? What's he after?"

"Everything."

"What can he wish for he doesn't already have?"

She shook her head and glanced at the door. "I've said too much."

"Bullshit. Answer the question."

She hesitated. "He wants to rule, like a god."

"He already does. And we're coding his apocalypse for him. What more does he want?"

"He wants us to use the drug, Anima, to assassinate the board."

"You, you can't be serious," he gasped.

She drew a deep sigh and brought a hand to her temple. "He never comes right out with it; he's too subtle for that. But it's the only thing that makes sense. He wants to be chairman, and he has enemies. Some of the board members are more ruthless, more insane than he is."

He grasped her by both shoulders. "Mitsuko, we can't let him use us for that. We'd be caught and terminated."

"We'll be terminated if we refuse."

Panic took possession of Blaise, and he blurted out his thought before considering it. "Then we've got to get out of here. Away from him."

She threw him an anguished look. "And go where?"

Could he risk telling her about Kristina and Amelia? About the Polyphemus worm? No. Mitsuko was too hard-wired into The Cloud for that. He repeated his mantra to throttle back his fear, so he could speak rationally.

"OK, point taken; there's nowhere to run," he conceded. "So what if we beat Minsheng at his own game?"

"How could we possibly do that?"

"What if we exposed his plot to the board?"

Terror flashed in her eyes. "He'd send the Mantis for us!"

"He's planning to assassinate them with Anima. Right? That's why he needs us. So just for the hell of it, let's say you use those Hong Kong contacts of yours to alert the chairman about what Minsheng's got in mind for him. Wouldn't the board be grateful to us?"

She tore herself loose from his embrace. "He has spies. He could reactivate our neurofeed. He'd catch us if we tried that."

"OK, calm down. We're just talking here, right?"

That seemed to reassure her a little, but he still saw fear in her eyes. "Yes. We're just—talking."

"OK. So just for shits and giggles, let's think this through. You say Minsheng and the chairman have been friends for decades."

"Yes. But they don't trust each other."

"Let's assume the chairman's been wondering when Minsheng might try something like this. If we were to confirm his suspicions, he'd have Minsheng terminated. And then the chairman, the whole board, would be grateful to us. We'd be eliminating a dangerous rival they already distrust."

"But if we betray Minsheng, they'll assume we're capable of anything and have us terminated."

"Just for argument's sake, let's say they terminate Minsheng instead of us. We're doing our final coding for *Gilgamesh V*, right? They need us alive till we wrap on that. So while we're coding, *we* could eliminate the board, with Anima, just like Minsheng's planning to do."

His heart pounded with terror at the risk of mentioning this, but he figured suggesting that he and Mitsuko collude in a plot, however unlikely its success, was the only way to win her over. "Isn't that what you want in your heart of hearts?" he pressed. "To murder them? I mean, every board member is male, right?"

"Every fucking one," she affirmed.

"Doesn't leave a helluva lot of room for a woman with your brilliance."

"The director calls Slags historical relics," she spat. "But he and the rest of those bastards on the board, they're the relics."

"You should be on the board," he asserted. "With me there, watching your back."

She considered that but then shook her head. "We could never pull it off."

He could see that fear of losing what she had was overcoming her. So he shifted his line of attack. "Look, we're just talking."

She nodded. "Our best bet is to do as we're told."

"So you don't think Minsheng's planning to terminate us after *Gilgamesh V*?"

"Of course not. He's mentioned the next series he wants us to collaborate on. Something to legitimize his reign as chairman. A patriotic series that will blame the Caliphate for assassinating the board, with a protagonist based on Minsheng himself."

He whistled, wide-eyed, to convince her he was knocked out by the possibility.

"Impressive. But let's assume things play out the way you say. We help Minsheng assassinate the board. How could he ever fully trust us after that?"

"I know him better than you do. He trusts me. He would have absolute power as chairman, and we'd have eternal life."

"If he lets us live."

"He will. He needs us."

"And if he stops needing us?"

She considered that before replying. "If I should be wrong about him, if he ever really did stop caring about me, then there's something else. Something we could use if we found out he was planning to terminate us." She cast a stealthy glance around the room. "There's one medical condition Lazarus-D can't eliminate," she confided. "Hypertension."

Blaise let out a guffaw. "Yeah, right. You're telling me Lazarus-D can reverse cancer, HIV, Parkinson's, brain tumors, diabetes, ebola, Marburg virus, a whole *Grey's Anatomy* of viral, bacterial, and genetic maladies, but they haven't licked high blood pressure? That's bullshit."

Mitsuko smiled slyly. "We can reverse every known disease. Replace the heart with a transplant from an involuntary Slag donor or grow a fresh, genetically-matched heart in an organ lab. But we can't eliminate the slim chance of life trauma spiking the blood pressure fatally."

Blaise shook his head. "Where do you get this from?"

"Lazarus-D research is a passion of mine. I'm a recipient, after all. The brain interests me particularly. It can't be replaced or transplanted, you see—only rejuvenated. For example, you can't upload the brain's content into another body. That's been tried. Failed miserably. The engrams reject the new host like back in the twentieth century when the first heart transplants failed. Human consciousness can only reside in the original brain, and the brain can only live in the original body, which Lazarus-D keeps alive forever. But even a rejuvenated brain in a healthy body is vulnerable."

Blaise flashed her a rueful smile. "Have you taken a special interest in the director's brain?"

Mitsuko played with a tress of her hair. "You might say that."

"I do say that. I'll repeat it. Are you planning something neurally lethal for our beloved director?"

Mitsuko stared into the middle distance, as if speaking to an invisible third person. "If a great tragedy or shock should spike the blood pressure beyond the brain's tolerance, a fatal aneurism could follow, especially in the case of someone Minsheng's age. Particularly since he snorts cocaine."

"Cocaine?" Blaise scoffed. "Why would the director resort to a prehistoric drug like that with his high blood pressure?"

"He needs relief from unbearable stressors. Stressors you and I couldn't begin to imagine. Pressures of power."

"But he's not stupid. He's getting regular Medco check-ups. That's mandatory. Surely his doctor's telling him to get off coke."

"His doctor is terrified of him. He tells Minsheng whatever he wants to hear."

Blaise shook his head. "Sorry. This is all bullshit. And this aneurysm theory won't fly."

"Why not?"

"You said a great tragedy or shock could spike the blood pressure beyond the brain's tolerance for it. Just one little flaw in that theory. Nothing shocks the director. He can't be traumatized by a tragedy, either, because he doesn't give a shit about anyone but himself. The rest of us are like ants crawling on a log, and he'd be happy to toss us, log and all, into the fireplace."

"You're wrong about him," Mitsuko retorted. "He does have something. . . someone. . . he cares about."

"Oh, yeah? Who? Other than his handsome one-eyed reflection in the mirror. I promise you, the man's heart is made of marble."

Mitsuko almost replied but changed her mind. "This subject's beginning to bore me," she sighed and brushed a long black tress from her eyes. "Let's talk about us. Our future. What if you're wrong about living forever? What if it's not a hell but something entirely different?"

Blaise rolled his eyes. "You don't listen so good. I told you. Repetition."

"But you assume there's a limit to the number of pleasures. What if we find infinite ways to enjoy ourselves? Undreamt-of ecstasies, discovered as we go. Pleasures beyond even VR."

Her liquid eyes met his, and he saw longing in them.

"So what do you want, Mitsuko?"

"To feel alive again. VR can never make you feel truly alive. Only another person can do that."

She kissed him tenderly, and then her kisses became urgent and desperate. Perhaps, he thought recklessly, if they were lovers, he could use Mitsuko to shield himself against detection while he uploaded Polyphemus. His chance of getting away with it might increase a tiny percentile. But as Mitsuko devoured his lips, a strange vision took possession of him. In a flash of illumination, he saw not Mitsuko but Kristina as she looked during their first night of love back in the Zone. Kristina had stirred a secret center in his soul, a place that had been cold and dark and hidden from him since he lost Cherry and Mei. It struck him that this vision was probably a curseil signal from Kristina.

When the vision passed, Mitsuko peered at him with the puzzled hurt of a spurned lover.

"Where were you just now?" she demanded.

Hard insight took hold of him. He knew Mitsuko well enough to grasp that whatever she said or did, she was an inferno of ambition. He would have to deceive her in a way that appealed to her imperial urge for conquest. So he returned to his lovemaking, as she whispered about hallucinatory pleasures they would enjoy together, now and eternally. Against his will he began to visualize them with breathless urgency. Perhaps pheromones suffused the air, or maybe it was simple animal need. In any case, Mitsuko's allure finally overcame him, and he lost himself in the scented mazes of her body like a rabid Theseus who had exchanged souls with the minotaur.

9

ON HIS WAY BACK TO L.A. WITH MITSUKO SUNDAY NIGHT, BLAISE peered out at gloomy stretches of desert, and it dawned on him that no matter how pleasant his interlude with Mitsuko had been, he had witnessed too much insanity in Minsheng's lair to delay the inevitable any longer.

After he dropped her off at Clint Eastwood Condoplex, he ordered the autobot to take him straight to the Mythoplex tower. The car dropped him off in front of the building, and he strode into the lobby with his customary arrogance and told the security android that he had some coding to finish in his office. His eye scan confirmed his Class I status, and he took the lift up to his floor. His heart pounded with terror about what he was about to attempt.

There was only one SWAT checkpoint on duty. The guards were tired and bored and waved him through. He reached his office, and the door clicked shut behind him. He stood in front of his holodeck, trembling. But he steeled himself, eased down in his cockpit chair, took the Polyhemus chip from its hiding place in his jacket, and inserted it in the upload slot.

"Upload module one," he commanded in a dry, cracked voice.

The upload ran smoothly, while hope and fear contended for control of his heart. When module one had completed, he removed the virus chip from the slot and stowed it in its hiding place in his jacket, hoping that Kristina was right about it being undetectable. He had three modules left, and he'd have to wait a week between each upload before risking one again.

Then everything went south.

His screen turned red, and a dry female voice chirped, "Server-wide security breach."

He heard pounding boots, and hoped desperately they were headed in another direction. Then SWATs burst into his office. Blaise shot out of his cockpit chair, pivoted away from the drawn laser burners, and caught one of the SWATs across the bridge of the nose with a Thai-style snap kick. The man screamed, dropped his burner, and grasped his ruined nose. With blood lust sharpening his senses to diamond precision, Blaise spun round for another kick, brought his knee up, flung out his leg, and caught a second SWAT at the base of the throat. As the second SWAT went down, another fired a security net over Blaise and glued him against the back wall. Another fired a sedative dart and everything went black.

When Blaise woke he found himself in a bright, lofty room he had never seen before. He lay naked on a white acrylic slab, and he couldn't budge. Invisible bonds glued him fast.

Acrylic slabs like his circled the room like a bizarre necklace. He recognized a dozen Class Is, also naked and motionless, glued to other slabs. Their pale flesh and flaccid penises looked ridiculous. A door slid open at the rear, and Minsheng entered in his cleanly-pressed director's jacket. He strolled the room, hands behind his back, lingering a moment at each slab before passing on to others.

"Last night we had a major security breach," he informed the imprisoned Class Is. "Someone tried to upload a dangerous worm that could have severely damaged our neural network. All of you have level five security clearances, and all of you were working late here when the breach occurred." He cleared his throat as he paced. "This was a sophisticated worm. We can't trace the point of upload. So what I want to know is, who's the traitor?"

"Director, this is ridiculous," a slender Chinese Class I man protested. "Nothing gets past our firewalls. Why would we risk our lives on such a stupid scheme?"

Minsheng smiled. "That's what we're here to find out." He lingered at Blaise's slab and then moved on.

He knows it's me, Blaise thought. *He's just toying with me.*

"Indeed, why would one of you betray us?" He stepped to the center of the room. "Discontent? Resentment? But why? You're the elite. The immortals. Whether or not you've had Lazarus-D disease-reversal injections yet, you're entitled to it and a place at the top. Forever." He paused to reflect. "Or should we blame this on insanity? I've reactivated all your neurofeeds on the chance that might be it. But aside from slightly erratic EEGs from fear concerning your present dilemma, everyone's EEGs appear normal. So why, then? Why try to destroy what you've worked a lifetime to create?"

The terrified Class Is blinked at Minsheng and then at each other.

"Director, none of us could possibly betray you," the Chinese Class I protested.

Blaise suppressed his terror at what was coming with the iron discipline of his mantra. If he could keep his EEG within the accepted range, he might be able to bluff his way through this, despite the fact that he had taken out two SWATs before they caught him. Kristina was right about Polyphemus being untraceable but dead wrong about its effectiveness. If he survived this ordeal, he would have to figure out why it had failed and recode it for another try.

"No confession?" Minsheng observed. "Well, then I have no choice but to extract the truth." He glanced at the back of the room. The door slid open, and the petite Japanese female android Blaise had seen in Minsheng's office entered with mincing steps in a flowing kimono.

Minsheng glanced from face to face with an opaque expression while the petite android approached one of the Class Is, the one who had spoken out. The android smiled, and from the folds of her kimono the blade of a sword gleamed.

"Since all of you are or will soon become immortals, I can inflict pain on you indefinitely, for years, for centuries if I care to," Minsheng observed. "So it would be better to confess now and end things quickly." He glanced around at the ring of terrified faces. "Still nothing?"

The android lifted her sword and sliced off the hapless Class I's foot. The man's shriek reverberated through the room. The android smiled sweetly. A panel opened in one of the walls, and medical repair spiders crawled out, mounted the stricken man's slab, staunched his bleeding, and cauterized his bloody stump while the man whimpered.

"You'll receive no painkiller," Minsheng told him. "Your pain will go on. And on. Unless you confess."

The android raised her sword and swung it like a scythe on the man's arm, which dropped with a thump to the floor. The man screamed louder while the repair spiders staunched the blood gushing from his ruined side, which reduced him to a blubbering animal that could no longer form words. The repair spiders staunched his bleeding, but his agony went on.

The android approached a new victim, who struggled with all his might to free himself. "It's not me, Director Minsheng," the man cried.

Blaise couldn't bear to watch Minsheng's casual torture, nor could he tear his eyes away from it. He felt the urge to confess that he had attempted the upload, to end the suffering of the others, but if he did, he would never get another chance with Polyphemus, and Minsheng's regime would torture the whole world forever.

After what felt like an eternity of the petite android's hacking and piteous screams, the room filled with the metallic reek of blood and the stench of shit as the bowels of the dying evacuated themselves. Minsheng approached Blaise with the android smiling sweetly behind him, blood-spattered in hacksaw patterns across her kimono.

"You've maintained your silence through all this," Minsheng observed. "That can only mean two things. Either you committed this traitorous act and somehow managed to keep your EEG normal in the face of what you've witnessed. Or you're innocent." He brought his face close to Blaise's. "I want to believe it was one of the others. Your work is far more important to me than theirs. And after all, why would you betray me when you have so much to gain?"

"I didn't betray you," Blaise said with as much calm as he could muster.

"A guilty man might fight as hard as you did to escape, mightn't he?"

"I'm not an idiot. I'd never attempt anything as stupid as a viral upload."

"No?"

"Director, I helped to program the quantum computers when we installed their AI firewalls. I know very well nothing could get past that."

"So your attack on the SWATs in your office was pure reflex, a PTSD reaction. Is that it?"

He's not buying this. He knows!

The petite android approached with her sweet smile and blood-spattered kimono. She twirled like a ballerina and executed elaborate dance steps as her sword sliced the air in graceful arcs. Her gaze settled on Blaise's naked leg. The medical repair spiders crawled up on the slab where he was suspended.

This is the end. I've failed, utterly.

Minsheng smiled. "I've had my eye on these others. Ambitious bastards, looking for their chance to assassinate me. Whereas you? You've always struck me as the pure artist. Someone for whom creation is the ultimate gratification: the cleanest escape from the agonies of your past." He stroked Blaise's hair in a fatherly manner. "But can I be sure of your loyalty?"

"Of course you can," Blaise reassured him in a voice he steadied through sheer force of will.

"I learned long ago that nothing in this life is certain, Blaise."

"Director, why would I give up my chance at immortality as the mythologizer who coded *Gilgamesh V* with an eternity to enjoy my fame?"

Minsheng considered him with pursed lips while the petite android continued her lethal twirls and swordplay, her kimono whipping the air like a multicolored flame.

"Why, indeed?" Minsheng wondered. "Unless you've been corrupted. We both know your father had to be purged, despite his work in refining the neural network."

"I'm not my father."

"True. Still, I wonder, could you have inherited some traitorous gene?"

Death was as close as the kimono twirling a few steps away. "Director, I barely knew my father. He abandoned us when I was seven."

Minsheng considered that. "Your mother, then. She was a subversive writer."

"She died when I was eight. She was a hopeless drunk. I understood very little about her."

Minsheng nodded. "True enough. Still, the human mind is capable of anything, even self-destruction. Perhaps on some level you harbor a death wish. Perhaps that's why you're such an effective killer."

Blaise was stunned to hear the very thing Mitsuko had brought up during their intimate interlude at Minsheng's estate. Had she repeated their conversation to the director? Had Blaise and Mitsuko been under surveillance despite Mitsuko's reassurance that the board member's wing of Minsheng's house was sacrosanct?

Blaise realized he would have to think like Minsheng if he wanted to survive. "Director, I'm the only one who can finish *Gilgamesh V*," he asserted. "Mitsuko lacks the finesse. You must know that. So why would I accept the singular honor of helping you obliterate the Slags and the Caliphate, and accept the gift of eternal life if I harbored a death wish?"

"An attack of conscience, perhaps?" Minsheng mused. "I've always known about your capacity for moral horror. I attribute it to your PTSD. Still, such horror might make you loath the idea of slaughtering billions."

"Director, you said yourself you didn't trust these others. This viral upload, one of them did it. Someone jealous of what we're accomplishing." Blaise saw a glimmer of interest in Minsheng's eye and pressed on. "Maybe they were in it together. A conspiracy to discredit both of us with the board so they could put themselves forward as saviors of the Anima initiative. A hopeless plan. But vanity and ambition blinded them to that."

Minsheng nodded in a way that suggested Blaise's reasoning had swayed him.

"Whatever the case, you've dealt with them all," Blaise pressed. "Here, today. Now we can reach our goal. It's what I live for."

Minsheng pursed his lips and chuckled. "I've apparently been a better influence on you than I realized. So be it. I'm going to let you live. I just wanted you to witness this in case a traitorous thought should ever cross your mind."

Blaise's restraints vanished, and Minsheng helped him sit up. The petite android stepped away then reappeared with a silk robe. Her arm touched Blaise's flesh as she helped him into it, and he noticed that distinct sponginess of flesh that gave her away as a VR projection.

Minsheng grinned. "Ah, so you've discovered my little secret. Yes, this one is pure VR. I've still got my flesh android back in my office. But this virtual clone of her embodies your recent coding breakthrough, plus my team's Mantis coding refinements, as you saw in my office. What the body believes becomes the body's reality."

Blaise's head reeled at the implications of what the director had just revealed.

"We can kill remotely far more effectively now." The director let that sink in before continuing. "Imagine the horror of a Mantis strike when our victims are so convinced it's real that they suffer actual physical damage as you've just witnessed. And we're exploring military applications: ways to break through the Caliphate's military firewalls. When we crack that, we'll send phalanxes of Mantises to slaughter them. A stopgap measure, of course; something to keep the Hadjis busy till you've completed coding Anima."

So this is what my life adds up to, Blaise thought as his heart sank into the abyss. *I thought I was an artist. I'm nothing but a mass murderer.*

10

Every day after the door slid closed and he settled into his floating cockpit chair, Blaise touched the fold in the cloth of his jacket where Kristina had hidden the Polyphemus chip. He ached to escape, to get back to her and recode Polyphemus for another try. But convincing Minsheng to grant him any leave, even a weekend, was unthinkable with the demands he placed on him and Mitsuko.

The director dropped by daily to gauge their progress, betraying nothing behind his imperial aplomb but the camaraderie of a co-conspirator in a vastly significant scheme. But Blaise scented, in the metal and gunpowder tang of Minsheng's sweat, desperation to see Blaise reach the goal. No doubt the animosities of Minsheng's fellow board members prompted these frequent appearances. The director's reputation, and probably his life, depended on showing the other board jackals that he could accomplish the Anima initiative.

Blaise noticed, on his bullet train commutes, how far along the L.A. incineration center had come. In the raked-back vista between two heliotropic towers, a geodesic dome had bloomed from the cityscape. Minsheng confirmed what Zuma had confided to Blaise at Minsheng's estate. The board was pouring billions into logistical planning and construction for centers like this in all Cloud-controlled cities, and specially-trained army troops would haul the bodies there from Slag Zones for tidy disposal. Minsheng bragged that Blaise was his stealth weapon and reminded him about the rewards and privileges he could expect when the Anima initiative was complete. He watched with pride as his plan for genocide gradually emerged on Blaise's holodeck screen.

Blaise loathed Minsheng's daily appearances, which affected him like a parasitic worm burrowing into his entrails. There was no escape from the endless coding the director demanded. Blaise chanted his mantra to stay sane, all the while racking his brain to think of some way to get away, to get free.

"You're doing a man's job," Minsheng intimated, placing a fatherly hand on Blaise's shoulder at the end of one crushing sixteen-hour shift. "How long till you finish this quadrant?"

Mitsuko, coding next to Blaise, managed to keep her expression neutral.

"Thirty minutes, an hour, tops."

"Good, good," Minsheng smiled. "I'll leave you to it, then."

"What are you up to?" Mitsuko demanded when the director was gone.

Blaise studied the holodeck screen. "What do you mean?"

"With the director."

He searched her face and saw raw terror in her yes. "I'm trying to survive this cluster-fuck. What are *you* up to?"

She shot a glance at the office door. "Have you been meeting with him, separately?"

"Oh, sure. That would really make sense."

She trembled, and her voice cracked. "Have you?"

Blaise gave her a dismissive guffaw. "Yeah. I shared a bottle of sake with him in his office and told him you're great in bed. He said I had excellent taste in women."

"Are you two planning something?"

"You mean, like, against you?"

"Answer the question!"

"Yeah, right, I'm gonna plot against the only games planner on earth qualified to help me finish this series."

"How do I know you're telling me everything?"

"Get a life, Mitsuko. Plotting against you with Minsheng is your kind of bitch move, not mine. Remember? We went through all the possibilities at the director's palazzo."

"If you're planning something with him, you'd better tell me. We still have time to make a separate deal with the board."

Blaise had to calm her down, or she might, in an effort to save herself, confess everything to Minsheng they had confided to each other at his estate.

"The smart move is to play Minsheng's hand out," Blaise pointed out. "He's going to reward us beyond our wildest dreams. Remember?"

She searched his face, obviously hunting for reassurance. He decided to try humor to allay her suspicions.

"Look, little miss paranoia. I learned a long time ago, never break someone's heart. People only have one. Break their bones instead. They have 206 of them."

"This isn't a joke!"

"No, but your suspicions are. Just chill, will you?" He let a beat pass before adding with a tender lilt, "I need you. You know that."

"Really?" she asked skeptically.

"Sure. And I'll show you."

"When?"

"Tonight. If this shift ever ends."

"Come to my place," she whispered with sybaritic suggestiveness.

Encouraged by the languid slant of her lowered lashes and the moist promise of her parted lips, he readily agreed. He rented an autobot to shuttle them home. On the way she attacked him with kisses that intensified in urgency until the autobot announced their arrival at her condo-pod. Mitsuko climbed out and tugged Blaise inside, pulling him past her grinning lobby bot into the lift. On the way up she pressed his hand against her wildly beating heart.

When the door to her condo slid shut behind them, she ordered him to wait for her on a cream-colored couch with red, square-shaped cushions emblazoned with gold Chinese characters.

"Where are you going?"

"No questions."

She left him to admire the intricate sandalwood embrasures flanking the doors, the quiet dignity of vases and floral-patterned dishes on the shelves, and the long white side table with a crimson silk cloth. In the illumination of square hooded lamps, he heard the bubbling of an oversized aquarium, its interior wreathed with sea fronds through which tiny, gold-fringed fish darted like inky after-images. Along another wall stood an elephant-eared plant with five heavy bulbs.

Mitsuko, in a red-fringed silk cheongsam negligee, glided in and slipped onto the couch. Her perfume sent him into delirium. But when he reached for her, she slapped his hands away.

"No," she hissed. "Not without permission."

"Bullshit," he scoffed, but when he reached for her again, she slapped his face so hard it made his head ring. He sprang back, shocked. Suddenly, she threw her weight against him, catching him off balance in such a way that she managed to force him onto his back. Grasping his hair, she brought her hard, pitiless eyes close to his. From a fold in her cheongsam a slender blade emerged. She pressed it against his throat, her face distorted by rage.

"You will not touch me, do you hear? Until you convince me, you'll never betray me." She punctuated her words with harder presses of the blade.

"You're insane," he gasped.

"Say it! Tell me you'll never betray me with Minsheng."

The blade dug into his flesh. "You have my word," he croaked with as much conviction as he could muster in his state of mortal terror.

"Tell me again. And mean it this time."

"I'll never leave you."

"And you'll never betray me. Mean it!"

"Never. I hate Minsheng as much as you do. Maybe more than you."

A few more reassurances of this kind brought a tender look to her face, and he was relieved to see her toss the knife onto the coffee table with a faint, resonant clatter. Then she drew him into a fever dream of lovemaking, light-years beyond the boundaries of civilized constraint.

She insisted he stay over that night, and soon it was nearly every night. When they dragged in together from work, bleary-eyed with exhaustion, she changed into a blood-red kimono and acted out his most sordid fantasies with the artfulness of a ballerina, the virtuosity of a contortionist, and the stamina of an Olympic gymnast. She altered their pleasures with countless variations and subtle surprises, so he washed ashore night after night in the tangle of her sweaty limbs like the survivor of an erotic hurricane.

He consumed a month of this addictive feast before a strange lassitude descended. He dismissed it as exhaustion from overwork. But as the days passed, he succumbed to a despondency bringing with it keen shafts of memory that burned like fire. Since he had little hope of getting back to Kristina, nostalgia for a lost paradise gradually took hold. Peaches and Mei haunted his memory with a sharpness and intensity he had never felt before. It drove him to work even longer hours and consume Mitsuko's body with greater ferocity. But his despondency only increased. Incorrigible sorrow tightened its pressure on his heart. Inexplicably, childhood memories returned to haunt him. One in particular made a deep impression and became a special kind of torment. Back before his father had been called away to Hong Kong, Blaise recalled a day when he and his mother sat in the yard outside their house in suburban Atlanta. It had been a warm spring afternoon when azaleas bloomed like pink popcorn and cicadas and crickets chirruped, a cacophonous drone in the humid heat. He and his mother had watched the family dog Knick-Knock as she gave birth to a litter of puppies near the brick wall in the front yard of their sleek suburban house. As each puppy emerged in its amniotic sack with a smell of warm puppy flesh, a sense of the miraculous had washed over Blaise. Knick-knock, a brown mongrel bitch, had licked the sticky brown, white, and spotted bodies afterward. The puppies had mewed with tightly-closed eyes and cautious paws, each an astonishing creation fresh from God's oven, as his mother called them.

"Mama, mama, what kind of puppies will they be?" he had cried. "Will they be boys or girls? Can we keep them?"

His mother had answered him with laughing green eyes. "Pick any one you like, darling, and that one will be yours."

He had picked the brown puppy and named him Booley, and Booley had been his dog throughout childhood. This memory tore at Blaise. It aroused an emotional response he couldn't define but which haunted him to the point where he dreamed about it. He saw an ocean of puppies floating like warm, sticky jewels that contained in their simplicity the answer to some question he couldn't remember but his heart ached to ask. This question seemed vitally important, perhaps the most important question anyone could ask. Yet he had no words to form it.

After this dream, the pleasures Mitsuko introduced him to dissipated into numbness and despair. He realized that if he couldn't find a way to get back to Kristina, he would spend eternity like this, trying to overcome the guilt of his complicity in annihilating billions by burrowing deep into Mitsuko's scented body. He suspected that not even a thousand years of pleasure with her could eradicate that stain. Eventually, guilt would drive him to kill himself. His desperation to avoid that, to find a way out, to figure out a way to get back to Kristina, prompted him to ask Mitsuko to share something about her life. Perhaps, he thought, it would create a deeper bond between them. There might be some slim chance he could use their intimacy to get Mitsuko to convince the director to give them both a vacation.

She laughed away Blaise's queries and distracted him with artful sexual techniques. But one night in bed he nagged her so mercilessly to share something from her childhood that she gave in to his request.

"Why would you want to know about me?" she scoffed.

"What was your mother like? Your father? Brothers, sisters?"

She slid her hand to his penis, but he pushed it away.

"Please," he begged. "It would mean a lot to me."

She settled into her pillow with a resigned look. "If you must know, my mother was an impeccably correct Japanese lady living in Beijing with my father. She was a fish out of water in that country."

"But what kind of person was she?"

"Honestly, Blaise. What's the point of this?"

"Indulge me."

"She managed the family finances, OK? It's common in Japan and China."

"And?"

"She was efficient. Orderly. Graceful. Highly regarded in the community, despite being Japanese."

"And your father?"

Mitsuko hesitated before answering. "Away most of the time. In the military and then his armaments firm. I hardly knew him."

"Were you and your mother close?"

Mitsuko let out a sigh. "She nursed me when I was sick, bought me beautiful clothes, sent me to good schools, and trained my brother and me in social graces."

This wasn't getting Blaise anywhere, so he pressed the point harder. "But did she love you?"

Mitsuko shrugged. "I have no idea. Mostly what I recall is her gliding kimono, her blandishments to excel in school, the hours she spent combing out her tresses before her mirror, two hundred strokes every night. And her silences."

"Silences?"

"My punishment. She never beat me. She simply erased me from her mind when I didn't make the best score on an exam, or failed to shine at some social function. I was ornamental jewelry. My brother got the real attention. My father expected him to follow as head of the firm."

Now Blaise knew he was onto something. "Were you jealous of your brother?"

Rage flashed in Mitsuko's eyes. "The first son is a family's hope, the daughter a distant second. We hear all that Cloud propaganda about women's equal opportunities. A ridiculous myth! And in Asia it's far, far worse for a woman. The first son gets all the focus. I was an afterthought. And there's the other thing."

"What other thing?" he pressed, sensing he had struck a nerve.

"A family needs the first son to marry well and build a career. He can't be socially awkward. So high-ranking families have a special way of instilling confidence."

"What's that?"

She bit her lip, and tugged at a tress of her jet black hair. "By letting him take his youngest sister's virginity."

Blaise couldn't believe what he was hearing. "Your brother raped you?"

"Don't let it concern you. It wasn't rape. My father ordered me to submit."

"Ordered you? What about your brother? How did he feel about it?"

"He seemed to enjoy himself."

"Unbelievable! What happened to that little prick? Did he inherit the firm?"

"He was killed in one of the Caliphate wars. My mother died of grief over it."

"How did you feel about that?"

"When we got the news, I felt . . . I may as well admit it, I felt avenged. But by then, the damage was done."

Blaise heard deep woundedness in her voice, so he eased back on his attack to avoid upsetting her too much. Reflecting on it later, it struck him that Mitsuko had endured suffering on a level that had left devastating and enduring scars, perhaps as bad or worse than Blaise's PTSD. And her humiliations continued at Mythoplex, where she endured Minsheng belittling her and refusing to grant the promotions she deserved. Blaise's feelings for her softened into something approaching sympathy. In light of her revelations, which she was unlikely to share with anyone else, he began to wonder whether their intimacy meant more to her than simple pleasure or was merely a means to spy on him for the director. Perhaps he had awakened something like love in her.

Their work together became more unbearable as the days ground on. There were unexpected coding complications and roadblocks, each of which took days or weeks to code around. They sweated through twenty-hour days to overcome these massive glitches, and the strain began to tell. Mitsuko showed up at work with bags under her eyes that no makeup could hide, and she fought with diminishing success to maintain her mental equilibrium while navigating an excruciating labyrinth of code. Blaise suffered pile-driving migraines that demanded daily treatment pricks from his Medco wall dispenser. Insomnia tormented him when he wasn't having nightmares, and he had to go on a bland diet for his ulcers. When Minsheng visited, alarm at Blaise's gaunt, hollow-eyed look showed through his usual composure. He recommended Chinese herbal supplements, sent Blaise to his acupuncturist, and scheduled a physical exam with his personal physician. The physical showed that Blaise had a sound constitution aside from the ulcers, but the doctor insisted that Blaise badly needed a rest to avoid nervous collapse. Eventually, Minsheng took pity on Mitsuko as well, and sent her to his same doctor, who reached the same conclusion about her. Still, the director refused to give her or Blaise any time off.

Then one day, Minsheng disappeared for a week, called away to Hong Kong for some emergency. When he returned, he informed Blaise and Mitsuko that war had broken out in the Sudan, the most threatening conflict in decades. Many army divisions and attack hovercraft had been diverted there, where the Caliphate had deployed a new nanobot technology that decimated entire regiments. This new weapon magnified the lethal effectiveness of an earlier nanobot technology the Caliphate had used for decades. Now the Hadjis had unleashed a new and more lethal version. Minsheng ordered Blaise and Mitsuko to complete the coding needed to weaponize remote Mantis strikes, adding that they had to find a way to break through Caliphate military firewalls so the strikes could have devastating effects.

Blaise worked with Mitsuko nearly round the clock for several weeks to complete the weaponization, and they succeeded in bypassing the firewalls, though the stress from it nearly cost them both their sanity. Minsheng told them he was very pleased, but he ordered them to shift back to Anima coding to honor their launch deadline.

Mitsuko broke down in tears at the end of one exhausting shift. "Director, please," she begged. "We can't keep this up."

"I can't push back the Anima deadline," Minsheng insisted.

"You're going to have to," Blaise put in.

Minsheng fixed his opaque gaze on Blaise, who glared back at him through bloodshot eyes. "She's right. We can't keep this pace up. Your own doctor said we have to have a break or we're not going to be any use to you. We haven't slept, haven't eaten, we're coding seven days a week. We're going to have a psychotic break if we don't get some rest. Then who'll finish your Anima coding?"

Blaise saw fear glint in the director's eyes. But it passed quickly.

"One week off," Minsheng conceded after a long pause.

Mitsuko's face brightened. "Oh, thank you." She dug in her purse for a tissue to daub her eyes but couldn't find one and excused herself to visit the ladies room.

"I suppose it's good timing," the director conceded after she was gone. "A vacation's in order. I suggest you and Mitsuko—"

"If it's all the same to you, sir, I'd like to vacation in the Zone alone," Blaise cut in, seizing his chance. "I know it's a doomed pastime, but I get sensual relief there. Besides, Mitsuko and I could use a break from each other."

Minsheng glared at him. "There's trouble between you two?"

"Not at all, sir," Blaise smiled. "She's wonderful. But you know how it is. Too familiar real flesh can grow tedious, can't it?"

The director's expression was as opaque as the abyss of deep space. Blaise felt certain he was going to refuse him. But Minsheng surprised him.

"A man is entitled to his pleasures," Minsheng conceded with a deep sigh. "And I certainly can't afford for you to have a psychotic break. But you absolutely have to be back in one week. Understood? One week. Everything depends on it." Half-jokingly, he added, "You wouldn't want me to have to send SWAT or the Mantis after you."

Blaise winced at the implied threat. "A week in the Zone will make a new man of me, sir," he reassured the director. "And then I'll get *Gilgamesh V* and *Anima* in the can. You have my word."

Minsheng considered that, then said, "I'll give Mitsuko a week, too. Your assistants can pick up the slack while you two are on break. Junior-level games planners won't be much use, but they can clean up a few blocks of code." Minsheng placed a paternal hand on Blaise's shoulder. "Besides, with so many troops diverted to the Sudan, we don't have enough available to haul away Slag bodies in quantity. I've discussed this with the board. I'm sure they'll agree to push back the *Gilgamesh V* release. I can probably get you and Mitsuko an additional month."

"Thank you, sir," Blaise replied gratefully.

Minsheng's smiled. "When you get back, I have a little side project I'd like you to handle. Nothing too strenuous. Something for the board. A surprise, actually. Something they'll enjoy after you've completed your epic. I want to present it to them at the next board meeting."

Blaise nodded complacently as if he had no clue how ambitious the director's plans had grown. Mitsuko had been right about his coup attempt. Minsheng had undoubtedly recruited a replacement board who would support his chairmanship in exchange for expansions to their own fiefdoms. But how long would his co-conspirators survive? For that matter, could any Class I under Cloud rule, including Blaise and Mitsuko, hope to survive long after Minsheng became chairman?

After the director left, Blaise used his holodeck to send the coded signal to Kristina that he would come to Reseda the following morning.

That night when they were in bed, Blaise broke the news to Mitsuko that he was vacationing alone.

"Don't you want me to come with you?" Her question trailed off into hurt.

"I'd love nothing better," he replied as convincingly as possible. "But I need some time on my own. It's only a week. You need a break from me, too. We'll come back refreshed and ready for each other again."

"Haven't I made you happy?" she whispered, pressing his hand to her breast. Her eyes glistened, and her mouth trembled.

"Deliriously happy," he lied with all the conviction he could muster. "But getting away from each other will be good for both of us."

"I see," she conceded and gathered herself up to her full imperial dignity. "I don't understand why you won't take me with you. But you're going to do what you want."

"It's what we both need," he reassured her. "And don't forget, we'll have eternity to enjoy what we accomplish together with Anima."

She gave him a dubious look.

"Told you," he whispered, stroking her luxurious hair. "I can't get along without you." And a pang of regret touched his heart for leaving this complex and perplexing woman whom he didn't think he would ever completely understand.

11

THE NEXT MORNING BLAISE BELT-BEAMED HIMSELF INTO A bullet train seat. Next to him lay a duffle bag with toiletries and several changes of clothes and shoes. He passed through familiar stops but didn't get off at Sepulveda Station, his usual destination. Instead, he drilled deeper into the Zone. From time to time, SWAT cops boarded. But his Class I blue silk jacket rendered him invisible to them. They only checked Slag identity swooshes, though, at one stop, they dragged a wretch off the train and shoved him into the arms of others who had apparently been searching for him. As the doors hissed closed, Blaise heard his cries from the beating they gave him.

The transport hurtled north by northeast, then to the northwest, judging by the holographic map on the wall across the aisle from Blaise. He passed stations he had never seen before, until at length, he arrived at Reseda, deep in San Fernando Valley. There was no escalator from the platform. A grimy flight of steps led up to a dilapidated lobby littered with the dust and decay of decades. His Mythoplex watch said 1730 hours, but the sun hung above the parched horizon like an angry orange eye. He found the street deserted. He waited for half an hour in the alcove of an abandoned storefront and heard nothing but the soughing of desert wind. He began to worry that something had happened to Kristina. Then he heard steps and spotted a Slag woman as she rounded a corner and hobbled toward him. She wore a shapeless hat pulled down low over her eyes and a gray, sack-like dress and lace-up boots. She had slung a plastic garbage bag over her shoulder and stopped to push open the top hatch of a rusting dumpster and dig around inside. He heard her muttering to herself.

Blaise stepped from the alcove and approached her. "Excuse me. Have you seen a young Chinese woman? I'm supposed to meet her here."

The woman kept her hat pulled low and gestured for him to follow.

"Where are we going?" he asked, but she shushed him with a finger and led him into a side street that shielded them from the bullet station. Then she dropped her garbage bag, whipped off her hat, and shook out her hair. It was Kristina!

"What the hell," Blaise gasped.

She had lost weight since he last saw her. Her cheekbones were more pronounced, and her arms looked thinner. She gestured for quiet, and he followed her, noticing how her gait carried all the grace of movement he remembered, with none of the stealthy cunning that Mitsuko's movements always had. Her hair, much longer than Mitsuko's, fell halfway to her waist. A stray tress touched her full lips.

"I did it," he declared "I uploaded the first module. But the fuckers caught me."

"Shhh," she whispered. "Wait till we're back at the warehouse. There may be surveillance cameras here."

They passed into what had probably once been a main street. Weeds grew in beds where trees had once flourished. Fissures cracked the ruined pavement as if an earthquake had passed through. Headless parking meters leaned over spaces sectioned off by faded paint. Gutted shops and restaurants yawned on either side. In one spot near a concrete curb, red ants swarmed like molten fire over an upended tarantula.

"Keep to the sidewalk if you don't want to get bitten," Kristina cautioned. "There are scorpions, too."

They turned into a lane and picked their way past abandoned fire pits with charred wood, the skeleton of a roofless hover-car, heaps of rubbish, and a dumpster spattered with birdlime. They came to another street, beyond which lay a warehouse district. Here the structures were built to last, and aside from decades of encrusted dirt and rust, they stood like enduring ghosts of a busier age.

Kristina approached a padlocked door, produced a key, and gestured for him to follow. She led him into the musty interior, down a corridor and into a storehouse with a rust-pocked aluminum roof supported by concrete pillars scrawled with graffiti. The storehouse had an odor of dry rot and stagnant time. Sunrays slanted vertically across swirling dust motes. Blaise sweated profusely in the stifling heat. A whining, industrial-sized floor fan barely cooled a circle of grim-looking women in metal folding chairs, dressed in jeans, work shirts, and boots. The women had pallid skin and ascetic figures and ranged in age from their twenties to fifties. They studied Blaise with an intensity that made him distinctly uncomfortable, this quorum of Slags like the ones he had passed so many times on the streets of the Zone: Mexican, Caucasian, Indian, Cambodian, sub-Saharan African, and Middle Eastern among them. Then he noticed one odd-looking Caucasian man with carrot-colored tufts of hair, who wore old-fashioned glasses with round lenses that gave him the look of a startled owl. Before Blaise could ask Kristina who they were, she wheeled round and delivered a short-arm jab to his belly. He doubled up on the floor from the force of the blow, which knocked the breath out of him.

Blaise tried to sit up, but a force like many invisible hands held him in its crushing grip. Kristina knelt beside him, grasped him by the hair and slammed his head into the concrete.

"Kristina, what are you doing?"

"My mother is dead," she spat.

"Amelia, dead? How?"

She slammed his head against the floor again. "The Cloud reverse hacked her, reactivated her neurofeed, and the Mantis took her before we could block it. She's dodged those bastards for years. Always ten steps ahead of them. Then suddenly they catch up to her. Probably with help from you."

"Are you crazy?" he gasped. "Why would I want Amelia dead?"

"Bring him here, to the circle," barked a slender black woman in her forties.

Invisible hands released him, and Kristina dragged him to his feet and shoved him into a metal chair. Then she sat a couple of seats down from the black woman in the circle. Blaise looked from face to face and saw nothing but malice in the cruel eyes that scrutinized him.

"Excuse me, do you have names?" he asked in an effort to break through their hostility.

"Yeah, we got names," the black woman answered. "And if you survive this little chat, we'll tell you what they are."

A Middle Eastern woman whipped back the hem of her jacket to reveal the butt of a laser burner. She took it out and laid it atop her blue-jeaned leg.

"Careful," the hatchet-faced man with the owl eyes cried. "He might bring the Mantis."

"I risked the Mantis to upload your fucking worm, and it didn't work!" Blaise blurted. He glanced at Kristina for support, but her expression was hard as an impenetrable mask.

"Those SWAT animals are about as subtle as MOAB bombs," the black woman snapped. "We all look alike to them. But sending in a covert agent; now that's a great way to ferret us out."

"Covert agent? Do you know how crazy that sounds? Kristina, tell them I'm not a spy."

"When did you sell us out?" the Middle Eastern woman demanded. "Was it after Minsheng had you arrested? Or before? When did you put them onto Amelia?"

"Your worm couldn't get past the AI firewalls. I got arrested, along with some other Class Is. I had to bluff my way out of getting tortured to death. I never sold you out."

"You made a deal with Minsheng to save your worthless ass," the black woman accused.

"That's ridiculous. I've been trying to try to find a way to get here for two months. To un-fuck this situation. But Minsheng's been working my ass off seven days a week on his genocide project."

"And you finished it?"

"No. Minsheng pulled me off that to perfect some weaponized Mantis military tech, from algorithms I developed to sharpen up VR feed. Then I had to break through some Califate firewalls. After that, it was balls to the wall on Anima again. I haven't slept in weeks."

"Tough life, crushed between the jaws of Mitsuko's pussy," the black woman scoffed. "And while you were coding with her, you gave away Amelia's location."

"No! Minsheng worked us both day and night. We kept running into glitches. We're still a long way from integrating Anima into *Gilgamesh V*. I did everything I could to keep it that way."

"Bullshit! You're breaking your ass to finish it, so Minsheng and the board can commit genocide against us. Then you get to enjoy eternal life with your hot little Beijing bitch."

"Where do you get all this shit?"

"Don't look so surprised, asshole. Think we stopped our surveillance on you? It ain't perfect but it's steady-state."

"I did what I had to do to survive," Blaise managed. He thought it distinctly possible they were about to kill him. He looked to Kristina but saw not even a hint of mercy in her face. "But I never sold you out."

The Middle Eastern woman leaned toward him. "So the director's working your Class I ass off round the clock, and stress is killing you, but suddenly Minsheng decides to give you a week off? Just when it's crucial to finish your Anima coding? And days after Amelia's assassinated? Now, why would he do that, shithead?"

"Maybe Minsheng sweetened the deal for you," the black woman put in. "Maybe he offered you a spot on the board. All you gotta do? Lead SWAT here. Or maybe fry us with the Mantis, now you got access to it."

"Wouldn't I have fried you the second I walked in if that's what I had in mind?"

"So what *do* you have in mind, asshole? Cuz things ain't lookin' so good for you here."

"Minsheng's scared shitless his demands on me might cause a psychotic break. He can't afford to have his best coder crash and burn. I convinced him I had to recharge in the Zone."

"You've spent your professional life enslaving the masses with VR. And when Amelia and Kristina give you the chance to redeem your worthless ass, you sell them out. You'd sell all of us out."

"That's not true!"

"You're Class I. You wouldn't know the truth if it bit you on the ass."

"But I'm here, a helluva long way from other Class Is, Einstein, risking my life to help you."

"Games planner lies ain't gonna work here."

"Lady, Polyphemus failed. Period. Through no fault of mine. So you'd better be asking how we're going to reconfigure it."

"You sabotaged that upload. Didn't you? And you're here to kill us."

It occurred to Blaise that nothing he could say would convince them he hadn't sold them out. They were going to assassinate him. In the face of such absurdity, he tried his last, best defense: humor.

"You got a lot of questions, lady. Well, I got one for you. What's black and sticks to a tree? A peeping Tom after a forest fire."

The black woman looked perplexed. "Think jokes are gonna save your ass?"

"Even worthless people can bring a smile to your face. For instance, when you push them down the stairs."

The black woman glanced around at the others in the circle. "Fuck this, let's start the probe."

Blaise tried to tell another joke, but the hackers hurled a wave of energy that pinned him against his chair with the crushing force of a tsunami. It rushed to his brain, flooded his thoughts and memories, and erased the possibility of reason. Terror penetrated him as they ripped off the masks he used to hide himself from the world and plunged deeper. They thrust into his reptilian brain like flaming swords. The burrowed into his innermost sensations and most humiliating secrets, and plunged deeper still beyond his individuality across seas of raging stars and nameless meridians of the infinite abyss until they reached his soul's core, the carnal womb of his gestation, which pulsed with the ultimate agony of being.

"S-s-t-op!" he managed, eyes clamped shut. Tears wet his cheeks with the unguent of infinite guilt. "Oh, God. Kristina, help me!"

Suddenly the tsunami evaporated, and he was no longer crushed and paralyzed but merely enraged and exhausted. He opened his eyes, gulped deep breaths, trembled and sweated in the afterbirth of his ordeal. The black woman gave a signal, and the hackers rose one by one and vanished into the gloom beyond the huge oscillating fan. It blew lukewarm breeze to him with a vacant hum.

Kristina approached and took him in her arms. He wept from the grief of having his soul stripped naked and burbled half-formed words clotted with the snot of his tears. He slipped off the chair, and she held him like a mother soothing a child's nightmare.

"It's over now," she whispered. "I'm sorry it had to happen, but the others insisted. They had to be sure. I had to be sure."

"Of what?" he gasped.

"That your soul hasn't been corrupted."

"What . . . did you do to me?"

"Curseil. We've made some breakthroughs since I last saw you. We're learning to co-exist on many dimensions. A skill we had to cultivate to fight Cloud mind control. We haven't perfected it. But one area we're getting pretty good at is soul assessment."

He blinked at her, tried to grasp her meaning.

Her smile, couched between two black tresses that tumbled about her slender shoulders, swept his fear away.

"Your soul is intact, Blaise. Now you can be part of what we're building."

12

KRISTINA LED HIM DOWN A HOLLOW, RINGING METAL CORRIDOR to her quarters, a former storage room. There was an unmade bed, a couch and faded rug, and a solar-powered kitchenette. A holodeck stood on a table near a couple of metal chairs and a standing floor lamp. Art prints relieved bare concrete walls. A hacker engineer had installed a heater that ran off energy stored from the same solar panels that powered the stove.

She made him lie on the bed, stilled his trembling hands, dried his tears, and whispered calming words until he fell into exhausted sleep. He dreamed of flying over virgin jungle in a tinfoil airplane before crashing into infinite green. The aroma of food woke him. Kristina had changed into a blue silk kimono. She brought him a steaming bowl of noodles on a tray with a cup of spring water, a napkin, and chopsticks.

"Don't get up," she urged. "You need to rest. You've no idea how badly Minsheng's drained your spirit." She brought the bowl close to his nose. "Pad Thai with zucchini squash noodles."

"Wonderful," he cried gratefully. Then a pang of guilt touched his heart. "Kristina, please forgive me for taking so long to come back."

"Not many people break free from a lifetime of soul slavery," she said while she fed him. Then something flitted across her face that made her look away. Uncertainty slipped into her tone. "That woman, Mitsuko. She must have been hard to leave, even for a week. She's so beautiful."

"Forget about her. What's important is, I had to see you again. We've got to find a way to recode Polyphemus. Turns out, this Anima genocide is just the beginning. Minsheng's planning to assassinate the board and make himself chairman. He's completely insane! He forced me to kill a man with the Mantis."

"Being human is a terrifying thing. But we can be so much more."

She pointed to a poster with a vista of gestating galaxies. The caption read: *We are not human beings having a spiritual experience. We are spiritual beings having a human experience. – Pierre Teilhard de Chardin*

"What does it mean?" he wondered.

"Be patient. I'll show you."

"Show me what?"

"Things you've always wanted to know without knowing you did. Things I learned from a great teacher."

He regarded her with amazement for her ability to remain calm considering what faced humanity at Minsheng's hands.

"You're incredible," he smiled. "A hacker, a terrorist, a master of disguise, with psychic powers, no less. There's a lot more to you than I saw in that stripper back in the Zone."

That made her laugh. She swept her tresses back from her face, which brought her high cheekbones and full lips into sharp relief. He noticed that one nostril rested a few degrees higher than the other, though not enough to make her nose malformed. He found such a tiny imperfection deeply attractive. It gave her a natural beauty he had forgotten about after his time with Mitsuko.

"You're so lovely," he whispered.

She whipped back her hair. "You're such a liar."

"It's true, Kristina."

"Men like you worship the look they see in holographic ads and VR series. Slag men are just the same. I don't have that kind of glamor."

"So how'd you convince me you were a hottie from 'Frisco?"

"I was in character. I studied acting."

She slipped a smooth, tear-shaped crystal with a blue flower suspended inside it from her kimono and plied it with her fingers, turned it this way and that, like a musician playing a strangely silent instrument. He was fascinated by the delicacy of her gestures, her slender wrists and arms.

"Acting? Where?"

"USC."

"USC's grown up in weeds."

"It's declined since its glory days. But The Cloud board never really considered replacing it with condo-pods. I think they want to turn it into a museum. Some former academics took over a few classroom buildings, hacked into the L.A. power grid, and gave us classes. That's where I learned acting."

"Doesn't SWAT sweep the campus?"

"They have bigger fish to fry."

He had other questions, but she silenced them with a kiss and caressed his hair with her fingertips until he fell asleep.

When he woke, he felt strangely refreshed. Kristina whispered code into her holodeck at a rickety table. Her lithe white leg peered out from the hem of her kimono.

When she saw he was awake, she smiled and glided over to him. "How are you feeling?"

"Like I've had my ass kicked. Where are we, anyway?"

"I've been here a couple months. It's a sub-level of the warehouse I took you to. I'll have to move soon. Keep a step ahead of SWAT."

"I remember now," he shuddered. "The others . . . that horrible mind probe."

She rubbed her nose against his. One of her tresses touched his face. "Tell me I'm beautiful again, and I'll tell you where the bathroom is."

He stroked her hair. "More lovely than I have words to describe."

She flourished a hand toward the door. "End of the hall. We passed it on the way here. Plumbing still works. I've even got recycled toilet paper. How's that for civilized? Why don't you clean up a bit? When you're done, we could do a couple of exercises."

Blaise's heart sank into the floor. "Please, not them again."

"No, not with the others," she laughed. "They're busy coding in their own hideaways. We're modifying the Polyphemus code to make it firewall-proof, and you'll help us. I'm talking about doing something different now. Yoga exercises. To clear your head. Give you some perspective. Freshen up, now, OK? I've got a bit of coding to finish."

Blaise found the bathroom, a prehistoric artifact with a cracked linoleum floor and toilets made from vitreous china. Lichen and ancient dust had blackened some, but a couple of shitters had been restored to working order. He relieved himself and made a sponge bath at one of the sinks, shaving himself in the triangular sliver of a ruined mirror.

When he returned to Kristina, he was surprised to find her kneeling naked on the faded Persian rug, eyes closed, palms on thighs. She was breathtaking, but in a less sculpted way than Mitsuko.

He dropped his backpack on the couch. She opened her eyes.

"Please kneel facing me," she instructed.

He had no idea what she had in mind, but he did as she asked. After he knelt, palms on thighs, he found the rug hard and bristly. His calf muscles pinched. He wasn't sure how long he could hold this posture.

"Would you mind clenching your fist?"

It struck him as a strange request. "Why?"

"A sensory awareness exercise. Please. Clench your fist and release."

He did as she asked.

"Good. Now clench your fist again. Release, then clench again. Notice how the bones, tendons, and muscles in your arm are rigid? Touch the veins in your arm. They're bulging like angry snakes, right? Now expand that awareness."

"Expand it where?"

"Throughout your body. All your fibers are connected, compressed, clenched up by anxiety, stress, fear."

His knees were starting to ache. "How do you know all that?" he asked, impatient for some relief from his pinching calves.

"It's the same with everyone. You're carrying a lifetime of stress in your body, from childhood traumas, from being taught you had to suffer to achieve. Society told you to dedicate every last gram of energy to beating the competition. You have to top yourself, time and again, or you're a worthless turd. Am I right? Plus, you're addicted to VR."

Both of his calves were pinching badly now. He wanted this exercise over.

"The longer you substitute VR for the real thing, the more you alienate body from soul. That's at the root of the despair eating you up since you lost your wife and daughter."

"How do you know about them?" he demanded.

"You told me about them the first night we were together."

"I don't remember that."

She saw the hurt in his face. "You were drunk on sake. You poured your heart out. You said it was very healing. For your soul."

"There is no soul," he shot back. "And my calves are killing me."

"The great fallacy of the Western mind."

"What? Calves?"

"The idea that mind, soul, and body are disconnected."

"You can't disconnect from something that isn't there. The soul is a fairy tale. We don't need it anymore."

"Then what do we need?"

It was embarrassing to kneel before her and discuss a superstition like the soul, a notion that had long since become a dirty joke.

"I need to get off my fucking calves. And my back is aching."

He heaved up and limped over to the couch, plopped down and tugged a blanket she had there up around his shoulders.

She pulled on her kimono and kneeled facing him. "Are you offended to talk about your soul?"

"Nobody believes that ghost in the machine stuff anymore," he asserted to re-establish his authority. "It's infantile."

"Why infantile?"

He wanted to stop her words with kisses and caresses, but this was an initiation of some kind, and he risked pissing her off if he didn't indulge her. She obviously expected him to debate the subject.

"Because, Kristina, the notion of the soul reflects our desperation to deny the finality of death. It's a futile attempt to turn the universe into something meaningful. There's no higher meaning. We're just animals. When you're dead, you're dead. Lights out. Fade to black."

Kristina placed her crystal on the rug. She arched her back, eased out of her yoga posture, propped herself up on one knee with her hands clasped over it, and studied him.

"You're quite sure of that?"

'This is boring, Kristina. Let's talk about something fun. Did you hear about that major new study? It found that humans eat more bananas than monkeys. It's true. I can't remember the last time I ate a monkey."

She laughed at that. "Pretty good. But let's not get distracted."

What did she expect from him? What was her purpose in this pointless debate? He had only a few days off before he had to face L.A., Minsheng, and Mitsuko again, and he didn't want to waste time philosophizing.

"What's with the crystal?" he asked, hunting another way to change the subject.

She crawled over to the couch with it, got under the blanket with him, and warmed him with her body and the scent of her hair. How he wanted her! But she wasn't ready for lovemaking yet. She ran a finger along the crystal's base, where the curved glass ended in a black irregular stub.

"You want to fuck me now, don't you?" she teased. "You're getting impatient for it, hmm?"

"Maybe," he teased back, swelling with desire.

"We'll get to the *carezza*," she laughed.

"The what?"

"The *carezza*. A tantric sexual technique. Patience, please," she teased and pressed the crystal into his hand. "This was an award Mythoplex gave my mom, back when she was a games planner. It had a base printed with her name and the date they awarded it. The base broke off. Cheap material. This was pretty much my only toy growing up. I used to think it was magic." She tapped the glass with a fingernail. "The flower in the center? No idea why it's there, but when I was little, my mom told me about a dying princess who could only be cured by the suitor who fetched her a blue rose from the underworld. This was her gift to me. Who knows? Maybe it is magic."

"I wish that were true, Kristina, but there's no magic," he observed bitterly.

She ran the smooth surface of the crystal along his cheek. "What about the laws of physics? The magic of photons. They can be waves or particles."

He couldn't help but roll his eyes. "Kristina, where do you get this stuff?"

She smiled and ran a teasing finger across his lips. "From Thomas."

He brushed her hand away, irritated not by her touch but by the mention of a stranger. "Who's Thomas?"

"My husband."

Dread spread through Blaise's body as if this mysterious Thomas had traipsed into the room and found them together, on the couch under the blanket.

She ran a finger through his hair. "Don't be jealous. He passed away six years ago."

"How?" Blaise asked, relieved.

"Natural causes," she replied. "A heart attack. He was a good bit older than me. And he had a strenuous life. He became a monk when he was a young man."

Her reverent tone prompted a new anxiety, something he hadn't experienced before. "Sorry, a what?"

"A monk. In what used to be a monastery in the hills above Malibu. The Cloud army razed it to the ground. Slaughtered every monk they could catch. He had to hide in the hills for weeks."

Blaise shook his head. "Sorry. Monastery?"

She slid from under the blanket, leaned back against a couch arm, and let him admire the musculature of her thighs, her slender calves, the luxurious sweep of her hair. He ached to make love to her. But now someone had come between them.

"Nobody remembers monasteries anymore," she lamented.

He shrugged. "I've heard the word somewhere. History class. The Middle Ages. Right? Back when there were Jesus-worshippers."

"It was a religious order. Monks lived apart from other people, to perfect spiritual disciplines. Meditation. Prayer. Yoga. Things like that."

"Sorry, a spiritual discipline?" Blaise asked.

"The yoga exercise we just did. That's a spiritual discipline. Centering yourself and eliminating body shame. A kind of meditation. Like that mantra you told me you chant."

"I chant my mantra to keep The Cloud Monitor from catching me. Look, just tell me one thing. Why are we sitting here philosophizing and not fucking?"

She chuckled at that. "Yoga re-centers you in your body. So you feel at home in it again."

Blaise found this view incomprehensible, but he didn't want to appear naïve, now that she had presented Thomas as an authority figure.

"Were these monks of yours some kind of, I don't know, what is it called? Mystics?"

"When there was a church, yes."

"And they practiced yoga?"

"Yes. It's a way of using your body to meditate. A kind of Zen."

This stuff was obviously important to Kristina, and Blaise was clueless about it. He felt like a rube, and he despised the dead man, Thomas, for making him one.

"So what exactly is Zen?" was all he could think to ask.

She grinned at the frustration in his face. "I'll explain another time."

"How long were you with this Thomas?"

Kristina's tongue touched the edge of her lips as she turned the crystal end over end. "You're jealous."

Blaise blushed and looked away. "How can I be jealous of someone who's dead?"

"We barely had four years together. I was eighteen when we married. He and my mom were friends. They had green thumbs."

"Green thumbs?"

She held the crystal up to the ceiling light and suppressed a laugh. "An old expression. We kept a vegetable garden out back of our apartment. I worked it with Thomas and my mom. Thomas taught me . . . so much. He was enlightened. It crushed me when he died. I thought he'd live forever. Thought mom would, too."

Blaise felt his own value recede into shadow. "Sorry you lost the man you love."

She studied his face, then smiled slyly, crawled over to him, slid up under the blanket and kissed him. "I've found a new man. And by the way, fucking is a wonderful way to top off a yoga exercise. Makes you so much more limber. Now about that *carezza* I promised you."

He was furious with her for teasing him mercilessly. But soon, his anger and jealousy of Thomas melted away in the sweaty jungle of her body. Afterward, she lay atop him, her eyes glowing with something he had seen before: an ethereal light from a place he couldn't name. It was beyond sex, beyond emotion. Something pure and precious that he thirsted for. Their lovemaking took far longer than he thought possible. She asked him to hold back his orgasm as long as he could and just feel their heart connection.

She nuzzled his neck. "You've been holding back energy trapped in your cells your whole life. It's disconnected you from your body. I just reconnected you. Shall we try more *carezza*? Maybe tomorrow?"

"Definitely tomorrow. Or later today. Or maybe right now?"

"Tomorrow. And every time we do, you'll find it sweeter, deeper, more meaningful, because it will come from the center."

"Well, it's wonderful," he whispered. But then a disturbing thought struck him. "What about Polyphemus? What's happening with that?"

"I told you, the others are recoding it. And we'll need your help. But I've been preparing you for something else just now."

"And what would that be?"

"Patience. You have to be in the proper state of mind to receive what I'm teaching you."

Something stirred in the quick of him: the conviction in her words, the vibration of passion, and, what was it, love? An emotion he hadn't felt since Cherry abandoned him, though Mitsuko had given him a convincing approximation.

Kristina taught him *carezza* for another two days. She told him it was a technique focused on tenderness and intimacy, which used delayed orgasm to heighten the spiritual connection between lovers. His attempts at it were clumsy and exhausting at first, but he soon warmed to it, and after each *carezza* session, they fell asleep in one another's arms like children who had been playing hard all day.

She led him through sensations he had never felt before. Each day brought a different kind of release, subtle electrical connections in his mind's marrow. After they napped and rose to go through yet another session, she had him kneel facing her, closer than before, so their knees touched. She was radiant. Her smile was so open and natural it brought tears of joy to his eyes.

"See me . . . feel me . . . touch me . . . heal me," she chanted.

"What's that from?"

"An old song from the twentieth century. Something my mom taught me."

The following morning she brought him biscuits and coffee.

"I'm going to show you something special today," she announced. "Our secret world. I think you're ready for it now. And after I do, we can join the others, and you can help us recode Polyphemus."

He realized with a start that he had only a few more days before he had to return to L.A. Minsheng's image and all the horrors connected with him reared up in his mind.

"What's wrong?" Kristina asked.

"I don't like to think about L.A."

She closed her eyes, sighed, and held his hand tightly. "I don't like it, either. But after today, you'll feel differently."

"Why?"

"I told you. Magic."

13

KRISTINA PUT ON A CLEAN BLUE COTTON DRESS AND SNEAKERS
and led him down a clanging set of stairs to a much lower sub-basement. They
passed control rooms with technicians who monitored consoles like those Blaise
had seen in neurofeeds about The Cloud regime's tech advancements. Blaise
wondered how the hackers had managed to pirate such technology without
getting caught.

They passed through a long corridor where the exhaust system hummed
from stretches of silver overhead pipes.

"How did you keep all this hidden?" he asked.

"Blind luck. That and our anti-hacking software. And we've got curseil now.
But of course, there's always a risk one of our own might give us away. People are
flawed and weak, and life's uncertain. The Cloud's corrupted some of our most
talented people. They hack into a holodeck and find one of us working on
something they can use. They approach that person and promise rehabilitation,
eternal life, just like they did with you."

"But no one's exposed this underground facility?" he wondered.

"We'd be dead if they had."

Something else occurred to him. "But The Cloud might let you continue
because it suits some purpose of theirs. They might let you think you're free until
you reach some milestone and then vaporize you. How do you know they don't
have you under surveillance right now?"

They passed through a corridor thrumming with the subterranean vibrations
of hidden machinery.

"Trust me, we'd know if we were," she replied. "We have a curseil team down here, working in shifts around the clock, blocking Cloud sweeps psychically."

That relieved him but doubts remained. "What about ground level?"

Kristina gave him a sharp glance. "I told you, we move continually to different locations up above."

"That's not foolproof."

Hurt showed in Kristina's face. "I know what you're thinking. Mom got caught. That was a rare piece of bad luck, Blaise."

"What about traitors? People who might like what The Cloud offers."

"When we catch a rat, we use curseil to execute the fucker. The Cloud Monitor loses interest after that. Case closed. On to new prey."

They came to a staircase painted industrial red. It led down several flights to a cavernous sub-level. At the rear of it rose an exposed vein of basalt, fluted with mid-Miocene rock. In the center of the rock stood a porthole ten meters high, with a metallic flange.

"That's the entrance to our hyperloop."

Blaise recalled the word but not the context.

A technician with a rolling gait and suntanned face approached, shook Blaise's hand, and gave Kristina a peck on her cheek.

"We're headed for the new city," she explained. "Can you hook us up?"

"Sure can," the cowboy technician replied. "Hyperloop leaves in ten minutes with construction workers and their families, and, I think, a couple botanists."

The hair on the back of Blaise's head prickled. He turned to face the owl-eyed man with reddish hair tufts, one of the hackers who had scoured his soul. Dread flooded Blaise's mind as if the man transmitted neurofeed on a chaotic frequency.

The stranger pumped Blaise's hand. "Glad you made it this far. We got Kristina to thank for that."

"Guess you're right about that," Blaise replied, not quite sure what to make of the man.

"John Lennon. Sixth of that name. Worked for Mythoplex back in the day, just like you. Shit-canned, exiled." Lennon glanced about and shrugged. "Now I'm here, such as it is. Hey, sorry for that soul-scouring. Wasn't personal."

"You did what you had to," Blaise rejoined, reassured by Kristina's smile.

"I'll let you kids go, but when you're back from the new city, you're invited to a barbecue out at my pod. I'll introduce you around."

Blaise looked to Kristina. She nodded.

"Sure, I've got a couple of days yet." Blaise smiled. But he felt a pang of dread at the thought of leaving this intriguing alternative world.

Lennon winked, nodded, and left.

The cowboy technician, at his holodeck, issued a curt command, "Admit two to hyperloop."

Resonant humming issued from the porthole. Blaise and Kristina stepped back as it swung open. Then Kristina led him down a tunnel bored into the rock for a hundred meters. They emerged on a platform edged by a scalloped tunnel that plunged deep into bedrock. Dozens of Slags milled about, among them children who poked and slapped at each other while adults ordered them to simmer down. On the tracks stood a missile-shaped train with a black nose. As Blaise and Kristina approached, a door thirty meters wide slid up to admit passengers to a car.

"How in God's name did you manage this?" Blaise gasped.

"Stole it from some early twenty-first-century geniuses. It's a hybrid design based on Elon Musk's hyperloop and the Japanese maglev train. We could've had an L.A. hyperloop twenty-five years back, interplanetary travel, too, for that matter, if they'd backed Musk's successors. But The Cloud only cared about power and personal immortality. So we hacked their servers and stole the designs. Been working our asses off to build it and drill the tunnel ever since."

"It's magnificent. But how'd you build it?"

"Three-D printing, same tech The Cloud uses. We've got an automated factory many levels below this sub-level. And we used stolen laser cannons to drill the tunnel."

They boarded the car and belt-beamed in near two women who secured rambunctious kids in their seats. Kristina explained that the seats faced the car's rear to diminish the effects of acceleration and deceleration at twelve hundred and fifty klicks an hour—twice as fast as a bullet train.

"So where we headed?" Blaise wondered.

"Doesn't have a formal name yet. Out in the desert, below what used to be called Arizona. We enlarged some limestone caverns there."

The door slid into place. The hyperloop vibrated, and the car shot into the tunnel. The crush of acceleration rushed blood to Blaise's head, but the pressure distributed itself cleanly along his body rather than with paralyzing force, as with the bullet train. Soon they reached cruising speed. The train moved soundlessly. Even the children were quiet.

Thirty minutes later, by Blaise's Mythoplex watch, the car decelerated. They reached a station in a plaza, part of a city inside a lofty cavern. The passengers Blaise and Kristina had traveled with laughed and chatted as they dispersed through streets that meandered past lozenge-shaped houses with undulant walls.

Deeper into the city, Blaise saw nearly-finished homes, fronted by multi-floored windows that curved around lawns with trees and shrubs. The houses were of variegated shapes, sizes and colors, and some had broad windows supported by columns that looked like plant stalks. Streets ascended and descended hillocks, and the playful shape of the houses suggested that an architect with a sense of humor had designed them. Laughter and humming machinery echoed from somewhere.

"It's sunny here," he remarked. "How'd you manage that?"

Kristina swept her arm in a graceful arc. "Solar panels hidden in the desert refract light here. There are shutters scalloped into the cavern."

Blaise scanned the cavern roof with its spiny crust of stalactites but couldn't make out anything beyond them.

"Does anyone live here yet?"

"Mostly carpenters, masons, and electricians putting final touches on everything. We're moving families here in groups of a hundred or so, so SWAT won't notice they've vanished from the Zone."

They entered a plaza shaped like a lotus blossom. Storefronts and apartments rose from vermiculate walls fronted by balconies like graceful lidded eyes. Spidery columns separated floors. Everything pulsated with life. The city looked like it was about to take flight as if Blaise had caught it in a pause between wing beats.

Kristina led him up a side street. Ahead he saw a curtain of green: a Douglas fir forest somehow transplanted from the Pacific Northwest to this cavern beneath the desert. They entered a glade where firs towered above, nourished by sunlight from hidden lattices. Blaise felt a breeze, smelled refreshing forest odors, saw squirrels and flitting birds. A delicious calm stole over him as if the trees sang on a subtle vibrational frequency.

"Looks like it's been here for centuries."

"We've been genetically accelerating growth," she revealed. "Laid in nutrient-rich soil to feed mycorrhizal networks. They're hyperlinked underground through fungal networks the mother trees regulate."

"Mother trees?"

His surprise amused her. "The oldest trees with the most fungal connections. They know when shallow-rooted seedlings in other parts of the forest need water and suck it up from their root networks to feed saplings and send nutrients. They can sense distress signals when neighboring trees are struggling."

"You make it sound like they're sentient."

"They are. But they move on a slow time continuum. Can't detect that in this holoscape we use to get around our three-dimensional world."

Blaise had more questions but forgot them as the fragrant forest swept up his spirit.

Later they strolled back to the city, refreshed by clean air and benevolent vibrations. As they climbed a street bordered by buildings with concave and convex walls, he saw what looked like giant lizards thrusting up from the horizon. They crested a hill. The lizards were towers rising from a tan-colored palace. Across its midsection were down-thrust buttresses with crowns webbed like bat wings. One tower thrust high above the others. Smaller spires soared up near the highest one as if a giant had dribbled them down as ornaments for a stupendous sand castle.

"What is this?" Blaise whispered in awe.

Deep joy registered in Kristina's voice. "Sagrada Familia."

"Sacred family."

"Yes. The Hadjis destroyed the original in Barcelona during a dirty bomb attack. We found digital blueprints on an old server in the Vatican in Rome after the Hadjis leveled the Eternal City. We used 3-D printing to reproduce the basilica, with marble mined from a Colorado quarry."

"How on earth did you get marble from Colorado?"

"An old freeway east of L.A., too insignificant for The Cloud to patrol since the Hadjis obliterated Denver with one of their dirty bombs. Our excavation crews sweated it out for years in an abandoned quarry to extract the raw stones. We used industrial lasers adapted from Cloud military models to carve out the marble and hauled them here on industrial hover-trucks stolen from the army."

"Without Cloud hover-gunships spotting them?"

"The former U.S. Southwest is worthless desert. Even if a Cloud satellite defeated our cloaking devices, they'd dismiss a hover-truck transporting marble slabs as a black market op. Like the kind Minsheng operates. He buys marble for his estate from smugglers with their own hover-truck fleets."

Blaise reflected on the Byzantine complexity of a world he had known nothing about before coming here. He felt as naïve as a child.

"You called this place a basilica," he commented when he found his voice again. "A temple for Jesus-worshippers, as I recall. I took a course in ancient mythologies at UCLA. Amazing. Didn't think there were any of them left. It's breathtaking."

"We spent decades transporting the marble here, section by section. Took an army of architects, engineers, masons, sculptors, laborers, Cloud exiles, and castoffs to build the basilica in twenty-four-hour shifts. We laid the capstone in place last December."

As she led him to the temple, Blaise's heart throbbed with, what?—something exquisite he couldn't name that vibrated from the structure itself.

"But why would you spend years building this temple? What purpose does it serve?"

"You'll see when we get inside."

She gestured for silence as they approached obsidian doors twice a man's height. They passed into a portico flanked by lofty windows with multi-colored glass panels. Beyond lay an echoing hall. Jointed columns spread out in rows on either side. The lofty windows threw fractured rainbows in kaleidoscopic patterns.

Blaise gazed up, where buttresses branched like leaf veins that culminated in granite flowers. At the hall's rear stood silver pipes notched with gashes, like a gigantic pan flute. Above rose a burnt-ochre cupola, and behind the cupola rose varicolored windows with jointed columns. Here, the air was more than air. It had a buoyancy redolent of incense, powdered stone, and waterfall vapor. He approached a window of multicolored glass and felt a giddy rush. Reality tilted as if he had landed in the hold of a storm-tossed ship. He stumbled back into the main hall, drawn to a pulsing presence. Voices harmonized in a nameless tongue, a quavering refrain from some spectral choir. From above the fluted pipes, layers of coruscating magma, light within light, opened like a molten flower, shattered his physical being, and splintered it into shards in a higher ecstasy that saturated him with joy upon joy. This oceanic tide erased the fleeting agonies masquerading as everyday life and consumed everything in the rapture of a limitless dimension.

When Blaise came to himself, he was on his knees, trembling. Kristina helped him to a seat in a row of benches. He noticed they weren't alone in the vast temple. Others, Slag workers mostly, sat or stood with faces uplifted with joy and rapture.

"What happened?" he gasped.

"There are no words; just trust that it's real," Kristina reassured him.

Her hair encircled a face transfigured by light, a presence he had felt before emanating from her but which revealed itself fully now in her slender form.

She's right. I see it now. It's real.

"Your soul—" he cried, overcome by tears.

Something was emerging inside him, a jewel of infinite value, birthed from the slime of his own soul, a presence pulsing from his center, and he knew he had to cling to it. He felt he couldn't possibly go back to L.A., whatever the risk, now that he had experienced this. Even if the Mantis came for him.

Kristina, sensing something from him, transmitted two words using curseil: *We am.*

14

BLAISE WOKE FROM A DREAMLESS SLEEP TO THE STRAINS OF
a stringed instrument he had never heard before. He was on the couch in
Kristina's room, a coarse blanket thrown over him. A solar heater glowed from a
corner. She knelt facing him across a scuffed coffee table. She had changed into a
sleeveless silk dress with pink orchids and gold brocade embroidered in the fabric.
A silver pin clasped her hair, and she had combed her black tresses down in glossy
heaps. A teakwood tray with a brown crockery teapot, cups, a wooden ladle, a
china bowl with dried tea leaves, and other implements stood on the table.

She trailed her fingertips across her mandarin collar. "This belonged to my
mother. She inherited all this stuff from my grandmother. It fits me, the dress,
don't you think?"

He was moved by her transformation, which emphasized her fine, feline figure,
and thanks to the makeup and eyeliner she had applied, her liquid eyes as well.

"Absolutely," he replied, his heart swelling. "And that music?"

"Urhu," she replied. "Traditional Chinese. I keep some recordings in my
holodeck."

"Perfectly beautiful. Like you."

"Liar," she laughed, blushing and obviously pleased.

She performed a tea ceremony with graceful gestures. He found the ritual
hypnotic. And when she finished, he felt utterly at peace until a dark thought
intruded.

"Kristina, I can't go back to L.A.," he confessed. "That new city you're
building. That's where I belong. Not in L.A."

Her smile grew troubled. "I know how you feel," she agreed as she poured them both more tea. "After what you saw, leaving must feel like being expelled from the womb of all things."

"You'll have to find someone else to upload your worm."

She set down the teapot. "You're just overwhelmed by what you saw today."

"I'll work in your hidden city as . . . a mason, a carpenter. I don't care what."

She picked up the tear-shaped crystal with the blue flower inside and turned it in her hands as he had seen her do before. "You belong here, with us. But first you have to finish what you started. Later today we'll meet with the others. They've made a lot of progress recoding Polyphemus. We'll need you for the final touches."

He shook his head. "I can't go back, Kristina."

"Of course you can," she encouraged.

"No. My whole life's been a bluff. I'm not like that Thomas you talk about. I've never had courage. Only ambition. And fear. Fear that I'm worthless."

She placed the crystal down by the tea service, joined him on the couch, and took his hands in hers.

"You know you've got to go back, Blaise."

He threw his arm across his eyes, as if to escape the horror of L.A. and all it implied. "No. I can't."

She tugged his arm down and met his eyes with a tremulous glance. "I don't want you to go. Can't bear to think of you with that bitch Mitsuko. But you have to finish what you started."

Thomas, the monk, flared up in Blaise's mind: a hallucinatory figure with incandescent eyes and a booming voice. Blaise knew he could never live up to that ideal.

"I'm not the right man, Kristina. I'm just a games planner."

"You're the only man," she retorted, her voice strained. "We've got nobody else with a level five security clearance."

Blaise heaved up from the couch and padded away, the concrete floor hard against his bare feet as he stepped off the rug. He knew Kristina was right. He couldn't stay here and let whole populations die. But he couldn't face the director again, either.

"You said your network's global," he offered. "Find someone else to upload Polyphemus."

Kristina joined him and turned his face to hers. "We've tried. Six tries. Six failures. The others wouldn't—couldn't—upload even the first module."

He took a long, deep breath and shut his eyes. "If I could stay here long enough, and you help me understand what happened today, I might find Thomas's kind of courage."

He looked at her and saw anguish showed in her eyes. "I want you to understand the source. But I don't have the words. Nobody has them anymore. The Cloud deleted all the sacred texts."

"What the hell is this 'source'? Some kind of electromagnetic field? A portal into a parallel universe? What?"

"Don't ask me to describe the source of all things. That never works. As soon as you open your mouth you falsify it."

He turned away from her. "Then why put decades into building a temple for something that can't be described?"

She took a deep breath and steadied her voice. "Building it *is* a way of describing it. Its sacred space, Blaise. Designed by Antoni Gaudí, a long-forgotten architect. We built the new city in his style. His architecture expresses something fundamental The Cloud tried to erase from human consciousness."

Her words were absurd. How could there be 'sacred space'? What was it? Where did it come from? Then a strange feeling crept into his heart, a hint of something from another level, the curseil level that gave her words coherence.

"Well, whatever this 'source' is, it's more real than my entire life has been up to now. So I can't go back to L.A." He sighed deeply at the absurdity of what he had just said. "It's insane, I know. Minsheng will send the Mantis for me if I don't show up."

Her eyes turned hard, as they had when the curseil circle scoured his soul. "I told you we're shielded from The Cloud down here. With curseil. But if you won't go back, I don't think the others will protect you. They'll kill you."

He blundered away from her and returned to the couch. Her room felt like a prison cell now.

"You can't explain what happened to me today. But you want me to risk my life for it."

She joined him on the couch. "Blaise, there's more to this than I've told you."

He gave her a sharp look. All his initial fears about Kristina, her hackers, and their intentions rushed back to him. She took her crystal from the coffee table and turned it in her fingers in a way that made him realize how he hated this habit of hers.

"Minsheng lied about why The Cloud wants genocide. The population isn't twenty billion. It's closer to seven. Nearly what it was a century ago."

"That's not possible," he cried.

"It's true, Blaise. Regrettably, we're to blame for many of those population losses. The Caliphate used nanobots we developed against The Cloud twenty years back, long before you fought in Nigeria. The nanobots wiped out billions before we found out and deactivated them. That unfortunately gave The Cloud an edge. And they were crushing the Caliphate till last year. That's when we decided to give the Hadjis back their edge. To buy time."

"Time for what?"

She stared into the crystal as if the answer might lie inside it.

"Stop playing with that fucking thing!" he barked. He snatched it out of her hand. "The truth. Right now. Or I'll smash it against that wall."

"Give it back, please."

"Not till I get the whole story."

She threw him a stricken look. "We needed time to find someone like you. So we developed a new weapon for the Caliphate, a super-advanced nanobot. Something The Cloud can't defeat. The Caliphate paid us a fortune for it. It allowed us to speed up construction here, so we can offer Slags a sanctuary."

"You helped the Hadjis slaughter millions of poor, dumb, brainwashed Cloud soldiers and, and then the Caliphate wiped out whole populations in countries they conquered. How can you justify that?"

"That's how we financed the hyperloop, the new city, everything. And it keeps The Cloud busy with unwinnable wars."

"You sold out to the Hadjis!"

She shook her head. "No. We gave them a military advantage we control."

"How the fuck can you control nanobots?"

"By giving them shelf life. Making them the kind we can deactivate."

He sprang up from the couch and stalked away as if she might be contagious. Then he spun around to her.

"If your nanobots are so advanced, why not wipe out the entire Cloud army with them?"

She glanced at the crystal and stretched out her hand. He hesitated, then approached and dropped it in her hands.

"Peace is our way, Blaise, except when we're forced to fight, or help others fight." She considered him, then made a decision. "Look, you still don't have the whole picture."

She gestured for him to follow her to the portable holodeck on the rickety table. She pulled up a holographic map of the world.

"Tighter aspect ratio on Africa," she ordered, and the continent filled the screen. "Scroll down." The image scrolled to the horn of Africa.

"We leave wholesale slaughter to the Caliphate," she said, glancing up at

Blaise. "They've overrun the Sudan and South Africa. And decimated millions. Something we didn't foresee"

"Tell me something I don't know. Minsheng dropped that little MOAB bomb on me last week."

"Did he tell you the Caliphate decimated twenty Cloud divisions?"

The figure shocked him. "No."

"The neural network portrays Hadjis as desperate men fighting out of caves. But they're quite advanced." She paused and spoke to the holodeck. "Zoom out forty percent." The African continent shrank, and he saw the Middle East, Eastern Mediterranean, Black Sea, and the great land mass above it. "The Caliphate's taken all of Russia and everything down through sub-Saharan Africa."

Blaise was aghast. "Russia, too?"

She nodded. "Yes. This week. Europe and Asia will be next, including Hong Kong. Then North America."

"My God, I can't believe this."

She smiled. "That word again: God. You use it a lot, ever notice?"

"It's just a figure of speech!"

His shout startled her, but she quickly recovered. "Sensitive subject, I see. Nevermind. The thing to remember is the Hadjis despise us only slightly less than The Cloud does. But they need our weapons. And they pay handsomely for them."

So many absurdities swirled around in Blaise's mind that he couldn't make sense of them. He pressed his palms to his eyes.

"Let's say I can bring down The Cloud with Polyphemus," he ventured, glancing up at her. "Wouldn't the Caliphate attack us afterward? Wouldn't we be trading one enemy for another?"

Kristina shook her head. "They can't attack us with our own weapons. Nanobots, Blaise. Silicon micro-plagues we can activate and deactivate." She took a deep breath and let it out slowly. "Without them, the Caliphate will lose their conquests; conventional laser weapons can't keep rebellions from springing up. But there's something else. The board thinks if they drive the Slags and Hadjis to mass suicide with Anima, they'll have time to get Class Is to cities they're building further inland . . . before the floods hit."

A fresh abyss loomed in Blaise's mind. "Floods?"

"Blaise, the Cloud Board can't reverse global warming."

"But if we reduce the population—"

"Global aspect ratio," Kristina ordered the holoscape, and the entire world materialized. "Illuminate global flood zones."

On the screen, city after city glowed aquamarine: L.A., San Diego, Miami, London, Cape Town, Hong Kong, Sydney, and all the other coastal cities that had survived Hadji dirty bomb attacks.

"The damage is irreversible," Kristina sighed, pointing to various cities. "All those cities will be lost forever."

Blaise, shocked, stalked away from the holodeck as if he might outrun it. Where did he think he was going? Back to the new city? Not likely. The hackers wouldn't let him. Not unless he completed his mission. Weariness and frustration overcame him, and he threw himself across the unmade bed.

"How long have you known all this?"

He heard Kristina's approach, the bed's creaking, and felt her fingers on his shoulder.

"Cloud scientists have known for years. That's why the board wants to move Class Is inland. To new towns and cities. Minsheng's building one."

He gave her a sharp glance. "But he runs VR programming. What does he know about building cities?"

"You caught a glimpse of Minsheng City at his estate. You told me about it. You just didn't realize what it was."

He recalled the silver spires he had seen from Minsheng's balcony the day the director had ordered him to terminate the Slag.

Kristina nestled close to him. "I should have told you all this when we first met," she sighed. "But mom said I should wait till you proved yourself."

"So Amelia didn't trust me any more than the other hackers."

"She was afraid if you knew about the floods, you might decide terminating the Slags was mercy killing. That they'd be better off incinerated than drowned. Afterward, you could move to Minsheng City, and you'd have an eternity with Mitsuko to forget what you'd done."

He thought that over, examined it from all angles, and decided Amelia had a point.

"You were right to doubt me," he admitted. "But if Polyphemus works, how can you possibly evacuate the Slags before the floods? Without The Cloud servers that maintain them, the seawalls will collapse."

His change of tone encouraged her. "We're going to move fast. We'll commandeer hundreds of military hover-trucks from the marine base at Camp Pendleton, south of L.A., to evacuate people, and set up tent cities in Reseda for the refugees. We've got similar plans for other coastal cities. We've been stockpiling freeze-dried food and water. We'll transport everyone in Reseda to the new city in groups of a hundred. We're excavating new caverns to make room. And we have a plan that could save the parts of the world that survive the floods. With The Cloud gone, we can build desalinization plans on the new inland coasts, to irrigate deserts and restore croplands and rain forests. That would lower global temperatures enough to keep the planet from becoming a lifeless desert."

He considered her plan. Hope for its success flickered but quickly died. The seawalls would probably collapse as soon as the Polyphemus worm crashed their maintenance servers, so no evacuations would be possible.

Then something else struck him, and he rolled over to face her on the bed. "If the Cloud board knew about the coming floods, why not just move Class Is to Minsheng City and let L.A. drown? Why build incineration centers?"

"The sea walls may, just possibly, hold out a few more years with Cloud servers maintaining them. But the Caliphate is winning the war with our super-nanobots. The Cloud's got to annihilate the Slags and Hadjis before their own army's destroyed."

Blaise's head spun with the labyrinthine complexities Kristina described.

"What about The Cloud divisions your super-nanobots are slaughtering? And the millions in Africa?" he demanded. "How do super-nanobots fit in with your dedication to peace?"

"We did it to buy you time the only way we could." She brushed his forehead with her fingertips. "You have to try that upload again, Blaise. Otherwise Minsheng will finish *Gilgamesh V* and Anima with Mitsuko, and the genocide will happen without you."

Blaise pressed his palms to his eyes, trying to shut it all out.

"The VR age is ending, Blaise. We're going to live in reality again. You've been to the mountaintop. You've seen the future in our new city. Now you've got to go back down that L.A. shithole and make sure it comes true."

Her words filled him with hope and dread. He glanced up at her. "You're right," he conceded.

Tenderness shone in her eyes. "And when you come back to me next time, it will be to stay."

She gave him a kiss that ran deeper than sexual desire or mortal love. It came from her center.

15

BLAISE AND KRISTINA SPENT A DAY, AND MOST OF A NIGHT, with the other hackers in a holodeck lab, putting the final touches on the upgraded Polyphemus. They ran the worm through hundreds of simulations, mimicking all The Cloud AI firewalls they had identified. They repaired glitches and coding loopholes and slogged on until early morning, performing debugging protocols to give the new version the best shot at bypassing everything Cloud quantum computers could throw at it.

After a sleepless night they sat side by side at street level on a rusting oil drum to watch the desert sunrise.

"You think it'll work?" Kristina asked.

Blaise sighed. "We'll know when I upload."

They grabbed a few hours of sleep in Kristina's room, and then drove out to John Lennon's afternoon barbecue in a stripped-down autobot the hackers had stowed in one of the abandoned Reseda warehouses. Lennon the Sixth lived in a restored ranch house twenty klicks out in the desert. Blaise recalled the drive to Minsheng's estate and how he and Mitsuko had lubricated their awkwardness with each other by drinking Pinot Noir. This drive with Kristina was very different. Her scent calmed him, and the sagebrush, cactus, and bulbous desert plants alongside the abandoned freeway were like the living tissue of a single, silent organism.

Nevertheless, despite the peace of their surroundings, lingering concerns tugged at Blaise's mind. Given their complicity with the Hadjis in developing weaponized nanobots, might bringing down The Cloud result in a hacker-controlled regime without the advantages of eternal life? But perhaps the hackers had cracked that nut as well, with pilfered Lazarus-D technology. And what about the Slags the hackers hoped to rescue? Would there be time for that before the seawalls collapsed? Even if they could evacuate the Slags, would hacker savvy bring lasting compassion, freedom, and equality after the novelty of rescue wore off, and the Slags remained, a generation of lost souls? Some could be trained; others couldn't be. For the uneducated ones, it would mean menial labor. And the "new" city might just devolve, in time, into another Cloud empire.

"Why the long face?" Kristina teased him. "Isn't the desert beautiful?"

"Just tired," he answered, not caring to voice his concerns on his last day with her.

Up ahead, Lennon's house stood atop a gully that terminated in the fan-shaped runoff from flash floods. He had replaced the orange roof tiles, but the walls had been worn away by sand and time. Blaise stowed the autobot under a shed at the rear, on the chance a Cloud drone might pass in a random sweep. When they climbed out of the car, the heat hit them. It was sweltering.

When they strolled in through the low-slung back door, marijuana smoke and a piquant herb odor greeted them. A vintage air-conditioner unit hung from a window. In the wood-beamed living room, Blaise saw several hackers who had scoured his soul. That alarmed him, but his anxiety passed after Lennon pumped his hand, showed him to a couch, and handed him a reefer. The weed gave Blaise a contact high that softened the smoky room festooned with native Indian designs and threaded crosses. The black woman who had interrogated Blaise brought him a plate of refried beans and tortillas with hot sauce. She and a Middle Eastern woman, also one of his interrogators, plopped down on either side of him. They wore coarse cotton skirts and blouses and reeked of cheap scent. Kristina joined a conversation with Lennon and other hackers across the room.

The black woman pointed to the fabric crosses adorning the wall. "Ojo de Dios—eyes of God," she informed him. "We make 'em from chopsticks and colored thread. They're traditional, from the Huichol Indians in an unflooded part of Mexico. I'm Toni Morrison, twelfth of that line, by the way. Glad you're with us, badass. Took some balls to upload that first module."

Seeing these ferocious women intended no harm, Blaise relaxed and let the weed knead his pleasure center like a deep-tissue massage.

"Zenobia the eighth," the Middle Eastern woman put in, seizing his free hand in a near-crushing grip. "Named after an ancient Syrian queen. Pre-Muslim. Third Century AD. Me, I'm pure Islamic."

"Sorry, did you say Islamic?" Blaise asked between bites of refried beans.

"Surprise, surprise, I'm a Muslim," she laughed.

"You mean——"

"An Allah-worshipper. A few of us survive here despite The Cloud. We lost the Koran when they deleted it from all the databases. But we still got the memory of it."

"Hadji's a racist term," Toni told him. "Islamic people are Muslims."

"Ain't many so-called Hadjis who are still Muslims," Zenobia explained. "The Caliphate's just a darker-skinned version of The Cloud. Their wars are political. And their Caliph worships nothing but power."

Across the room, Kristina let out a rich laugh at something Lennon said.

Zenobia nodded to her. "Kristina, now. She's a believer. She got it from that monk dude, Thomas."

Blaise wasn't sure how to respond. To him, Muslim and monk were words lifted from prehistoric fairy tales.

"Kristina tells us you really got the chops," Toni chimed in.

"Chops?"

"The balls to go back and try another upload."

"She talked me into it," he laughed.

"Fuck that. You talked yourself into it. And we're grateful. Kristina's mom Amelia spent a helluva long time looking for somebody like you."

Blaise felt his neck prickle from the approach of a mildly disturbing presence: Lennon, with a steaming mug.

"Kombucha mushroom," Lennon explained. He shoved Toni over so he could sit next to Blaise. "Sweetened with tea and sugar. You'll like it."

"Is it hallucinogenic?" Blaise wondered. "I'm already stoned on this weed."

"Hell, no, this ain't no cartoon drug," Lennon laughed. "It's healthy and natural." Lennon elbowed Toni further away. "Hey, why don't you and Aretha go light up a bong?"

"Name's Zenobia, asshole!"

"Whatever. The two of you look like your heads are about to come to a point. Why don't ya stop being ballbreakers for two minutes and lemme talk to our boy here?"

The women rolled their eyes, heaved up and sashayed away, hand in hand, to another conversation.

Lennon threw Blaise a careless smile. "How're those refried beans?"

"Good. Haven't had any since The Cloud put us all on tofu and salad."

"Grow 'em myself, make the tortillas by hand." Lennon grinned in a way Blaise found unsettling. "Hey, listen, dude, ask you something personal?"

Blaise set his plate down. "Sure thing."

Lennon glanced at the others, some of whom scrutinized them. "When you were back in L.A., and they hit you up with the fact that being a Class I means getting to live forever, how'd that grab you?"

"Minsheng mentioned the Lazarus D project, but it wasn't till later—"

"What did it feel like to know you'd never have to die? Just go on fucking Mitsuko, living off the fat of the land, for all eternity. Some people'd say it's against nature. Still, upgrade your organs every ten years, reverse diseases, and you're good to go. Right? So how'd it feel to get the offer?"

Blaise didn't like Lennon's tone or breath, which stank of alcohol and weed.

"If you must know, I loved the idea," Blaise answered. "Until I got a taste of eternal life in The Cloud. Trust me, you wouldn't like it."

Lennon flashed a toothy grin. "Oh, that's good. Eat great food, cruise around in a hovercar, snag an estate like Minsheng's someday, and those trips to Hong Kong? Where the girls melt in your mouth like vanilla ice cream? Pretty sweet."

"Repeated century after century, even pleasure becomes nauseating."

"Where'd you get that from? That pie in the sky shit Kristina preaches?"

"No. I got it from personal experience."

"Come on. They offered you eternal life and you turned it down. I wanna know why."

Before Blaise could utter another word, a laser beam burned through the kitchen, incinerated one of the hackers, and ripped out a manhole-sized hole in the back wall.

Everyone hit the floor.

"What's happening?" Blaise wailed.

Toni crawled into the kitchen through plaster and powdered shingles and peered out a window over the sink. "SWAT!" she cried to the others in the living room. "They're dug in out there with a laser cannon." She crab-walked back into the room. "Lennon, is there a back way out, a tunnel?"

Another beam bored holes through two walls and cut more hackers in half. Burned flesh mingled with the fetor of charred plaster. Lennon kept his head low, like the others, but grinned like the Cheshire Cat.

"No way out of this but me," he snickered.

"What does that mean, you little weasel?" Toni demanded. "Did you sell us out, you piece of shit? Do they know about the warehouse? The hyperloop? The new city?"

"Naw. I'm buying eternity in installments."

Another laser beam burned through the room, lower this time. Everyone pressed their heads to the floor.

"Told 'em enough to get 'em here. You'll flesh out the details after I stop that laser cannon."

"You traitorous piece of shit!"

"You got sixty seconds. Then they take the roof off this place. Oh, and don't think you're gonna use curseil on me. No time."

Kristina, face covered in plaster dust, crawled to Blaise's side. "Stop them!"

"How?"

"Minsheng said you could summon the Mantis. Do it!"

Another blast ripped through the roof. It brought a chunk of ceiling down and crushed another hacker. Everyone coughed up dust. Reluctant to exercise a power he loathed, but knowing Kristina was right, Blaise crawled through the rubble into the kitchen and peered out the window over the sink. Outside, in the cruel heat of late afternoon, a SWAT hover-truck was half-hidden in a gully. On the turret, a SWAT stood behind a black shield, manning a laser cannon trained on the house. Other SWATs in black tactical gear had dug into position around the house with laser burner assault rifles.

"I'm calling the shots, God dammit!" Lennon shrieked. "My signal'll stop 'em. Just swear you'll tell 'em what they want."

The cannon unleashed another beam. This time it hit the kitchen wall and gouged out termite-infested wood and a half-century of rot and debris. A section of plaster struck Blaise in the face and knocked him off his feet. Driven by the razor-wire panic of knowing the laser would soon incinerate everyone in the house, Blaise climbed out from under the debris, crawled to a gaping hole in the wall, and focused on the hover-truck with lethal intensity. Out of the sunny desert coalescing lights swirled into being with a chirruping cry and an enormous apparition of jointed green. The SWAT manning the laser cannon raked the beam across it, but it passed through the Mantis without effect. Its spiny legs had a surprising nimbleness as it crawled toward the cannon, which fired beam after beam. It pierced the Mantis at killing points that would have eviscerated a whale but hit nothing but vapor from a VR projection of appalling focus. The Mantis stretched out its claw as the cannon operator fired into the green carapace between its jeweled eyes. Nothing could stop it.

As Minsheng had taught him, Blaise hurled a single thought: "Kill! Slaughter!" Other SWATs leapt up and fired their laser burners. Thanks to Blaise's new VR coding, refined by Minsheng's programmers who used it to weaponize the Mantis, the claw found the SWAT turret gunner's head and snapped it off. Other SWATs kept up their fire, but the beams passed through the Mantis like chalk lines through a green shadow. Blaise steered the creature toward them, and the Mantis pursued their screams and curses with prayerfully folded claws. The SWATs used tactical training to roll and dodge, bounded up and raked the advancing horror with more laser fire, but they couldn't wake from this nightmare because the Mantis pursued them through their neural implants. Blaise's heart pounded and adrenalin pumped through him as he got caught up in the chase and relished the rush of power. The SWATs fired again and again, but they couldn't equal the creature's lethal purpose. One SWAT hid in a declivity between two rocks. The Mantis lifted the dangling SWAT with one claw, and speared his forehead with the other. It chased down the survivors until nothing remained of the SWATs but food for ants and scorpions. Then the creature folded its claws and hovered in the desert's burning silence a few moments before it dematerialized.

Trembling with exaltation from the slaughter he had wreaked, Blaise picked his way through the stench of lasered flesh into the sweltering living room. He was covered in plaster dust and caked in sweat. The attack had reduced the room to rubble, except for two roofless walls. Kristina, with the surviving hackers, had backed Lennon into a corner.

"They made me do it. I never wanted to hurt a single hair on none of your heads," Lennon whimpered. "They threatened to kill me!" He sank to his knees. "I ain't had shit for a life. Nothing but setbacks and fuck-overs since I was a kid. I wanted to live. They promised me eternal life!"

As the hackers focused their curseil powers on Lennon, Blaise felt himself drawn in as their energy pierced Lennon's mind with crushing force and plunged deeper, deeper until his brain winked out like a blown match.

16

BELT-BEAMED IN HIS SEAT ABOARD THE CLOUD SPACE SHUTTLE, Blaise peered out a parallelogram-shaped window at the earth's curvature. It shimmered against blackness pricked by millions of stars. The shuttle was roomy enough to seat two hundred, but only a couple dozen Class I executives were aboard. Mitsuko, in a seat facing him, grinned at his sheepish expression.

"First time on a shuttle is special," she observed, nodding to the window. "Quite a light show."

Blaise glanced at the front of the cabin, where a clot of executives at the whiskey bar were absorbed in conversation. One executive's blue silk jacket blocked Blaise's view of Minsheng, belt-beamed in a row of seats that faced the back. When the executive moved, Blaise saw that the director was asleep, lips parted, face slumped against a cushion so it emphasized his creased forehead, artificial eye, and pig-like jowls.

"Puts things in perspective, doesn't it?" Mitsuko commented.

"I'm sorry, what?" Blaise rejoined. He thought she meant Minsheng.

She nodded at the star-scape. "A hundred thousand galaxies out there, each five hundred million light years wide. And the Milky Way's just one of a hundred billion supercluster galaxies. They call it Lanieakea. It's Hawaiian. Means immeasurable heavens."

"And we're stuck down here," Blaise laughed.

Mitsuko tossed him a feline shrug. "With infinite possibilities."

"Infinite slavery's a better way to put it."

"Really, Blaise, what can five hundred million light years mean to us? Nothing, except to remind us we're nothing. No-thing. Nada. Infinitesimal specks in a vast, indifferent universe."

"And that makes you happy?"

"Of course. Because our speck of a planet offers an eternity of pleasure. Ultimately, all we have to cling to . . . is each other."

She crossed her legs to afford him a view of creamy thighs in black silk stockings. Blaise rolled his eyes. Sex with Mitsuko was the last thing on his mind. Why had the board called them to this Hong Kong meeting? Minsheng usually handled such assignments alone. Why would the board want two subordinates to tag along? Had the Hadjis attacked the Chinese mainland or North Am east coast? If they had, perhaps the board would order Blaise and Mitsuko to accelerate their Gilgamesh production schedule yet again. But if they were so desperate to stream Anima to billions of future suicides, why hadn't Minsheng given the order to fast track coding back in L.A.?

Another thought crossed Blaise's mind. Was it possible Minsheng had fallen out of favor with the board? If so, what did they have in mind for the two sycophants who'd come with him?

"You look so serious," Mitsuko laughed. "Come on. Hong Kong is breathtaking."

"If you say so."

"You're worried about what happened on your vacation?"

He shot her a burning glance. "No. Of course not."

"It was nothing. You got sexually entangled with a Slag stripper and black market smuggler. SWAT came to take down her gang. You got caught in the crossfire and terminated the SWATs to save yourself. Really, Blaise. Losing a dozen SWATs? A minor inconvenience. They're only Slags themselves."

Her words reassured Blaise to a degree, but there was also worry about the fact that he had uploaded the first module of the new Polyphemus virus before he had left for Hong Kong. He had waited with heart in mouth for The Cloud Monitor to detect the breach, but the hackers' new coding kept prying cyber-eyes out. If his luck held out, he could upload the remaining modules and bring down the entire neural network. But how long could he hope to outwit The Cloud's AI? For all he knew, the Monitor had detected his breach, and Minsheng knew everything but hadn't retaliated for reasons of his own.

Despite Blaise's worries, the shuttle's thrumming ventilation system allowed him to drift off to sleep eventually. In his dream, he and Kristina stood hand in hand by a river that flowed like limpid music. The current was so clear that Blaise saw polished stones through the refracted light of the silty riverbed.

When he woke, the shuttle had begun its descent. Friction screamed as the atmosphere tried to burn the shuttle to cosmic dust. Terrifying shudders and jolts forced everyone to belt-beam themselves in. But the shuttle held together.

When it broke the cloud cover in dead of night, Hong Kong's skyline took Blaise's breath away. A city with nowhere to build but the sky, this megalopolis demanded engineering cunning that allowed the board to throw up skyscrapers higher than any dreamt of in L.A. Rainbow-colored cells glittered with devastating beauty in towers rising like jewel-encrusted spears high above the earth. They formed giddy crystalline masses along coastal waters where tiny ships twinkled in the black. Beyond Lamma and Po Toi islands, a seawall encompassed the clinquant land masses like the pupil of a giant's eye.

Blaise spied two burning tracts of fire that cut deep into the New Territories. As the shuttle descended, this image resolved itself into an endless runway. Blaise glanced forward and saw Minsheng peer out one of the windows. When the director noticed Blaise noticing him, his expression assumed its customary opaqueness, like a species of one-eyed fish with a nictitating iris. For some reason, this opaqueness disturbed Blaise in a very specific way. Minsheng's face had an android's flat affect, with a depthless eye that regarded Blaise as if he were a bacteria. For an instant, Blaise wondered if the director actually was an android, but that didn't fit Minsheng's limitless ambition and Byzantine cunning.

The shuttle landed in what felt like a controlled crash. Deceleration threw Blaise forward so forcefully he feared he would be hurled across the cabin. Mitsuko clenched her eyes shut and clutched her armrests. The runway was far longer than Blaise anticipated. Deceleration lasted too long for his taste, as if the ship were passing through parallel dimensions separated by resistant membranes. At last, it slowed to bearable speed and taxied toward a stupendous terminal. Over the roof flew the Hong Kong flag, with its white Bauhinia Blakeana orchid and The Cloud's official K-Spot logo against a red background. Beside the flag loomed a holographic billboard with *Homo Deus* emblazoned across its surface in seven languages, to show every visitor that he or she had entered the world of immortal gods. Behind red carpet, hovercars waited. The space shuttle taxied to within several hundred meters of the reception committee, and its engines ground to silence. The executives on the shuttle bowed and stood aside to let Minsheng deplane first. Blaise and Mitsuko pushed through them and caught up with him. The three descended a long flight of steps to the tarmac. On the red carpet, garlanded girls in silk dresses placed bauhinia and herbarium leis over their heads. The air brought the scent of sandalwood, a Hong Kong fragrance since the days the city manufactured incense. Now the city pumped sandalwood into the air through hidden ducts strictly for aesthetic appeal.

Minsheng's status guaranteed him an opulently appointed hovercar. After they climbed in, pipa music washed over them. As the car glided off, Blaise saw the car bypass the geodesic dome of the airport terminal. That meant no customs delays. Minsheng informed them their baggage would arrive separately in a wing of the Forbidden City. The board had dismantled and carted the labyrinth of courtyards and palaces from Beijing to Hong Kong, where they reconstructed and expanded it by many orders of magnitude befitting their global capital. Blaise had seen photographs, but he never imagined he would walk those legendary corridors himself.

"You're wondering why I've brought you two," Minsheng intoned with his customary gravitas.

"Yes, actually, we were," Blaise responded. His heart raced at the possible scenarios about to unfold.

"Deputy Director of the Board Zuma, whom you met at my villa: I'm afraid he's been assassinated by Hadji forces in Johannesburg. And I replace him."

Mitsuko gasped. Blaise, unsurprised since Kristina had revealed the military realities to him back in the new city, complimented Minsheng on his promotion.

"We're delighted with your elevation," Mitsuko seconded Blaise. Zuma was dead; the only thing that existed now was Minsheng's ego.

"You will both be promoted to full director status, with a security clearance of six, and expanded staff," Minsheng continued. "I needn't mention that you must never divulge what I'm about to discuss, on pain of vaporization." Minsheng let his threat sink in before he continued. "Our Caliphate enemies are using a new super-weapon: highly advanced nanobots. They've decimated our troops in the Sudan and South Africa."

"That's horrible," Mitsuko cried, while Blaise did his best to appear appalled.

"The board can't afford to sacrifice Africa. Priceless mineral rights are at stake, including South African diamond fields."

Blaise noticed that Minsheng failed to mention the loss of Russia. Why? Perhaps to minimize the scope of the disaster?

"It grieves me to report that the Hadjis plan to invade India, China, and the rest of Asia."

Mitsuko turned pale. "Even Hong Kong?"

Minsheng nodded.

"Will we be able to stop them?"

"That will be my task. I'm in board meetings all this week. Also, I'll be in strategy sessions with generals and scientists looking for ways to neutralize the nanobots. In the meantime, we're deploying Mantis-led surgical strikes." Minsheng glanced at Blaise. "You'll recall me mentioning a special project. This trip affords the perfect opportunity. Your suites are attached to a holodeck room. You're to collaborate on an Anima demo for the board."

"You want us to—give the board—an Anima VR feed?" Mitsuko stammered, as if she hadn't heard properly.

Minsheng gave her a stately nod. "Yes. So the board can experience it themselves."

"But why?" Mitsuko fretted. "With invasion facing us, why not complete the series first and destroy the Hadjis with Anima?"

Minsheng rolled his eyes. "Some of my colleagues doubt, even at this date, whether Anima can actually precipitate mass suicide. Even those who do believe question how we can enslave entire Hadji armies with it. I've argued myself sick to convince them Hadji troops have their own version of the K-Spot, that their lives are short and filled with senseless suffering, that they'll take to Anima like ducks to water. But nothing will convince the skeptics till they've experienced Anima themselves. You have five days to produce a beta module."

Blaise knew very well Minsheng meant to assassinate the board with his Anima demo, but there was nothing he could do to prevent it without putting his own life at risk.

"If I may say, Deputy Chairman," he pointed out. "We've still got an enormous amount of work to do to finish the series. Extracting Anima for this demo could cause serious delays."

"I'll take that risk. You can't present the full version of Anima for the demo because you haven't coded it yet. What's needed here is simply the most immediately lethal blocks of code. Something fast-acting, totally immersive, pleasant at first, but quickly deadly. We'll pull the board members back from the brink, of course."

Minsheng's good eye softened at the sight of red walls looming ahead.

"Ah, we're approaching our pavilion. I suggest you both get a good night's sleep. You start refining your Anima demo module at zero dark thirty tomorrow morning. Blaise, stick to your coding. Never leave your pavilion. But you, Mitsuko: I may need you to fetch some colleagues of mine here, under the radar, so to speak." He produced what looked like a red credit chip imprinted with the white petals in the Hong Kong flag. "This is an access key to the autobots parked on the imperial palace grounds. I'll explain later how to get to the parking area. I may not need these colleagues before our Anima demo, but if I do, you're not to mention to anyone that you're fetching them; and bring them straight to my quarters." He handed her the chip, and she slipped it into her purse. "Oh, and no questions," he added.

"Yes, of course," she replied. "I won't disappoint you, sir."

So this was Minsheng's power play. Blaise's and Mitsuko's special project coding would cause a regime change in which Minsheng seized power. Would he let the cyber-assassins who brought him to power live? Immediate termination wasn't likely. Minsheng needed Blaise and Mitsuko to complete *Gilgamesh V.* Their termination would come later. Maybe with a level six security clearance, Blaise could find a chance to upload more Polyphemus modules here in Hong Kong.

Minsheng settled back in his seat, quite pleased with himself. "Blaise, I forgot to mention, you're to be given a special honor: a visit to the Hall of Heroes. Mitsuko will fill you in on the details. I assure you, it will make a deep and lasting impression."

17

BLAISE AND MITSUKO SWEATED IT OUT, TRYING TO MODIFY enough code for the Anima demo. Their suites, on the second floor of a Forbidden City annex, overlooked a lobby with gold and red inlaid walls accented by red columns with crests that spread into gold ceiling transoms. Chandeliers drooped like jellyfish above a tiled floor. Sandalwood scent sifted through the wing, effluvium of a decadent empire that had endured many centuries.

New-generation androids guarded the lower floor, dressed in Qing dynasty gold jackets, red conical hats, and blue skirts. Like humming statues, they stood at intervals with laser burners slung. Blaise glanced down at them with an anxious heart tug when he and Mitsuko emerged, exhausted, from their first day of coding. Mitsuko complained of eyestrain and a tension headache. Blaise felt depleted from the stress of the deadline Minsheng had imposed.

They descended a curving staircase. Their steps echoed along a corridor hung with chandeliers. They chatted, relishing the luxury around them as they passed a gold-inlaid teakwood couch and chairs. A Persian rug ran beneath, bordered by live trees in ceramic pots. They entered a red-columned dining hall with tasseled lanterns floating at a dizzying height. Teakwood partitions sectioned off dining areas, where tables of Class Is enjoyed Sichuan fare. Mitsuko and Blaise found a booth that afforded privacy. Two female androids in red Hong Kong silk served a fragrant feast. They washed it down with bottles of hot sake, legal here. Though they didn't speak about it, Blaise felt sure Mitsuko wondered where Minsheng could be at that moment, and what would become of them after they completed the Anima demo. Minsheng had undoubtedly struck bargains to secure his rise to chairmanship with the assistants, major-domos, and other retainers the board oversaw, not to mention military and civilian advisory committees. No palace revolt would follow. But the other board members' unscrupulousness matched Minsheng's. Wasn't it possible they knew about his plan? But that wasn't credible. Minsheng would already be dead if they knew. And their terror of Hadji slaughter had probably convinced them to accept the Anima demo as their path to survival.

Blaise tried to set these worries aside long enough to find a good moment to upload another Polyphemus module, but that was impossible with Mitsuko at his elbow, churning and burning at their holodeck under the glitter of jeweled surveillance eyes embedded in walls and ceiling. Blaise had to face that his upload opportunity would come, if at all, back in L.A., not here.

He and Mitsuko strolled back after dinner with minds softened to agreeable fuzziness. Their suites were catty-cornered at the end of a blonde-tiled corridor. Both entrances were framed by red and gold wood carvings. Blaise wished Mitsuko good night and retired.

Under a scalloped ceiling, red and gold lacquered walls and mirrors ran along both sides of the room. The support staff had set out bottles of California wine on marble tables supported by red hangings with embroidered designs. Beyond the pillowed couches, a maroon-colored enclosure framed a wood embrasure inlaid with gold filigree. A bed with a black coverlet embroidered with golden koi beckoned. Blaise pulled off his shoes and tossed his jacket and trousers on a chair. As he reached for the globe lamp, a rustle of silk made him glance at the door. He was surprised to see Mitsuko slip into his room with a figure hidden under a gold sheet. She whisked it away to reveal a slender, naked young Chinese woman with reddish-brown hair and a face with an upturned nose and liquid eyes. Before Blaise could object that he was past exhausted, and in no mood for Mitsuko's games, Mitsuko cut him short.

"Take a closer look."

The girl glided to one of the mirrors. The nails of her scarlet-painted toes brushed the carpet's gold-circled dragons. Blaise had the uncanny feeling he knew this girl but couldn't place her. She knelt on the couch and breathed into the mirror, frosted the glass, and brushed it with the faintest of kisses, her lips like molten rubies. Blaise's irritation with Mitsuko's subterfuge dissolved into lust as the woman's orchid scent reached him, accompanied by a subtle odor he couldn't name, but which made him suspect pheromones had seeped into the room. Or perhaps Minsheng had instructed the chef to infuse his dinner with a hallucinogen. His suite dissolved into a continuum of color and pattern that included the fragrant girl at the mirror with her dark-flamed hair and Mitsuko, who shed her robe and approached. His body felt as insubstantial as a dandelion.

"This is my daughter, Kiana," Mitsuko whispered. "She's just turned twenty-one, and she's taking her school vacation to be with her mama and learn about life."

Blaise joined them on the couch, where Mitsuko guided his hand to Kiana's fragrant flesh, bringing a blush to her daughter's cheeks. Mitsuko gave Blaise teasing kisses. Then both women caressed him until his exhaustion dissolved into a derangement of sensual bliss. He glanced in the mirror and saw their reflection multiplied into infinity. The women urged him onto the bed, pushed him down, and melted his mind in a lunar synthesis that erased all sense of himself. He became a single prong in a three-spoked wheel of passion that whirled in endless revolutions. Despite dozens of lovers, both real and VR-generated, Blaise had never been with two flesh-and-blood women at once. They taught him a language as arcane and incomprehensible as the Chinese they whispered to one another. He elided into an androgynous being with the breasts, lips, and orifices of a woman, a melding that expanded to the fabrics, textures, and colors of the suite until he was no more.

18

BLAISE AND MITSUKO ENDURED A WEEK OF SOUL-SAPPING
labor. By Friday noon, they had nearly completed the Anima beta module. Blaise
had pushed his brain past sane limits. He submerged in his addiction to Mitsuko
to relieve stress concerning the implications of what he was doing. Her body
became essential, and he accepted the mysterious Kiana, too, who was actually a
flesh-bot android with a face, body, and scent designed to blend features of his
dead wife Cherry and Mitsuko. Once he recovered from the bizarreness of that,
he accepted Mitsuko's invitation to sink deeper into decadence. She brought in a
Japanese flesh-bot to enrich their orgies with Kiana. Mitsuko called them the
gang of four.

When Blaise depleted his body to the point of inner annihilation, Mitsuko
whispered, "This, darling, is our eternity."

Minsheng visited their makeshift office to scrutinize their coding on Friday.
Pleased with what he saw, he declared, "I think you can wrap up the remainder
tomorrow. I'll schedule the demo for Monday, just to be safe. You will witness
your triumph, by the way. You will accompany me to the boardroom. My
colleagues want to meet the geniuses behind this groundbreaking VR
technology. In the meantime, Mitsuko, why don't you escort Blaise to the Hall
of Heroes this afternoon? I think he's earned it."

Mitsuko gave the director a tight smile and shuttered an emotion behind her
lashes. A bit later, while she and Blaise enjoyed dim sum, Mitsuko told him as if
from rote memory he was about to enjoy one of the greatest honors afforded a
Class I.

"The Hall of Heroes is partially real-flesh, partially VR, but we won't have to reactivate your neurofeed," she explained. "In the Hall, imagery and sound feed directly into your K-Spot."

"So what's it like? One of those holographic cathedral extravaganzas?"

"More interesting," she countered with the tiniest hint of irritation.

"You don't sound that convincing."

"I've seen the Hall of Heroes, Blaise. And after today, you'll be able to say you've seen it, too. It's a rite of passage. Your admission to the inner circle."

"Thought we were already in the inner circle."

"This puts an indelible stamp on your status."

Blaise heard something forced and anxious in her voice. But on the other hand, maybe he was projecting his own exhaustion and paranoia onto her. So when they drained the last of their lunchtime sake, he followed her down a corridor to a wing of the Forbidden City he hadn't seen before. They entered a throne room with red-tiled columns, gold-inlaid ceiling squares, and, beneath an archway framed by heavy red and gold curtains, flights of steps leading to doors framed by gold dragons. At the top, Mitsuko issued a curt command, and the doors hissed open. They entered a car that dropped precipitously to a level many floors below the one they had left.

Blaise followed Mitsuko down another corridor that seemed out of place in the Forbidden City: Rococo walls carved with arabesques and Cupids more befitting eighteenth-century Versailles than twenty-second-century Hong Kong. The floors had interlocking gold circles that thrust into the distance like squirming clots of serpents. Oil portraits of Eastern and Western kings and emperors, stiff with imperial dignity, adorned the walls. The corridor drew itself out thousands of meters, telescoping seemingly into infinity under a tessellated ceiling. Eventually, he spied a pair of brown doors inlaid with gold embrasures. As he and Mitsuko approached, they passed android guards dressed in imperial gold, blue, and red. Marble benches lined the walls.

Mitsuko uttered a crisp command. The doors swung inward. Beyond was a brilliant lozenge-shaped room with marble walls that glistened with polycarbonate frosting. In the center stood a high-backed marble chair. Beyond it, in a fan-shaped pattern, were five marble sarcophagi shaped like lotus petals, as in the Hong Kong flag.

"The Hall of Heroes," she revealed in a tone that strained to muster conviction, as if she were a tour guide who had brought guests here many times. "Those are cryogenic sleep chambers, housing our five founding fathers. They passed away before we had the Lazarus-D project, but we preserved their bodies by deep freezing them at two hundred degrees below zero. Molecular nanotechnology reanimated their minds, and we kept their bodies intact using cryoprotectant. You may approach and view each. Then wait in that chair for your visitation."

"Visitation?"

"You'll see."

With that, she slipped away, and the doors swung shut behind her with a resounding clang. Unsure how to feel about this womb-world, Blaise decided there was nothing for it but to inspect the sarcophagi. No irregularities marred the walls, but he was certainly under surveillance, and there could be no thought of avoiding this privilege. As he stepped up to the cryogenic sarcophagus on the far left, he heard thrumming, like an old-fashioned refrigerator but with deeper resonance. Under a frosted glass pane, he saw a moon-shaped Chinese face with a receding hairline and mole under full, sensual lips: Chairman Mao the First, reposing in his Peoples Republic collared tunic. His name was inscribed on the glistening marble in English, Mandarin, Cantonese, French, Russian, and Japanese. Blaise wondered how long he had been frozen—since his death in 1976? Incredible to think cryogenic technology had been that advanced back then.

At the second sarcophagus, Blaise saw the pale, bloodless face of Adolf Hitler. His hair was combed like a knife blade across his forehead; his mustache was plumped in cosmetically restored flesh, eyes shut in simulated sleep. He wore his chancellor's jacket, shirt, and tie. How could Hitler be here? Back at UCLA, Blaise had seen photos of the chancellor's charred corpse outside his bunker in 1945. But perhaps those photos had been faked, crude precursors of present-day VR affronts to reality. He stepped to the third sarcophagus, where he saw the prominent forehead and mustache of Joseph Stalin the First under the viewing panel. The fourth sarcophagus contained the pink, prematurely wrinkled visage of U.S. President Brent Cadwallader the First. His burnt-orange comb-over hairdo floated above his sleeping forehead. In sarcophagus five lay Vladimir Putin the First, with his thin jaw and receding hairline.

Why had The Cloud singled out these five political monsters? Other strongmen from the twentieth and twenty-first centuries sprang to mind: Idi Amin, Saddam Hussein, Benito Mussolini, Francisco Franco, Muammar Gaddafi, Mobutu Sese Seke, Nicolae Ceaușescu, Kim Jong-Il, Pol Pot, and Augusto Pinochet, among others further back in history's abysses. So why these five? Was it purity of obsession, manipulative cunning, the sheer numbers they oppressed, or something else? Clearly the board had ruled out Hussein and Gaddafi because they were Allah-worshippers. But the five honored ones' offenses against humanity varied wildly. Still, here they were, favored psychopaths preserved forever in frozen death.

Blaise knew his next step was to sit in the marble chair for what Mitsuko called his visitation. So he did. He half-expected to hear a voice boom from the heavens or something equally cinematic; there was nothing but humming, but then came tickling in his K-Spot. A warm inrushing presence brushed his mind. The hall fragmented into globules of pink, orange, blue, and white. He floated before two circular bands of fractals that crossed and re-crossed each other. They turned in mandala-like arcs, one clockwise and the other counter-clockwise, and changed hue and dimension as they circled an interlaced center within a center within a center. Then came articulate vibrations that gradually dissolved into words, and he discerned their meaning: *Your whole life, since you swam in amniotic bliss in your mother's womb—everything you have known has been the foreboding of a sleeper who will soon awaken; everything you thought, felt, saw, smelled, tasted, and touched has been a dream within a* dream. *But now, see this hairline fracture split open the delusional gestalt. Widen that fracture, unchain yourself and walk into the sun of higher reality. Expand yourself into the limitless power you were born to wield, you with us and us with you.*

He felt the moist, hungry souls of the dictators, oligarchs, demagogues, and mass murderers latch onto him in a telepathic leech-hold. He felt the awful burden of their greed, hunger, and desperation, and he grasped that their only relief from the unendurable agony of their entombment lay in sucking him into the void that imprisoned them. They were like dying stars falling backward forever through gestating galaxies into a limitless void. Blaise screamed, "God help me!" with all his failing strength, a fruitless cry to a deity he had never known, as the oligarchs inhaled the flame of his soul. Then from far away, from impossibly far, came an answer. A warm, fertile, female presence entered his marrow with cleansing warmth and purgatorial flames. An answering force pushed back the hungry ghosts trying to suck his soul dry. It was Kristina. Her essence joined the essences of others whose minds melded with hers, and beyond her presence and theirs, he saw the coruscating light from Sagrada Familia and knew for the first time completely what it meant to be curseil. He was fully alive, on every level, right through to the core of himself.

Then he was himself again, in the marble throne of the womb-like hall, surrounded by thrumming flower-petal-shaped cryogenic coffins. Tears trickled down his cheeks as he realized he was still whole, still alive, and hadn't merged with the madmen entombed before him.

19

IN THE HALLWAY, HE FOUND MITSUKO ON ONE OF THE MARBLE benches. She saw his trembling, consoled him with vacuous bromides, and led him back to their wing. He said nothing until they ascended to the upper level and reached their suites.

"What just happened to me?" he asked.

"A visitation. From the founders."

"Founders of what? What are they? I saw nothing but corpses of famous dead psychopaths. What were they trying to do to me?"

"Take some of your essence. Their bodies died, but their minds have survived in cryogenic sleep. They communicate with each other telepathically in a sort of hive mind. When a Class I visits them, they take some of that person's mental essence. It gives the founders energy. And they guide us in return."

"You're saying those cryogenic ghosts are tapping into me now? Sucking energy from me?"

"Yes. They'll be connected to you forever, taking energy from you and all Class Is."

Blaise tried to grasp the implications of her words, but his mind wasn't equal to it. "I need to get the fuck out of here," he told her. "Visit the city. Be around ordinary people. This is too insane."

Anxiety clouded her face. She nudged him inside his suite and closed the door behind her. "That isn't possible, Blaise."

"Minsheng said we have till tomorrow. You've got an electronic pass and hovercar access. I need a few hours. I want to see . . . I don't know, Kowloon Park. Trees, flowers. Anything but this place."

Mitsuko followed him to the closet and watched with horror as he removed his blue silk jacket from a hanger and pulled it on.

"Minsheng won't permit it! He'd be furious! And the park is closed. It's nearly sunset."

She took his arm and tried to pull him toward the bed, but he snatched his arm free. "I've bled myself dry with his Anima coding," Blaise snapped. "I've seen his fucking Hall of Heroes. I'm going into the city if I have to walk."

"Blaise, you can't leave me here," she pleaded. "Everything depends on us staying together until . . . afterward."

"After Minsheng sucks my soul dry like those psychopathic ghosts in his Hall of Heroes? Well, fuck Minsheng, and fuck you. I'm out of here."

Mitsuko turned pale. "Blaise, please. We're so close to getting everything we want."

"What YOU want!"

She threw herself into his arms and held him like a barnacle fending off a tidal wave. "You want what I do. Can't you admit it? Can't you see that . . . I love you?"

He shoved her away. "Give me that access chip. And all your cash."

She searched his face for signs of weakness, but he was furious at her for trying to deny him temporary respite from his ordeal.

"Please, don't," she implored him. "Minsheng forced me to take you to the Hall. I had no choice."

He advanced on her. "Everyone has a choice. Now give it to me or I'll take it."

His threatening tone convinced Mitsuko to produce a translucent red chip and cash from her jacket pocket.

"Promise you'll come back before you're missed," she begged. "After midnight, auto-surveillance reports any overdue hovercars."

"Yeah, whatever," he retorted as he snatched the chip from her.

He passed android guards in echoing corridors and groups of whispering Class Is clustered outside a conference room before he reached a hallway he and Mitsuko had passed through several times during their coding breaks. It led to a door with a red exit sign in English, Cantonese, and Mandarin. He swiped the access chip he had taken from Mitsuko, spoke his voiceprint ID to the small holoscreen in the door, and it clicked open and released him into the dry, spice-scented warmth of a Hong Kong autumn evening. His Mythoplex watch showed twenty-four degrees Celsius/seventy-five degrees Fahrenheit. Perfect weather for drinking and whoring. The hovercars were parked in a football-field-sized lot near the red wall separating the Forbidden City from the rest of creation. There were no guards, but he saw scanning laser cannons at intervals atop the wall. He steeled his expression so hidden surveillance eyes would pick up nothing more than a Class I on some official errand. He chose a car and opened the door with Mitsuko's chip, climbed in, and ordered it to take him to a nightlife neighborhood.

"Please specify," the feminine voice chirped.

"I don't care," he spat. "Someplace with sake bars and strip clubs."

"I require a specific district, sir."

He ransacked his memory for a name based on his hasty research before boarding the shuttle back in L.A.

"Lan Kwai Fong district," he barked. "What kind of whiskey do you dispense?"

"Only the best twenty-five year aged."

"That works. I don't care which brand."

He settled back in the plush as the car glided out of its spot and hummed toward a gate in the wall. He drained his glass and had a second; he was going to tie one on tonight, and there wasn't a moment to spare. The gate groaned open and revealed a blood-red sun seeping into the horizon. The hovercar headed south. He tried to outdistance his thoughts, but his personal nightmare spread black wings over him. He cursed himself for a life spent enslaving others with a technology that would soon empower mass murder. He would add to his body count when Minsheng slaughtered the board, and after that, entire populations unless Blaise finished uploading Polyphemus. But even if he succeeded, there was no guarantee it would work. And if it didn't, the Cloud Monitor would discover his failed attempt, and the Mantis would come. Mitsuko would figure out a way to launch *Gilgamesh V* without him, and live forever, take other lovers by the hundreds, and he wouldn't be a blip on her inner radar. The Cloud would trace him to Kristina, annihilate her and the hackers, and obliterate their new city under the desert. And with no one to deactivate the hackers' nanobots, the Hadjis would sweep across Asia, Europe, and North America and achieve their global Caliphate.

Blaise dreaded the prospect of losing Kristina and the hackers. They were the new hope, the new ships, and he ached to be with them. But part of him longed to be with Mitsuko, too. He savored the exquisite pleasures he had sampled with her, despite his fury at her for delivering him to the Hall of Heroes. It was insane. How could he love Mitsuko and Kristina, such diametrically opposed souls? Then it struck him that something else lay behind his attraction to Mitsuko: she was female power in a corrupt, male-dominated world. She was a salve for patriarchal oppression, and she assuaged his guilt for becoming its willing priest. And there was something else. Whether he cared to admit it or not, he was deep in collusion with Mitsuko. When she had spoken of overthrowing the board and seizing power herself, Blaise had visualized himself at her side, building a matriarchal empire from the ruins of a goatish old regime. The oligarchs who assaulted his soul in the Hall of Heroes were the essence of crucifying maleness that had polluted nature beyond repair. They had plunged the world into eternal war and turned humanity into a race of VR idiots. Perhaps when all was said and done, Mitsuko's hatred for the patriarchs offered a more salvific path than Kristina's. Why not plunge into an eternity of sexual bliss in a freshly-minted society where Mitsuko ruled and shielded him in amniotic safety from the torments of a male-dominated world? Why not enjoy eternity with her in the second womb that Project Lazarus had created for Class Is? But then another, more horrifying thought struck him: with absolute power and eternity to enjoy it, how could he and Mitsuko keep themselves from devolving into the same monsters who slumbered in the Hall of Heroes?

He turned these thoughts over until the car pulled off the freeway and descended a ramp. He caught a vista of Hong Kong's skyline before the car swung onto a street of iridescent neon signage that flashed yellow, red, green, and blue. Dance clubs, restaurants, and bars were tucked into alcoves at the foot of skyscrapers that surged up like electric phalluses. The district had a seedy, lived-in look as if its glory days had long since passed. The streets were crammed with gaunt Hong Kong denizens, rail-thin hookers, and harassed-looking workingmen in cheap linen clothes who plied their trades as street vendors, pimps, or numbers runners. Blaise noticed the occasional silk class II jacket on patrons going in or coming out of rundown establishments. They reassured him that he had found Hong Kong's Slag Zone. His heart leapt with ill-founded hope. He knew no one here and had no idea how he would be received by these Hong Kong bottom feeders. But in his present state, the only way to cleanse his soul from the Hall of Heroes lay in mingling with these oppressed throngs. He let out a bitter laugh at the lie he had told Mitsuko about visiting Kowloon Park. He didn't crave cultivated nature; he wanted uncultivated flesh.

"Stop here," he ordered the hover-car, which dutifully edged into a spot at a grime-spattered curb. "Return to your pod," he ordered as the door slid up.

A distinctive stench greeted his nostrils, a blend of alcohol, fish balls, and beef brisket, and under everything else, a gutter stench soured by piss and vomit. These were different smells than the L.A. Slag Zone, but they had a hominess that appealed to Blaise, like a woman's armpits after a night of love. Amid the mixture of Chinese dialects that assailed his ears, he heard snatches of English, Russian, French, and Japanese.

A street sign alerted him that he was on Lockhart Road. Ahead, Jaffe Road cut across it. This was Hong Kong's red light district, but the tourist vids he had scanned back in L.A. had given it a glamorous ambience, light years away from this ratty reality. Still, this was preferable to the Imperial City. He spotted the hologram of a naked Chinese girl gyrating on the sidewalk under a crimson neon entrance: CLUB CELESTINA. Before he could reach it, he heard the low-pitched whine of a hovercar. He ducked into a restaurant alcove, where he had a clear view of the teeming street and sky. Scanning the surrounding buildings, he spotted, in a gap of night sky between two towers, a red SWAT car with the five-petaled white logo of Hong Kong on its underbelly. The car shot out of view, but that was no comfort. It could easily have spotted him with its satellite lenses. And indeed, a moment later, the hovercar floated into view blocks away. It glided his way, ten meters above the brick pavement. As it swept the street with searchlights, he bolted for Club Celestina and shouldered aside pedestrians who cursed his rudeness.

He flew up tan steps with brass borders, a knockoff of the gold leaf that embellished so much of the Forbidden City. He used the cash he had taken from Mitsuko to pay the greasy thug with gold teeth at the entrance grill and rushed into green luminescence from a ceiling crisscrossed by emerald light bars. A Japanese disc jockey with a tonsure spun the neo-Metallica favored in Asia. Black-bikini-clad Asian girls danced in packs before iridescent neon stages. Judging by the patrons' spandex jackets and scuffed shoes, this was a down-at-heels club. It reeked of cigarettes mixed with stale sweat and menstrual musk. Here was the desperation, futility, hopelessness, and lust that made Blaise feel at home like nothing else. He scanned the crowded entrance, afraid Hong Kong SWAT had followed him. He was so distracted he collided with a gaggle of dancers.

A girl caressed his face with red talons. "Me! Me! You come with me!"

He barely had a nanosecond to flash her a smile before he spotted them: SWATs in red uniforms with the white Hong Kong logo over the chests, crimson boots, and night vision goggles. For an instant, Blaise thought of summoning the Mantis to take them out; but he was, after all, in Minsheng's entourage, and rash action would cause embarrassment for Minsheng and termination for Blaise. Instead he grasped the wrist of the skinny, black-maned girl who had attacked him and whispered, "Take me someplace private. A thousand dollars for you."

The girl grinned and led him to a door that opened on a hallway with curtained rooms.

"No, take me to your place," he urged. "Two thousand dollars if we go there."

"Cash?"

"Take me to any ATM. I'll give you three thousand. I swear to God."

She considered his silk jacket, the elegant cut of his trousers and boots, and replied, "Five thousand from the ATM."

Intercut with hammering metallic tracks that the DJ pounded out back in the club, Blaise heard sharp cries, protests, and screams, one of which shouted, "SWAT!"

He smiled at the girl to instill confidence. "You got it, babe, let's go."

She led him to a green empty patch of polycarbonate and touched it with a red lacquered nail. A maw opened and admitted them to a dazzling corridor like the inside of a syringe. It plunged into a basement with numbered apartments. She pointed out an old-fashioned ATM and waited while he eye-scanned himself and got the cash. Behind them, a laser beam burned away the door they had passed through and cut the girl in half before it slammed into a wall a hundred meters beyond. Her body gushed intestinal gore as it slammed into the wall. Blood and organ spray splattered Blaise's jacket and blinded him before he could blink it away and run for his life. SWATs poured in from the outer club, cursing in Mandarin and Cantonese. Blaise sprinted into the sterile brightness with no hope of an exit, no illusion he could escape.

A laser beam singed his jacket at the right shoulder. He spun out of the line of fire and pitched onto the floor in a rush of clean white terror. Pounding boots and curses approached. Wire mesh engulfed his body with nearly imperceptible electric shocks. He heard labored breathing and thudding boots as they smashed into his back and sides. He felt the sting of a sedative dart in his arm before everything went black.

20

BLAISE THRASHED HIS WAY UP FROM A DREAM IN WHICH worms of corruption burrowed into his flesh and found himself naked in bed. Bruises and welts scarred his body. A medical repair spider balanced atop his chest on wire-thin legs. Its diamond proboscis emitted a soft beam that repaired a laser burn on his shoulder. The cut morphed from deep purple to pinkish and finally restored flesh, and then the spider crawled to a purple bruise and repeated its treatment.

Mitsuko studied the spider's progress from a couch, her eyes bright with fear. She wore a red and blue silk kimono, her hair piled up Japanese style. A purple bruise marred one cheek.

"What happened to you?" he demanded.

She touched her cheek and lowered her lashes.

The spider finished mending Blaise's flesh, crawled into a compartment, and vanished behind a lacquered panel. Mitsuko rose and approached to help Blaise slip into a red silk smoking jacket. It took a minute because his whole body ached.

"How do you feel?"

"Like SWAT beat the shit out of me," he groaned.

She winced. "Excessive reaction by incompetent thugs. Minsheng ordered them to return you safely. The Mantis has terminated them, and your . . . adventure . . . never happened. All surveillance vids erased. You were here with me all night."

"Fabulous," he sighed. "Now I suppose we finish our coding."

She glided back to her seat on the couch with geisha grace.

"Minsheng wants a word with you first."

"Not in the mood."

The door swung inward and Minsheng strode in wearing an imperial blue jacket with a swordfish collar pin identifying him as a board member. Blaise glimpsed stone-faced android guards behind him in the corridor. The door closed, and Minsheng drew up a throne with red plush cushions.

"Well, you're back," he observed. "And none the worse for wear." He indicated Mitsuko. "She sat up with you all night. But that won't stop her, or you, from completing your mission."

Blaise pointed to Mitsuko's black eye. "How did she get that, Director Minsheng?"

"Deputy chairman is my correct title," Minsheng retorted.

"Still like to know how she got it."

Minsheng leaned toward him, and his voice became ominous. "What she got is her life. Something I wasn't inclined to let her keep considering last night's events."

"I made her give me her access token."

"I'm not here to discuss trivialities," Minsheng snapped. "Our Anima demo is scheduled Monday at nine hundred hours. And it must come off perfectly. Tomorrow you two will conduct a test run, and—"

"And Monday we help you assassinate the board."

Minsheng's face colored in a way that Blaise had never seen before. His thick fingers gripped his pant legs. It took effort to calm himself enough to throw Blaise a cold stare from his one good eye. Blaise had the impression Minsheng might explode like a MOAB bomb. But the blast never came. Instead, Minsheng tapped into whatever resource he used to restore inner equilibrium. His good eye went opaque as he shifted his bulk in Blaise's direction.

"You will never speak like that to me in this life again," he stated quietly as if he were describing some statistic from the neurofeed. "Is that clear?"

To emphasize his point, he gestured to a corner where a tornado of sparks coalesced into a towering green horror with prismatic eyes that glittered like star-scratched infinite space. The Mantis crawled toward Mitsuko. It scraped like crickets and cicadas smashed together in a blender and magnified a thousand times, a chittering scream of chaos. She raised her knees to her face and pressed back into the couch, trying to melt into the cushions, clawing at the air to fend off the advancing claw.

"Father, don't!"

Blaise leapt up from bed despite his sore, protesting muscles. "Take me instead!"

Minsheng glanced at him, and a smile creased his face. The Mantis shifted its mandibles and spiny claws toward Blaise. Then it melted into the void from which it had emerged.

"Hmm, encouraging," Minsheng quipped. "You've changed, Blaise. Imagine that. You're actually capable of sacrificing yourself for someone else." He heaved up from his throne and clasped his hands behind his back. "I'll leave you two to it, then. You'll be wanting breakfast, and you have a long day ahead."

With that, Minsheng slipped out the door, and it swung shut behind him. Blaise rushed to Mitsuko and embraced her while she sobbed into his shoulder like an abandoned child. It took him a few minutes to grasp that he was still alive, and even then, his shaking didn't stop. He had seen the abyss and lived to ponder it. He kissed Mitsuko's hair and lips with the desperation of a condemned man. Then they made love on the bed, he thrusting into her through his soreness, despair, terror, and pain, feeling, sensing, knowing they would soon have to murder or be terminated themselves.

Later, after they dressed and ate and sat side by side at their holodeck, Blaise studied her face with a question burning in his gut. She glanced at him, trying to suss out what lay behind his expression.

"Is it true?" he asked. "What you said? About Minsheng?"

"I'll explain another time," she answered in a perfectly calm voice. They both knew Minsheng had installed surveillance now that he had lost trust in them.

She turned back to the holodeck and resumed coding. He watched, then chorused her commands with his in the synchronized manner they had established to help each other through the final stretch.

21

BLAISE AND MITSUKO, DRESSED IN BLUE SILK JACKETS WITH seahorse logos on their lapels, followed in Minsheng's procession down blue and purple marble tiles. Their entourage included four Class I sycophants assigned to Minsheng in his new role as deputy chairman. Android guards in imperial gold, blue, and red stood with laser burners at present-arms as Minsheng's entourage circled a veined marble slab imprinted with the five-petaled Hong Kong logo. They climbed to a teakwood portico encrusted with dragons, under a roof with red and gold beams.

Two gates swung inward. They passed into the Great Hall of the People, an auditorium with inlaid wood floors and rows of maroon leather seats, which formed a half-circle around a raised stage and podium. The back wall slanted over the stage and featured a global map of The Cloud Empire, similar to the one in Minsheng's office back in L.A. The North Am, African, and Eurasian continents glowed with translucent hues that shifted continually. Blaise noticed the capitals of the Sudan and South Africa were lit up in Cloud colors. He wondered whether those cities would go dark given the recent military disasters. The chairman's chief of staff, Klugman, a pasty-faced man with a double chin, delivered an interminable speech about tin production in South America and its effect on global military spending. According to Mitsuko's whispered account earlier that morning, Minsheng had bought the chief of staff's loyalty by promising him deputy chairmanship. After the Anima demo, Klugman would announce that a Hadji cyber-attack had incapacitated the board. Some would believe the story; others whom he had made deals with would tolerate it as a necessary fiction to legitimize Minsheng's rise to the top.

Minsheng's four retainers peeled off to find seats against the back wall. Blaise noticed that a capacity crowd had gathered. Generals and their adjutants in black uniforms crowded the back rows. In the lower rows, a sea of blue silk jackets loomed: senior executives, governors, and ministers from throughout the empire. Blaise glanced at the balcony, which overflowed with executives' families, the women decked out in meretricious gowns and bouffant hairdos.

A thump, thump, thump invaded Blaise's mind: his heart. It pounded so hard he was convinced everyone gathered could hear it. Every casual glance from a Class I struck him as a cruel betrayal. They knew! They knew what he was about to do! Any second, they would rise up in a mass to overwhelm him, Mitsuko, and Minsheng and drag them away to torture and death. The auditorium took on an electric dazzle from the pulsing of his fevered brain. He thought he might pass out. He had to repeat his mantra until the panic passed.

Blaise and Mitsuko processed down to the mouth of the maroon center aisle behind Minsheng, whose opaque expression and fatty up-thrust chin never varied a millimeter from imperial dignity. Minsheng swung right at the lip of the stage and passed under the podium like a graceful floating barge before he mounted a flight of steps. The stage could have housed a sports arena. The chief of staff's assistants scurried about at mini-holodecks in a sort of orchestra pit behind the podium. Blaise heard murmurs and whispers in the cavernous hall as Klugman droned on about the productivity of North Am military contractors during the last fiscal quarter. Minsheng heard and saw nothing; he was oblivious to the darts from thousands of jealous eyes. He approached a pair of golden doors with guards. The doors swung open to admit him, Blaise, and Mitsuko to a corridor at the end of which other doors ushered them into the boardroom.

Blaise's legs trembled with terror at what he was about to participate in. He muttered, "No, no, no," to himself as if that vain incantation could somehow extract him from the reality of coming to murder gods. Then came a stunning surprise. What he had imagined beforehand as a vast lair of power was, in fact, a narrow, low-ceilinged, stuffy room with a gold-scalloped ceiling featuring a Tibetan mandala.

Behind a conference table and twelve chairs, six on either side, were rosewood bookshelves with jade and china vases, Buddhas, Quan Yins, and sculptures of other Chinese deities. The board sat erect in rosewood chairs: clean-shaven, middle-aged Asian and Caucasian men in blue silk who wore expressions of the same opaque vintage as Minsheng's. Blaise's heart pounded in terror. These were masters of the universe, The Cloud incarnate, wielding power over billions. Blaise found them more horrifying than the cryogenic ghosts in the Hall of Heroes because these monsters breathed and cast indifferent glances at him, as if to say, "Yes, we are what you expected, and you tremble before us, but it's of no interest to us whatsoever." At table head sat the chairman, a German named Voigt, a former European finance minister with an elegant physique, feline eyes, and bloodless, wafer-thin lips. Behind Voigt, a rosewood frame curved around a smaller room with French windows. Blaise glimpsed outside at the Hong Kong tower-scape and hovercars that flashed like trails of mercury across the skyline. An effluvium of stale time sifted through the dust of this chamber, where toxic mentalities such as these had, for decades, twisted and disfigured the destinies of billions.

Minsheng took his seat next to Voigt. Blaise and Mitsuko sat at the opposite end of the room, in chairs placed for the occasion. The Anima feed would come directly through everyone's K-Spots, so there was no equipment to set up and no explanations. Voigt, however, had a few words of introduction.

"Gentlemen, I thank you for coming today from six continents and as many capitals," he intoned, letting Germanic breaks between words slip into his English. "What you are about to experience is well worth the rigors of your shuttle flights. Anima is, and I say it without exaggeration, the greatest VR weaponry breakthrough in twenty years. The sample you will experience today will be infinitesimal in its effect, next to the impact it will have on Slags and Hadjis. They will succumb, in short order, to self-imposed starvation and suicide. Caliphate armies will collapse. Their cities will become catafalques of rotting corpses. This will spell the end of the Caliphate and mark the total victory of the *Homo Deus* age. As I said, this demonstration will be at low amplitude and perfectly harmless. You will have to imagine the crushing force of it when it strikes the K-Spots of so many useless billions. And now, gentlemen, I give you Anima."

Blaise glanced at Mitsuko and saw a glint of fright in her eyes.

Voigt gestured to a technician, and the boardroom vanished, replaced by a Babylonian banquet on the portico of a columned terrace festooned with trees and vines, lined on one side with flowerbeds and on the other by a low wall overlooking the Tigris-Euphrates. Above this river-level terrace loomed the Hanging Gardens of Queen Semiramis. High, broad walks towered over the river in terrace after terrace, each recessed behind the ones below, the entire structure built of mud bricks and supported by massive stone pillars. Amid the screams of peacocks and the cries of birds feeding on the gardens' plentiful fruit, stands of mountain fir trees grew beside aromatic flowering shrubs, all this myriad lushness cunningly irrigated by a fifty-kilometer aqueduct that watered the entire city and fed this preposterous edifice stretching to the heavens.

Beyond spread a city of temples and soaring ziggurats. The courtyard revels brought laughter from bearded men in green, vermilion, and maroon robes, accompanied by black-haired women in diaphanous gowns, their slender necks circled by necklaces of gold and lapis lazuli, limbs scented with myrrh, frankincense, and cypress. A naked priestess with braided hair encircled by gold ringlets floated down marble steps. She sang verses from the *Epic of Gilgamesh* while a robed magician strummed a lyre decorated with a head shaped like a golden bull.

The priestess finished her song and held an emerald vessel high. "I bring you Anima, nectar of Ishtar."

Temple prostitutes fanned out among the revelers, each carrying an emerald flagon. When the board members, who embodied courtiers at this revel, drank Anima, pleasure transported them into rapture, wave upon wave of bliss that annihilated thought and motivation and brought certainty that everything was forgiven. Anima redeemed every deceit, betrayal, and murder and solved every problem because there could never be a problem here; it healed every wound because there could be no wounds; it gratified every desire because there could be no desire for anything but this obliterating ecstasy.

Blaise's, Mitsuko's, and Minsheng's Anima VR feed was cut off by pre-arranged code. They reoriented themselves to the drab boardroom. They looked from face to face to verify that Anima had possessed the board members with its annihilating pleasure. Minsheng turned to Voigt. A thread of drool dripped from the chairman's lip, his expression as vacant as a deactivated android's.

"You seem a bit distracted, Voigt," Minsheng laughed.

Voigt didn't move.

None of the board members moved. The room had become a mausoleum of respirating corpses.

"I think we should send for paramedics," Minsheng chuckled. "Our board has suffered a cyber-attack."

He rose, approached Blaise and Mitsuko, and gestured for them to stand. He embraced them and gave each a firm handshake.

"Well done," he congratulated them. "You may remain in the rear of the assembly hall with the rest of my staff to hear the announcement that I am now chairman. Afterwards, enjoy the pleasures of your suites for the rest of the day. Tomorrow you shuttle back to L.A. to complete Gilgamesh V. Blaise, you replace me as director, and my Mythoplex staff will report to you. Mitsuko, you are assistant director."

Blaise nodded toward the board. "What will happen to them?" he wondered.

"Why ask?" Minsheng guffawed. "You know very well what will happen to them."

"I meant today, now."

That prompted another chuckle. "Don't fret needlessly. Nothing can possibly go wrong. The board members will be taken to an ICU, where surgeons loyal to me will place them on IV drips with no medicinal value but which will look good in vid-feeds. Thanks to your fruitful coding, the effects of their Anima feeds are permanent and irreversible. We don't have to wait for them to starve themselves. The magnitude of today's feed obliterated their minds, I saw to that. Neurofeed will broadcast their images globally to show everything possible is being done to reverse the neural cyber-attack. Within a week or so, their bodies will shut down from organ failure. Imagine the grandeur of bringing that oblivion to billions of Slags and Hadjis."

"Grandeur is certainly the word for it," Blaise rasped, his mouth dry with fear at the risks that lay ahead for him and humanity.

22

BLAISE AND MITSUKO GOT THROUGH THEIR FIRST WEEKS BACK in L.A. by sheer force of will. Over three hundred games planners and support staff reported to them now. They were executive producers for seven VR series and served in advisory capacities for two dozen more. The hours they put in to complete *Gilgamesh V* alone would have crushed more fragile egos, but they also had to contend with the cunning and malice of subordinates: climbers who had deluded themselves into believing they would someday take Minsheng's place as director of programming. Mitsuko crushed covert dissent by snooping on her staff's neurofeeds and EEGs and never hesitated to send the Mantis to terminate Class IIs who couldn't completely suppress their hatred for her.

Blaise, on the other hand, found neuro-monitoring loathsome. He had always valued his hard-won privacy of mind, so he only monitored others enough to satisfy minimum requirements and despised himself for doing it. But it was the pressure to complete *Gilgamesh V* that drove him to the precipice of despair. The release date was weeks away. Programming teams were debugging and beta testing modules as he and Mitsuko completed them. Blaise did what he could to slow the pace of coding, tormented by the fact that he needed only ten minutes alone at his holodeck to upload the new Polyphemus virus modules, but he was never alone long enough to do it; Mitsuko watched his every move with the stealthy gravity of a serpent. He was constantly called into production meetings, and Minsheng's jowly face popped up from Hong Kong on his holoscreen at daily intervals, demanding progress reports.

Facilities had moved Blaise into Minsheng's former suite on the top floor of the Mythoplex Tower. From his new perch, he considered downtown L.A. and the San Fernando Valley beyond. When the Santa Monica seawall collapsed, the distant foothills would be beachfront dunes, and the glittering spires around the Mythoplex tower would devolve into curiosities rusting at the bottom of an aquarium two hundred meters deep. *I fantasized about L.A. drowning when it seemed impregnable,* he reflected. *Now I can't bear the thought of losing it.*

He knew that without Cloud maintenance servers, the sea wall might last a few months or a few minutes. Millions would perish unless Kristina's hackers could engineer a speedy evacuation with pirated hover troop carriers, a slim possibility after Polyphemus crashed The Cloud military power grid. This worry made it hard to hide his inner turmoil from Mitsuko and the legions of programmers he managed.

Mitsuko stuck to him like skin, reminding him between devouring kisses about the magnitude of their triumph when they completed the most significant VR series ever conceived. Whenever his thoughts strayed, and they often turned to Kristina and the new city, Mitsuko dragged his attention back to her. He knew his obsession with her was insane, that she and Minsheng were sharks circling him in ever tighter circles. Yet at times, Mitsuko made him ache to believe in the incomparable future she promised, though he knew in his heart of hearts that the web she spun around him was nothing more than the sexual cannibalism of a black widow spider. Her cries of "Darling!" when they plunged into the abyss together made him want to believe her. But he recalled her shriek of "Father!" back in Hong Kong. How did that cry fit into everything else in his psychotic episode of a life?

One night at Mitsuko's condo pod, as they lay sweating in the aftermath of love like two sticky earthworms roasting in a forest fire, everything came to a head. He rolled off her, pulled on a red silk smoking jacket she had bought him, and threw himself into a chair across the room, hair disheveled, eyes bloodshot from sleeplessness.

"What's wrong?" she demanded.

His feelings were so confused he could only shake his head and pull at his hair. Then rage and frustration prompted the inevitable question.

"Why the lies?"

She drew the sheet up around her like a shield. "What lies?"

She had the crushing attraction of a giant gas planet's gravity field. He couldn't bear to think of losing her body, which had become essential to him, but he blurted it all out nonetheless.

"Stop playing innocent!"

"What's the matter with you? You're frightening me."

"Why didn't you tell me Minsheng was your father?"

"What difference would that have made?"

"It might have convinced me you weren't using me to shore up his power."

Her lashes slipped closed. She sucked in a breath and let it out slowly, luxuriously, like cigarette smoke. Then she laughed bitterly; whether at him or herself wasn't clear.

"I didn't love you in the beginning," she confessed. "He told me to seduce you, draw you in, ensure your loyalty. But then—"

"You fell for me, right? Come on, Mitsuko. I've seen that scenario in a hundred VR series."

"But I do love you."

"You want to rule, and you're using me to get there."

"No, we're using him so we can rule."

She crawled out of bed and knelt at his feet, all feline grace and female scent. Her beauty nearly blunted his resolve to have it out with her.

"Blaise, please listen."

Part of him wanted so much to believe her. But then Minsheng's image imprinted itself on her face, and he shoved her away so hard she stumbled back against the bed.

"I want the truth, God dammit! About you. About him."

Her eyes filled with tears.

"Don't even go there, Mitsuko," he warned her. "No acting. No bullshit about your hard life. Tell me the truth, or I'll make a separate deal with Minsheng and cut YOU out of the equation."

"How could I tell you . . . he was my father?" she sobbed.

"By opening your fucking mouth."

"He would've terminated me."

"What do you think he's planning for me?"

"There's no reason to terminate you now that he's chairman."

"How about to keep me from frying his brain with Anima?"

Mitsuko shook her head. "I know him, Blaise. You're too valuable. So am I."

"You told me you wanted him dead. You said you wanted to replace him on the board. Don't you think he might suspect that? Don't you think he's planning to terminate us?"

"If he wanted that, he'd have done it after the Anima demo. He could bring in other mythologizers."

"Nice try, Mitsuko. He can't bring in anyone else because we're the only two who can hit that launch deadline. He's got Hadji armies to contend with, billions of Slags to vaporize. But after the launch? We're irrelevant."

"Blaise, I've known him all my life. In his own way, he . . . he loves me."

"He's treated you like a dog bitch. Passed you over for every promotion. Humiliated you. Turned you into my whore. Where's the love in that?"

"He's incapable of expressing affection, but I know he feels it."

He leaned toward her, fists clenched. "Not enough, apparently, to keep you from wanting to assassinate him."

Mitsuko lowered her head, ran her hands through her hair, grasped knots of it with her fists.

"Yes, alright, I do want him dead. I have my reasons. He—"

"He what?"

"Raped me."

"Get your story straight," he shot back. "Your brother was the rapist, remember? Or did you lie about that, too?"

She clenched her fists, pressed them to her eyes, and sobbed. "I thought saying it was my brother would make it easier to accept."

Her tears looked convincing, but Blaise wasn't buying it. He yanked her hands away from her eyes. She tried to free herself from his grip, but he forced her to the floor and plumped down astride her so hard he knocked the breath out of her.

"I want the truth!" he screamed.

"He still fucks me," she gasped. "He always has. Since I was little."

He slapped her face, hard. "Liar!"

"Please don't. Don't be like him."

Shocked at himself for his sudden violence, he got to his feet and staggered away. "You . . . you let him fuck you? Even now? Why? Why would you do that?"

She shook her head, overcome by sobs, and refused to say anymore. She crawled back into the bed and slipped her hand under the edge of the mattress.

"Looking for your knife?" he asked. "I took it."

She glared at him with a wounded expression. "Where?"

"Got rid of it. In case you ever wanted to use it on me again. But right now, looks like you might want to use it on yourself."

"That was the idea," she admitted and crawled under the covers like an oyster retreating into its shell.

Blaise had a jarring insight. If her story about Minsheng was true, and it very well might be, given his depravity, there could only be one reason she tolerated his abuse. Because she wanted ultimate power and was willing to pay the price to get it. So where did that leave Blaise? Why had he offered his life in exchange for Mitsuko's back in Hong Kong? Was it love? How could he possibly love a sociopath like her? There could be only one conclusion. On some level, he wanted ultimate power himself.

"I'm carrying your child," Mitsuko sobbed from under the covers.

"Liar!" he screamed, and, desperate to escape her, he dressed and headed for the door.

As he sprinted for the lift, he heard her shout. "Blaise, come back!"

He heard her approaching steps and ducked into the lift car in time to cut off her pursuit.

In her pod lobby, he ordered an autobot.

"Would that be on Miss Mitsuko Brown's account or yours?" the lobby bot asked with a conspiratorial grin.

"Mine," Blaise snapped, glancing at the lift door to see if Mitsuko had pursued him. "And hurry up with it!"

He ordered the autobot to take him to the Mythoplex tower. It hummed along with a Beethoven sonata playing at low volume as it passed through streets designed to attract Class IIs. There were miles of pachinko parlors, towering holographic posters with trailers from VR series, and floating banners in red, gold, and vermilion, with erotic taglines such as, "Yuna's yoni's wet for you—VR channel 237." As he passed into the business district, immaculate greenspace and pristine towers predominated, and he had a déjà vu about what he was about to attempt. He wondered if it would end the same way as the last time.

It wasn't until he cleared the SWAT station on the top floor and shut the door of Minsheng's former office behind him that he realized this was real: he was going to do it. He slipped into his cockpit chair. Glancing about to reassure himself that Mitsuko hadn't followed, he slipped the Polyphemus chip from its hiding place in his jacket sleeve and inserted it into the slot.

"Upload," he ordered with his heart in his mouth.

His holoscreen lighted up. Polyphemus glided up the screen in an aureole of glittering code.

"Access denied," chirped a sleek feminine voice. And the screen went dead.

Blaise stared at his holoscreen in disbelief. The nothing that had just happened roared in his ears louder than the alarm that never came. There were no pounding SWAT boots. No sticky net or paralyzing dart, no waking up in Minsheng's torture chamber. Just a blank screen. Blaise stared at the wall where facilities had mounted his namesake's recursion formula, which had replaced one of the floating mountainscapes Minsheng favored. But it was no help. Nothing could help. He had no way to save the billions Anima would exterminate.

"Explain access denial," he ordered, hoping for a miracle.

"Level seven security clearance required for non-pre-authorized uploads," the cheerful voice answered.

His level six security clearance, the clearance Minsheng himself enjoyed, wasn't high enough for him to upload Polyphemus! He couldn't remember any mention of level seven access in all his years at Mythoplex. Minsheng must have ordered the AI developers to install it in case anyone dared to repeat what Blaise himself had attempted with the initial Polyphemus version. So the painstakingly-coded firewall bypasses Kristina's hackers had created with Blaise's help had come to nothing. And with the *Gilgamesh V* release date weeks away, Minsheng would never give Blaise even a day off in the Zone to regroup with Kristina and the others.

He slumped in his chair, drawing deep hopeless breaths. He glanced at the bonsai, Zen fountain, and the seven onyx sculptures of gradually increasing scale. He had started his journey toward genocide here, and he would end it here. A line from a poem his mother used to quote when she was drunk returned: *This is the way the world ends, this is the way the world ends, this is the way the world ends, not with a bang but a whimper.*

23

ONCE A WEEK, BLAISE AND MITSUKO SHARED LUNCH WITH THE games planning staff in the commissary to generate goodwill and feign comradery with their subordinates. Blaise hated playing the glad-handing leader whose upbeat presence promised that you, too, could rise up the corporate food chain if you bled your soul dry. Aching to escape these sycophants, he watched the occasional executive hover-car streak by the picture window and was stunned to see a young Chinese woman with a burnt-orange helmet of hair, chatting with a junior games planner at a table in a corner near the window. He blinked, hard, to convince himself he wasn't hallucinating. Unquestionably, it was Kristina under that wig.

Irrational speculations flooded his mind. This was an android, a hologram, or a telepathic projection Kristina had somehow managed with her curseil powers. But none of those possibilities struck him as credible. Plainly she was here, chatting with a Class III, wearing a shrink-skirt and corporate blouse, with a linen Class III jacket draped over the back of her chair. Her forearm had one of the self-mutilation scars stylish young women favored. His heart pounded. This cunning, resourceful, shape-shifting woman had risked everything to come here, in all likelihood, to help him complete his mission. But she would certainly be caught and vaporized. He glanced around for signs that someone had seen through her disguise, and noticed Mitsuko's glance, which prompted him to flash her a smile.

"Could you escort our little entourage up to your floor?" he asked. "This stretch of coding I'm dealing with needs solitary concentration. I'll be in my office."

"I always code with you," she pointed out.

"Just need some solo concentration time, OK? A little space. I'll ping you later this afternoon, and we can go over today's progress."

Mitsuko smiled politely, shoved her hand between his legs under the table and squeezed his balls. "You want some privacy to fuck that orange-haired bitch over there?" she hissed.

Blaise shoved her hand away, smiled, and whispered back. "I'm the director. I don't have to explain anything. Do as I tell you."

Mitsuko glared at him, rose with dignity, and ordered the staff to follow. Blaise stood, shook a couple of subordinates' hands, smiled, nodded, and strolled over to the organic fruit juice dispenser, where he caught Kristina's eye. Then he made for the exit, allowing some Class III assistant games planners to stop him for a chat. When he reached the corridor, he glanced back to verify Kristina had followed, then eye-scanned the door to his private lift and stepped inside with her just behind. Unsure whether the lift had hidden surveillance eyes, he said nothing, and Kristina followed suit. Then the door hissed open, and they stepped into his suite, which, Blaise knew, Minsheng had surveillance-proofed during his tenure as director.

"What are you doing here?" Blaise demanded. "How did you get past SWAT?"

"I'm a hacker," she laughed and took in the artwork, bonsai, Zen fountain, and onyx sculptures. "Nice digs, Blaise. Impressive view."

He noticed her forehead was stamped with a K-Spot, and he wondered if she had been captured, compromised, and brainwashed. But that couldn't be. Capture would mean termination. So he checked her eyes to verify she wasn't an android.

"You scanned me like that when we first met," she teased. "Remember?"

He held her at arm's length. "How on earth did you manage this?"

She gave him a wry smile, plopped down on a couch and propped her legs on the coffee table. "Where there's a will there's always some bitch crazy enough to find a way."

Her bluff manner reassured Blaise enough to sit next to her. Love for her flooded his heart, yet angst gnawed at his entrails, too, because he was sure they would be caught and vaporized.

"How did you get into the building?"

"Told you I'm a great actress," she replied. She tapped her K-Spot. "Fabricating one of these was dead easy for our techs." She slipped off her spandex jacket and held up her arms to show off her self-mutilation scars. "These? Makeup effect. Created 'em myself. Not bad, huh? So what have you been up to?"

"There've been some complications," he sighed.

Kristina dropped her bluff manner, slid her legs off the couch, and faced him squarely, jaw clenched. "Complications?" she scoffed, surveying his luxurious digs. "Yeah, I see the complications."

"Kristina, the upload failed."

"You mean you didn't upload it."

"I tried. They raised the access requirement to level seven security clearance. Polyphemus couldn't get past that."

She shook her head and laughed. "Oh, you're good. Very good. I almost believe you. But your recent history flies in the face of that story."

"I swear it's the truth."

"Such a tough life. You shuttle over to Hong Kong. Help Minsheng take out the board. Get yourself promoted to director. And continue your fuck-fest with Mitsuko."

"Kristina, everything went south on me. The pressure was unbelievable."

She lunged at him and struck him across the face. "Pressure? You self-pitying son of a bitch! I'll tell you about *pressure*. SWAT made another sweep through Reseda last week. They slaughtered everybody."

"Oh, my God."

Her eyes burned with rage. "Blew the shit out of our warehouse complex with MOAB bombs. Took out our computer center, research labs. Everything. Carpet bombed the whole town. Used laser burners on survivors. Thirty years of agony and hard work are gone. So many people I've known and loved, dead. If you'd kept your promise, SWAT couldn't have made that strike."

He placed his head in his hands. "It was Minsheng. I'm sure of it. The bastard doesn't trust me. He had that level seven security clearance installed." Then something else occurred to him. "What about the new city? Did they find that, too?"

Tears clouded Kristina's eyes, but she wiped them away and kept her expression hard as granite. "We made it out on the hyperloop millimeters ahead of SWAT. Blew the tunnel up behind us. Train's intact, but it's got nowhere to go now. The new city's safe until The Cloud finds it. We've moved thousands of families there from the Zone, a few hundred at a time over the past few months, plus a lot of computer and engineering equipment before the SWAT strike. And we can drill the tunnel back open with laser cannon if we live long enough."

"Thank God!"

"Blaise, I see in your eyes you meant to do the right thing," she admitted in a softer tone. "I've been telling the others that for weeks. But you stalled too long."

"Couldn't get a minute alone to try it till last night. And I can't hack past level seven firewalls."

She studied his face and then sighed. "I believe you."

"You haven't told me how you got here."

"I flew."

"How? With what?"

"Our engineering team reconditioned some old-model hovercars and programmed them to mimic Cloud frequencies."

"How'd you manage to fly out of hacker city?"

"Through an old nuclear missile silo from the days Arizona was in the United States. Used a hacked authorization to get here." She grinned at his shocked expression. "Car's recharging in the hover-bay up on the roof. Don't look so surprised. We're growing our curseil powers. We threw up a psychic shield that makes me undetectable."

"That won't last. We've got to get you out of here."

"I am leaving, Blaise, with you."

"We'll never make it out of the building."

"Yes, we will." She placed a reassuring hand on his arm. "Despite my doubts about you, I convinced the others Minsheng might block the upload. So we created new bypass protocols and loaded them onto a brand-spanking-new Polyphemus chip." She slipped a tiny box from her sleeve and took out a chip. "Takes half an hour or so to run through the new protocols; maybe longer to find the right algorithms to crack that level seven access; but the virus is automatic and irreversible once the launch sequence starts. We'll be long gone before then."

"Maybe," he sighed. "But it could fail like our earlier tries. And if The Cloud network goes down before we reach Arizona, we'll crash in the desert."

She laughed. "Never underestimate people with nothing to lose. This new Polyphemus should work. As far as getting out of L.A., we've got our own guidance system. Kicks in when The Cloud goes down. We'll use your flight authorization. Same one that got me here."

"How'd you get my authorization?"

"We're hackers. Remember?"

Kristina slipped a slender black cylinder from her jacket sleeve into her palm.

"What's that?"

"Your courage. A covert ops laser burner. I hope you'll do the right thing. But if you don't, I can't risk you stopping me."

"OK, I'll give it a shot," he replied after a beat. "But we'd better haul ass afterward. Mitsuko could show up any time. She's tag-teaming me on the Anima coding."

Blaise heaved up from the couch, stepped to his desk, and settled into the cockpit chair. He took the updated Polyphemus chip from Kristina, inserted it in the slot, and ordered "Upload."

Spiny glisters of orange light flashed across the holodeck screen as the Polyphemus upload surged past firewall after firewall. It was working! Code flitted across the holoscreen, a school of electric eels surging through the global Cloud network. Kristina placed a hand on his shoulder.

"Are you going to miss her?"

He glanced up at her. "She told me she's having my child."

Kristina rolled her eyes. "There's no child. That's Minsheng's mendacity, dreamed up to super-glue you to that bitch."

"What if she's telling the truth?"

"A compulsive liar who learned it from the father of lies?"

"He *is* her father."

"What?" she asked incredulously.

"He's been having a bedroom rodeo with her since she was thirteen. A child with me would be the perfect way for her to spite him."

Kristina shook her head. "She'll say anything to keep you here. And I know they offered you eternal life with her. A pretty sweet deal. And you're only human." Her eyes glistened, and her next words came hard. "But I'm offering you my heart."

Her glance pierced his soul, and he knew his soul and hers were linked at a level beyond the power of words to describe. "Your love is the only meaning left to me."

"And your love is all I have," she whispered and gave him a kiss of such exquisite tenderness that he forgot for an instant the mortal danger they were in.

Then he raised his eyes to the screen, where he saw the Polyphemus code attain level six and breach more AI firewalls.

Kristina had placed her slender laser burner down on Blaise's desk. "I'll show you something better than eternal life in The Cloud. The Omega Point."

"The what?" he asked, studying the screen, wondering if Polyphemus would fail them yet again.

"The Omega Point," she explained. "Our ultimate destiny. The final soul refinement that begins with curseil. Our way of recovering spiritual insights lost and found again and again through the ages. I'll explain it all. When we get back to the new city."

He glimpsed a radiance in her eyes he had seen before. Shame scalded his heart for his previous cowardice. Yet even now, with strength dawning, resistance remained. His desire for Mitsuko, his greed for eternal life, and desperate hope for the child she carried swelled up in a hurricane surge that threatened to drown his resolve.

"I believe you, Kristina, I believe," he managed in a hoarse tone. A line from a poem his mother had read him as a child returned: *Strength beyond hope and despair, climbing the third stair.*

"Here," Kristina urged. She showed him a chip he hadn't seen before. "Back up all your access codes on this, everything that gets you through Cloud firewalls."

"You said nothing can stop the Polyphemus upload."

"That's what our simulations show. But just in case."

He peered out at the vista of aureate towers interspersed with streaking hover-cars, the hive where twenty million souls milled and loved and struggled and died. Would this upload save lives or drown them when the seawalls collapsed? But without Polyphemus, the Slags would die anyway. Class Is and IIs would flee to Minsheng's new city in the desert, and The Cloud would go on forever. He took the backup chip, inserted it in a slot, and downloaded his passcodes. Then he started the upload.

He heard his private lift door slide open behind him. He spun round in his cockpit chair and was shocked to see Mitsuko stride in, as breathtaking in her blue silk jacket and kimono skirt as the first time he had seen her. Behind her loomed two enormous SWATs in black tactical gear. One pointed a sticky-net launcher at Blaise.

Mitsuko glanced at Blaise and then focused pitiless eyes on Kristina. "Kill her," she ordered one of the SWATs. "Him we need alive for reconditioning."

"Mitsuko, if you ever loved me . . ."

Her eyes burned with purpose. "I love my father. Now step away from the holodeck. I'm terminating that upload."

"Nothing can stop it."

Mitsuko signaled the SWATs. One drew a laser burner and fired at Kristina, who dropped like a stone and rolled clear. The beam raked a furrow in one of the Persian rugs. Blaise calculated the distance between himself and the second SWAT, who trained the sticky-net launcher at him. Drawing on his military martial arts training, Blaise cartwheeled clear of the net, which spewed out and engulfed Blaise's cockpit chair. Blaise landed, got his balance, pivoted, and rushed the SWAT. He spun round in a wheel kick. The SWAT darted clear and whirled round himself to give Blaise a roundhouse kick to the neck. Blaise pivoted out of his reach and, seeing the SWAT draw his laser burner, reacted with the desperation of a doomed man by giving the SWAT a deep front kick to the knee. The SWAT screamed as his kneecap shattered. His leg folded, giving Blaise enough momentum to thrust out his leg as he swung round and caught the SWAT in the throat, hard enough to crack his neck. The other SWAT fired his burner at Blaise, who whirled out of the beam's path so it barely singed his arm.

"No!" Mitsuko screamed to the other SWAT. "I want him alive!" She focused on Blaise. "I'm bearing your child. We belong together. Forever. So step away from that holoscreen and stop this madness."

Kristina, meanwhile, charged the second SWAT. She made a flying leap, hurtling through the air feet first. She smashed into the SWAT's back and sent him flying. Mitsuko lunged for his laser burner as he smacked the floor and scooped it up in her hand.

Turning it on Kristina, she shrieked, "Hacker bitch!"

Kristina caught Mitsuko's eyes with her own.

"What . . . what are you . . .?" Mitsuko gasped as her body lost all capacity for movement.

"It's called curseil," Kristina smiled. "You're not going to fire that burner. You're going to drop it."

Mitsuko struggled to free herself from invisible bonds, but she was frozen like a fossil in stone. "Let . . . go of me!" she shrieked with the rage and horror of someone long accustomed to spinning webs around others, but who now found herself caught in gossamer she could never have imagined.

Blaise heard a groan and saw the SWAT that Kristina had kicked prop himself up on his elbow and draw a backup burner from his pocket. Blaise rushed to his console and scooped up Kristina's slender burner. He raked the beam across the SWAT'S chest and abdomen in a clean arc that burned through his lungs and heart. His guts spilled out like a mass of smoking, blood-soaked snakes.

Mitsuko's face flushed from her effort to free herself from Kristina's curseil hold, but it was nothing doing.

"Come, death!" she screamed when she had utterly exhausted her strength.

In a corner a tornado of fireflies whirled round a green apparition that solidified into a green-winged horror with a black-ribbed thorax and prayerful claws, scraping like a million crickets. The Mantis swung toward Kristina, balancing on powerful legs, which dipped and rose as its antenna whipped, as if hesitating, perhaps held in check by the curseil counter-force Kristina projected.

"Stop it, Mitsuko!" Blaise screamed.

"This is the only way," Mitsuko reassured him. "I'm carrying your son."

Mitsuko trained her eyes and will on Kristina, and the Mantis advanced.

Blaise's relationship with Mitsuko flashed before his eyes in a flood of tender longing. He couldn't bring himself to laser her with the covert burner in his hand.

"Kristina!" he screamed as he lobbed it through the air.

Kristina lunged and caught the burner in mid-air. In one swift movement, she rolled clear of the Mantis and hurled Mitsuko against the lift doors with the beam. The Mantis crackled and vanished. Mitsuko's body slid down the door panels, smearing blood from a hole in her belly that gaped as if she had given birth through it. The stench of charred flesh made Blaise's stomach heave. He broke out in a cold sweat as he tried to cope with the shock of throwing away immortality and colluding in the death of his child's mother.

Kristina approached, panting and sweating from her exertions. "Let's get out of here," she managed when she could speak.

He drew a deep breath and let it out in increments. "My lift will take us straight to the roof."

She reached for her slender burner.

"Better let me hold onto that," he explained. "I know this building, and we'll have trouble getting to the hanger."

He slipped her burner in the sleeve of his jacket as they approached the lift. They had to step over Mitsuko's corpse. He slipped on the blood, lost his balance, and Kristina had to steady him. Mitsuko's bloodless face looked exquisitely beautiful in death. Horror, regret, and the agony of losing a flawed love overwhelmed him as he tore himself free from the life he was leaving behind. Then the lift doors slid open and closed behind them. He ordered the car to the roof, and repeated his mantra to summon the sangfroid he'd need to help them escape from the building. The lift opened on a short corridor. At its end, a pair of SWATs in black uniforms snapped to attention behind a table with a small holoscreen. Blaise gave them a dismissive frown as he sauntered up with Kristina. One of them eye-scanned him with a portable scanner.

"Meeting at Vidracom," Blaise informed him, then nodded to Kristina. "My new executive assistant."

The second SWAT stepped into his path as Blaise approached the door to the hovercar hanger.

"We have to eye-scan her, too, sir."

"New employee. Not in the system yet."

"Sir, you know the protocol," the SWAT replied, resting his hand on the butt of his laser burner.

Kristina's slimline laser burner slipped into Blaise's palm from his sleeve, and he lasered off the SWAT's head, which rolled away like a blood-soaked cabbage as the other SWAT groped for his weapon. Blaise lasered off his arm. The man collapsed, screamed, and writhed as he bled out.

"I don't have door access," Blaise cried, his mouth dry as a desert.

"Give me the burner and stand back," Kristina ordered.

She used her burner to melt open an oval large enough for them to squeeze through. The polycarbonate door was resistant but slowly succumbed to the fierce heat of the beam. A slab from the access door crashed into the executive hover-bay, accompanied by a shrieking alarm. No guards patrolled the hanger. It stood on a covered rooftop with an open bay higher than the surrounding towers. Blaise knew a SWAT backup team would burst through the door behind them at any moment. They bolted past double rows of hovercars that all looked alike to Blaise, but Kristina quickly found hers.

"Authorization two-seven-eight-echo-five."

The car door slid up and they climbed in and belt-beamed themselves tight.

"Return to coordinates 8850A-7Q."

"Command completed," the female voice lisped, and the car lifted off.

The jeweled tower-scape streaked past with ever greater velocity as they gained altitude. Blaise peered at other hover-cars. He expected to see an Air Force gunship. But the cars offered only glimpses, behind transparent side panels, of pallid Class I executives. Their car reached cruising altitude, and they saw nothing but infinite blue and the fulgent sun.

"Try to relax," Kristina advised. "Even if the air patrol scrambles, The Cloud will be down soon. Besides which, they'll never spot us. Our curseil circle is focusing psychic energy to serve as a stealth device."

Everything connected with Mitsuko flashed through Blaise's mind: his infatuation, his pride in coding *Gilgamesh V* with her, his hopes for eternity with her. He felt naked, abandoned, defenseless, yet reborn into a giddy freedom.

"How soon can we get there?" he wondered.

"We're looking at a fifty-minute flight." She threw him a look. "Forget about L.A., Blaise. Forget about her."

"What about those we're leaving behind?"

"We'll shoot out bulletins on our pirate neural network soon as The Cloud crashes to let people in the Zone know there won't be a functional laser burner anywhere in the metro area. My guess is, they'll overrun every Class I live/work/play pod and slaughter anyone in a silk jacket. Assuming the seawall holds, we'll send in teams to help people sharpen up their survival skills while we evacuate them. They'll need those skills after the food rots in the supermarkets. Our San Francisco and San Diego cells are organizing similar evacs. Same thing overseas."

He had many other questions, and she did her best to answer as they scudded above the clouds, glimpsing, far below, the desert and the gold and white stripes of the Sierra foothills. He was impressed by how thoroughly the hackers had thought through their strategy for replacing The Cloud. His shock from the day's events receded, and he got caught up in the excitement about life in the new city. Kristina assured him his coding skills were needed to refine neural tech and communications networks. As she spoke, he saw himself hand in hand with her in Sagrada Familia, sharing the light she had shown him there. Then he noticed that half an hour had passed since they fled L.A. The final upload should have disrupted The Cloud network by now. But two black dots rose through sky behind them, and a laser beam raked within a thousand meters of their hover car.

"Air Force gunships!"

Kristina turned pale. "How? The upload should be finished. And our curseil circle's supposed to cloak us."

"Well, it ain't working, babe. AI firewalls must've blocked the upload again. Now they're going to blast us out of the sky."

Kristina shot him a determined glance. "No, they won't. They'll force us to ditch if they can. They need you alive. With Mitsuko gone, you're the only one who can meet that *Gilgamesh V* deadline."

Another beam streaked by within five hundred meters.

He glanced back at the gunships, which looked like glittering needles shooting out wires of white heat.

"I think this is more of a wanted dead or alive scenario. It's probably fine with these air force fuckers if they kill us both. How far to the new city?"

"Thirty klicks."

"We'll never outrun them. We've gotta ditch and duck through those canyons, dodge 'em till we can make it to base."

"And if we do?"

"I'll figure out how to code around those level seven firewalls. Use hacker tricks to smash through them."

Another beam crossed their bow and streaked deep into the empyrean. Kristina screamed.

Blaise grasped at the only straw he could think of. "Contact your curseil circle, if you can. Get them to focus all their energy, everything they've got, on those gunships."

A beam grazed their car, and it spun out of control. The canyon below rushed toward them.

"Auto-pilot: controlled spin!" Kristina ordered. "Find a level landing spot!"

The gunships circled for a strafing run. The auto-pilot kicked in, but the laser hit made it impossible for the car to level off. The best they could hope for was a controlled crash. Kristina clenched her eyes to focus her curseil energy. Blaise tried to patch into her frequency, but panic interfered. A laser beam gouged a deep red trench in the canyon below. Their car plummeted to within thirty meters of the ground, then barely leveled off and smacked into the canyon floor, spinning out in a shriek of protesting metal before coming to rest.

The door glided up and canyon dust hit them in the face. They gasped and coughed, choked for air. Kristina grabbed an emergency backpack with water, protein wafers, and survival supplies before they stumbled out, plummeted down an arroyo, and tried not to twist their ankles on the scraggy ground.

They covered fifteen hundred meters before Kristina shouted, "They're coming!"

A hover-gunship far behind dropped a MOAB bomb on their hover-car. The blast knocked them off their feet. They tumbled over and over like paper scraps in a tornado, while a mushroom cloud rose behind like a giant fist protesting the sky. Dust washed over them, a suffocating wave that left them exposed like extruded rocks. When it cleared, they saw gunships circling, hunting for level ground to touch down.

24

THEY SLOGGED THROUGH THE CANYON FOR HOURS IN THE deepening shadows of late afternoon, fleeing the sharp commands of air troopers searching the canyons behind them. Engines roared overhead from gunships seeking their heat signatures. They did their best to dodge their pursuers, ducking behind boulders and scrambling down ravines. A gunship's laser cannon churned up a piece of canyon wall behind them, to drive them out in the open. It caused an avalanche, but as luck would have it, a cougar, as startled to see them as they were to see it, galloped away from the collapsing rocks and dashed through the canyon in the opposite direction. The gunship followed its heat signature and fried the cougar with a dead center laser shot, churning up fur, earth, and rock. Blaise and Kristina lay face down in a ravine without moving, barely breathing, until the gunship sped into the distance.

They leaped up and reached a furrowed gulley with walls too high to allow gunships to track their heat signatures and blundered across the uneven ground for several kilometers, doing their best to avoid injury. Eventually, they emerged on a red and gold plain with scrub grass and a forest of cacti with arms upraised like a praying congregation. The blazing October sun settled into the foothills. Blaise and Kristina were badly dehydrated. The emergency backpack she had salvaged contained only four liter-sized water flasks. Neither Blaise nor Kristina had taken desert survival training. Their chances were slim.

A gunship roared past in the distance. They flattened themselves in the undergrowth until it vanished behind a peak.

"We travel by night," he warned. "Otherwise, the sun will fry us, or those gunships will take us out."

"This time of year, we'll freeze to death," she protested. "There's only one thermal blanket in my emergency pack."

"We'll take breaks. Share our body heat and hope tarantulas won't mistake our armpits for burrows."

"Ha, ha. Ever spent time riding the range, badass? Or do you get that stuff from VR?"

"Nature video I saw at UCLA."

"That's what I figured. Truth be told, scorpions and rattlesnakes are the real nighttime dangers. But you're right. We wouldn't last a day in that sun. Problem is, at night, our heat signatures'll stand out like flares."

"Then we'd better find a hole deep enough to hide from those fuckers."

A gunship at the horizon fired its laser cannon, then streaked away.

"How good is curseil with directional guidance?" Blaise wondered.

"We're getting better, but we're infants at this. I guarantee our curseil circle's hunting for us. I got off a psychic distress signal before we crashed."

"So what's our ETA to that missile silo of yours if we travel all night?"

"Two nights if we haul ass and don't freeze first."

The sun vanished behind the foothills, and a belt of stars flickered beyond the half-moon.

"Wrap yourself in the thermal blanket," he offered. "Women feel cold more than men do."

She tossed him a dubious look but threw the blanket over her shoulders as they threaded through patchy ground. Gunships blazed past in the near and far distance, which forced them to dive into gullies and flatten themselves on hard ground, then leap up and scurry ahead. Fortunately, they weren't the only nocturnal animals that attracted attention: the desert teemed with foxes, feral pigs, coyotes, and cougars that gave off heat signatures close enough to humans to attract the gunships. The night passed in fits and starts. Occasionally, the wind carried the stench of charred animal flesh when a laser beam incinerated some hapless creature nearby. Blaise's and Kristina's legs cramped. Boils formed from their city shoes chafing against hard ground. The cold penetrated their bones. They had no choice but to push past endurance, and their efforts kept them from freezing. Finally, after stumbling through nettles and enduring cuts, abrasions and exposed rock, they couldn't take another step. They collapsed under a dusty berm like clay-colored aborigines. Despite fear of detection, Blaise relished mammalian contact with Kristina, that affirmation of being only touch can bring. He spooned her as he once did Cherry. Something stirred in him beyond physical need: his spirit waking from a long sleep as if their bodies were shadows of some higher, more precious, unnamable flesh.

"I and thou," he whispered.

"What's that?"

"From a book my mom read to me. It means your soul is speaking to mine."

"Incredible woman, your mother."

Under the half-moon, her eyes glistened. She kissed him softly, her lips salty with sweat. Theirs was a kiss of deep connection, a sharing of souls very different than the animal kisses he had shared with Mitsuko. The peace it brought allowed exhaustion to carry them off to sleep.

When he woke hours later, the morning sun slanted in from the east, and the desert had a spectral glow as if a flash flood had drenched the tumbleweeds, thick-veined plants, and petrified ground. He shook Kristina awake. She blinked, groaned, and her eyes opened. They shared a protein bar and a few sips of water.

He scanned the horizon. "How far to that missile silo?"

She fished a holographic compass from her backpack and consulted it. "About twenty klicks."

"What do we do when we get there?"

"There's a camouflaged blockhouse near the old missile silo. I've got the access code. An elevator will take us down to the new city."

"Twenty klicks," he considered. "We won't make five when that sun gets up. Is there any other way?"

"We've got jerry-rigged hovercars like the one I flew to L.A.. If our techs have a few more running, they could send an air evac."

"That's a pretty big 'if'. Better grab some more shut-eye, and we'll head out again tonight."

"And if the gunships find us?"

"Then, doll-face, we're fucked."

They endured the hallucinatory brilliance of the desert in the stink of sweat and fear, while gunships skirted the horizons. By noon, they had sweated off so much water weight that nothing existed for them but thirst. It took all their willpower to keep from draining the water flasks. Then, adding to Blaise's torment, a female voice brayed in his brain: "The board of directors announced a stunning victory against Hadji forces in the Sudan. Caliphate forces are on the run and will soon be decimated. Details at six. In other news, the Bureau of Consumer Affairs reports our North Am Quadrant scored record productivity gains for the third and fourth fiscal quarters in all industries."

"They reactivated my neurofeed," he groaned.

"Can't you block it?"

He focused on that, but the bleating voice reeled off endless statistics, commercials, and VR series announcements, including a coming-soon spot for *Gilgamesh V.*

"I can't, dammit!" he swore. "Minsheng's behind this. Now those hover-gunships will home in on me for sure."

"If you can help me block that Cloud neural signal with curseil, it might do the trick. I'll link my frequency with yours."

The gunships that had circled in broad arcs earlier narrowed their sweeps. Clearly, they had locked onto Blaise's neurofeed. He struggled to patch into Kristina's curseil frequency. It was like trying to isolate a water droplet in an ocean of noise. No matter how hard he focused, the neurofeed disgorged more productivity statistics, military victories, and praise for the sex-slaughter indexes of VR series. He glanced over the lip of the berm and saw a gunship streak toward them. What a fool he had been to think he could bring down The Cloud. They would laser Kristina to death and fly him back to L.A. Minsheng would force him to complete *Gilgamesh V* and then terminate him. The hackers' rebellion had come to nothing. Soon, he would be nothing, all memory of him erased, the new city obliterated, whole populations reduced to ashes, and The Cloud's hold on humanity fixed and eternal.

They had no place to run, so they clung together like desert burs. A laser beam struck their berm. Blaise and Kristina heaved up and hurtled through space with the disintegrating mound while the laser raked below them, gouging open a fissure in the earth like a ragged black vagina that swallowed them whole. They tumbled and rolled at a sharp angle down a pit that scraped, bruised, and cut them until they thudded to rest on some unforgiving surface like two fractured vessels, their screams silenced by dust and rubble in their mouths.

25

SUNLIGHT FROM A FISSURE WOKE BLAISE FROM A DREAM IN which he lay dead, eaten by worms. The fissure above him cast enough light for him to see he had landed in the belly of a limestone cave roofed by gold-sawtooth stalactites. Stalagmites marched toward him across the uneven floor. Kristina lay covered in dust and rubble a few paces away. He crawled to her, gasping from a knife-wound of pain in his side. He reached trembling hands to her face and neck and was grateful to find her breathing. She had a nasty cut from forehead to left ear. A purple bruise discolored her neck. He scrambled for the backpack near her and dug inside till he found a tactical flashlight. It cast a brilliant beam. Using it, he dug around and found a first aid kit in one of the side pockets, an old-school affair with bandages, adhesives, and antiseptic. He crawled back to Kristina, brushed the dust away from her face and clothes, and cleaned her cut with antiseptic. She blinked, groaned, and tried to sit up. He slid his legs under her and gently lay her head in his lap.

"Just rest," he soothed. "You took a hell of a tumble." He applied a surgical bandage to her cut and secured it with adhesive. "How bad's the pain?"

"My whole body hurts, but I don't think anything's broken. You?"

He grimaced as he touched his tender spot. "Think I cracked some ribs. But no compound fractures. I can still walk. Can't guarantee anything as far as internal bleeding, though." He peered at the sunlight pouring through the fissure. "Why didn't they come down here after us?"

She heaved up and inspected the gold dusty gloom around them. "Curseil. I got a telepathic message. Our circle concentrated all our power on that gunship, seized the pilot's mind, and forced him to shift into manual control and crash into that berm. He and his crew are nothing but charred bones."

"I thought maybe Polyphemus had crashed The Cloud, finally."

"No. That's one challenge still ahead of us."

Blaise peered around. "How far down you figure we are?"

"Gotta be sixty meters deep." She shot him a look. "What about your neurofeed? There are still other gunships out there."

"Must be getting better at curseil. I stopped it."

"Good! If you blocked it, maybe they'll think we're incinerated."

He rose groaning with pain and limped over to the fissure where the sun shone in. "Hope you're right."

"We've got something else going for us," he heard behind him. "A former airman who came over to our side told me pilots are scared shitless of the desert. Their gunships are designed for urban warfare. They hardly ever fly this far out. Limited fuel cell range. They may have hauled their asses back to L.A."

"Sounds plausible," Blaise laughed bitterly as he limped back to her. "But hard on the ego. Thought I was a person of some importance. Worth hunting for. Now I get to starve to death in a cave."

She laughed until the pain stopped her and then rested her head on the palms of her hands.

"You OK?" he asked as he eased himself down beside her.

She nodded. "I'm good. But my head feels like somebody drove a spike through it." She glanced up and flashed him a dust-caked grin. "Look at the bright side. Minsheng's probably got your whole programming team jamming on *Gilgamesh V* now. He probably grabbed a shuttle back from Hong Kong to oversee final coding himself."

A black umbrella of despair spread over Blaise. "There's nobody to stop his genocide now."

She considered that. "If our luck holds out, we'll get you back to the new city in time to figure out another upload."

She took the tactical flashlight from him and raked the beam across the cave. "We've still got emergency rations. A little water. There's got to be another passage to the surface."

They spent the next hour tending each other's wounds with the first aid kit. Kristina removed his dirt-encrusted jacket and shirt, inspected his bruised ribs, and wrapped antiseptic gauze around his waist.

"That'll have to do," she concluded. "You hungry?"

They shared a protein bar, and after Blaise pulled on his filthy shirt and jacket, Kristina slung the backpack, and they limped through the cave's rear, guided by the flashlight and an overwhelming urge to escape. After about forty meters, still close enough to the fissure behind them to cast some of its rays ahead, they entered a semi-circular chamber with smooth red walls and a ceiling of stalactites that curved in serrated clusters around a surface shaped like the palm of a hand. Someone had scratched drawings into the stone wall at head height: crude stick figures, dominated by a man with a rod held high above his head, and two smaller figures on either side. Above the human figures loomed two shapes like serpents coiled around their own tails, a design that formed circles of descending size. Horned elks and smaller deer-like animals appeared above, below, and beside these shapes at crazy angles, as if floating in the air.

"I've seen petroglyphs like this before," Kristina marveled, shining the flashlight at sections of wall. "These are from one of the ancestral Pueblo tribes." She pointed to the figure holding the rod above his head. "He would be the shaman. Those two smaller figures are his assistants. The spiraling serpents are ancestor spirits. The shaman would go into a trance and enter the dream time, where the ancestors gave him guidance for the tribe: what to hunt, where to look for water, medicinal plants, new hunting grounds. We're in sacred space here."

Kristina's rapturous tone moved Blaise. He felt something indefinable sifting into the dream-space of his mind, a presence. But the presence of what? Then he realized it came not from the crude drawings on the wall but from the radiance of Kristina's voice. Something emanating from her moved him so deeply he took the flashlight from her and shone it on her bandaged face. Her hair was a mess of scattered tresses, knotted in clumps, her face bruised and smeared with grime and dust. Her clothes were torn. She was bleeding from cuts and covered in welts. But she looked more beautiful than he ever remembered. He took her in his arms, sore as he was, and gave her a kiss so deep it lingered outside of time, and he recalled something his mother had read to him as a child: *What might have been and what has been point to one end, which is always present.*

"If we're going to die down here, I want you to know how much . . . " His voice faltered. He kissed her face and hair with desperate urgency. A fissure in his heart opened upon limitless vistas of joy and sorrow.

"You love me?" she whispered, returning his kisses.

"Oh, God, yes," he blurted. "I only realized it completely now that we've lost all hope. There's more goodness, more courage in your little finger than in my whole body."

They embraced until weariness and pain brought them to their knees, and then they rested against the cave wall and clung to each other, beneath the scrawled drawings by remote ancestors who had lived, loved, and died here as they soon would.

She whispered in his ear. "Never thought I'd pry you loose from Mitsuko."

He laughed bitterly. "That was a hollow love, a fantasy. Everything is real with you."

She sobbed, nestled against his shoulder. "I'm sorry I praised Thomas so much. I was jealous of Mitsuko. I wanted to make you jealous."

"I understand," he whispered, kissing her forehead and hair. She lay down the flashlight so that its beam cut into the gloom behind them. "He was a great love, but he wasn't like you, Blaise. He never had to live in the world till after they burned his monastery. And when he saw all that horror first-hand, it broke his heart and body. You, Blaise, you're the survivor. You have a great soul. A strong heart."

Blaise was grateful to know Kristina returned his love. But what could it mean now when they were going to die with the bitterness of knowing his mission had failed, and billions would perish?

"*Carezza*," she whispered in his ear, and they gingerly made love on the cave floor, sore and bruised as they were. For a few precious minutes their caresses lifted them out of their bruised and weary bodies.

Something stirred inside him as if one of the ancestral spirits passed by. But it was more than that: a breeze, freshening the air of the dusty chamber.

"Do you feel that?" Kristina gasped.

"An air current!"

"Of course!" she agreed. "If this was their sacramental chamber, there must be a way out of here."

The flashlight illuminated a cleft in a corner behind a stalagmite.

"Was that there all along?" Kristina cried.

"Come on," he cried.

The cleft led to a narrow passageway, almost too narrow to pass through. The air current issued from there.

"Can we get through?" Kristina wondered.

"We have to. I'll go first. If I fit, you can, too."

She took his arm. "I'll go first. If it's too narrow, I'll be able to get back out."

He tugged himself free. "I'm going first, and I'll have to take the flashlight," he insisted. "There's enough light for you to get back to that other chamber."

She tugged at his arm. "Blaise, please—"

"We're going to make it," he assured her and squeezed through the cleft.

After several meters the ceiling inside the passage dropped so low he scraped his head against it. But he pushed deeper, and the freshening breeze from up ahead urged him on. The passage descended, and the walls converged into a narrow slit. It would have been no trouble for Kristina to get through, but he had to inch along ragged walls pressing him front and rear. It was such a tight squeeze that the serrated stone shredded his tattered silk jacket and tore at the skin of his chest, back, and legs. He reached a place where the walls were so irregular and tight he couldn't move forward. He stuffed the flashlight in his trouser pocket and contorted his body to squeeze through. The strain exhausted him and set up a fiery pain in his cracked ribs. His strength was rapidly draining, and he was overcome by terror of being buried alive in this limestone coffin. But his spirit cried, "No!" and he managed, by force of will, long after hope had deserted him, to push forward until he cleared the narrow declivity. The walls fell away, and the passageway slanted up again. He stumbled ahead, stinging and burning from a host of bleeding cuts, and reached a large open chamber flooded with light and the scent of open desert.

"Kristina, it's OK, it's safe!" he shouted behind him.

He shouted again and again until he heard her faint echo reverberating up the narrow tunnel. "I'm coming!"

He placed the flashlight at the lip of the entrance so its beam would illuminate her way, and slumped against the cave wall, exhausted almost beyond his limits until he heard her grunts and struggling steps grow nearer. He was delighted to see her burst into the clear space with torn and ragged clothes and several new cuts. He grunted, rose, limped to her, picked up the flashlight, and shone it up the passageway ahead of them.

"That's where the breeze is coming from."

She hugged him so tightly he cried out in pain. "Let's get out of here," she wheezed.

They were both limping, but they saw light ahead streaming in like a song of life. They hobbled toward it, supporting each other as they climbed a gentle incline toward sunlight so raw it hurt their eyes. The incline leveled off into a smooth passage with rounded walls. They saw the cave's mouth and limped toward it.

They staggered out into the late afternoon heat and sank to their knees, weeping, sweating, and grateful to be free.

"Let's keep moving," she gasped, clearly in pain. "We're exposed here. Look, there's an arroyo where we can hide while I send a curseil distress signal."

They hobbled ahead, supporting each other, fighting off the urge to collapse, and passed between two towering cacti with arms stretched toward them. Abruptly, a hover-gunship loomed over the hill above the cave mouth behind them. A laser beam raked the ground and splintered one of the cacti, its beam passing so close that Blaise barely had time to shove Kristina away before it raked his tattered clothing and hair and singed him with its wrathful heat.

This is the end.

But it wasn't. Because as the gunship veered away and returned for another strafing run, Blaise glimpsed a hovercar pop up over the horizon. Suddenly he could feel curseil power pulsing in his brain. Instead of hovering over him for a clean kill, the gunship spun in an insane circle, hurled forward like a madman trying to escape confinement, and smashed into the mouth of the cave they had just left. The MOAB bomb it carried detonated, and Blaise and Kristina were swept up in the impact of the blast, hurled through space, and thudded to the ground like two fractured vessels, carried off into blackness by searing pain.

26

HE WOKE TO THE SCENT OF CEDAR, FIR, AND PINE IN A ROOM with a window giving onto a cityscape of undulating walls and mushroom-shaped houses. Beyond, a fir tree forest stretched toward a cavern roof. Pain pierced his side as if a bullet had lodged there. Duller pains throbbed throughout his body. A door hissed open, and a young Middle Eastern woman with warm brown eyes and olive skin approached.

"Am I dead?"

"No," she chuckled. "You're very much alive."

She caressed his mind with warmth, and her Mediterranean scent reassured him.

"Where am I?"

"The new city clinic. I'm Aaliyah, one of the doctors here."

"Where's Kristina?"

"In a room down the hall. You're both badly dehydrated, and you cracked some ribs from that landing you took in the desert."

He became aware of an IV in his arm and monitoring equipment.

Suddenly, everything rushed back to him in all its terror. "I need to get to a holodeck."

"Of course," Aaliyah soothed. "But we're safe for the moment. Those hover-gunships can't find us this far below ground."

"They were tracking us pretty closely."

"And we were tracking them. We used curseil to crash the gunship that nearly finished you when you blundered out of that cave."

He pushed words through pain, exhaustion, and despair. "You don't understand. I've got to re-upload Polyphemus."

He tried to rise, but her mind took him in its grip and restrained him.

"Look, please, whatever your name is—"

"Aaliyah."

"Arabic, isn't it? Don't you realize they'll annihilate everyone here, and all your people, too? I've got to get to a holodeck."

"And you will. But now you have to rest. We're using genomic tech to repair those ribs of yours."

Aaliyah made an adjustment on one of the flickering devices, and he drifted into oblivion with a half-formed protest on his lips. He slept deeply, and when he woke he felt refreshed, and his pains were gone. Kristina slipped into the room in a hospital gown, drew up a chair, and took his hand.

"We made it, my love," she whispered, and they held each other like two long-separated orphans. "Our curseil signal worked. They got a hovercar through for our evac."

"How long was I out?"

"Three days. Your injuries were more serious than Dr. Aaliyah let on. They've been repairing both of us with pirated Medco tech. We're pretty much good as new now."

"Then show me the nearest holodeck."

"You can try that upload later today. Our programmers have been trying to hack past that level seven security around the clock while you and I were out cold. But before you give it a shot, come with me to Sagrada Familia. It'll give you strength."

"That won't help me make that upload work."

"Yes it will."

He protested, but she wouldn't take no. And so later, after Dr. Aaliyah authorized it, they left the clinic and strolled to the basilica, where they sat in a row of benches behind several dozen hackers and Slags. Particolored light from high windows and soaring, plant-like columns brought Blaise unexpected peace. Hope welled up, and he believed, he knew, in that timeless space beyond the reach of his angst, that they still might defeat The Cloud, however slim their chances.

Afterward, they walked streets lined with flower beds. He saw adults and children who had once been angst-ridden ghosts haunting the Slag Zone. They looked well-fed, and many smiled. Several stopped to shake his hand.

"Can they use curseil?" Blaise asked.

"Not all. But word's spread about you."

They approached a lotus-shaped building with a window curving around the façade. Inside, Kristina introduced him to hackers in jeans, women mostly, a few men among them. Blaise recognized several from the curseil circle that had scoured his soul back in Reseda. They greeted him with tense smiles. One, Toni, the black woman who had led his soul-scouring interrogation back in Reseda, showed them to a room with a conference table and a holographic wall map of L.A. and the seacoast.

"We're glad you're both back on your feet," she conceded after she seated herself. Then she threw hard looks around the table. "I've been advised to break things to you gently. But we got no time."

"What's happened?" Blaise faltered.

Toni gave him a smoldering glance. "The Cloud launched the *Gilgamesh V* pilot. Minsheng left the deputy chairman in charge in Hong Kong and flew back to L.A. to oversee it."

Blaise placed his face in his hands, his heart black with despair.

Toni dug in the knife. "Anima addiction's catching on, too."

"Oh, God," Blaise groaned.

"There's another little problem, chief. Minsheng keeps reactivating your neurofeed so his gunships can telemeter in on us here. Everyone at this table's focusing curseil energy to block that, but it's exhausting us. You need to unfuck this situation. Pronto. Deliver the goods, or this city's a boneyard."

"Toni, please, don't," Kristina pleaded.

"Don't what?" Toni shot back. "He's to blame for all this. If he hadn't coded *Gilgamesh V* in the first place, we wouldn't be in this mess."

"If he hadn't coded it, someone else would have."

"Don't make excuses for him!"

"He risked his life to upload Polyphemus."

"Sure, after you pried him loose from his China doll. Otherwise, he'd still be banging her and letting us all die like our friends back in Reseda."

"Don't you dare insult him. We both nearly died getting back here."

"And we're about to be toast because of him. So he damn well better deliver the goods, or he's expendable."

"You could be a little kinder. Blaise is our only hope."

"That's your mom talking," Toni mocked. "The great hacker philosopher. 'Recruit a Class I to save us'. Well, Amelia got Mantised to death for her trouble, didn't she? And a lot of good people got blown to shit, including my Zenobia." She leveled a finger at Blaise. "We should've offed your lily-white ass when you first showed up in Reseda."

Kristina was livid. "He's worth a hundred of you!"

"He's poison. So was your mother, a dangerous, delusional idealist. The smart move was always to just keep selling enhanced nanobots to the Hadjis and let them take out The Cloud. But Amelia wouldn't have that. No, we had to recruit this asshole to hack in and fix everything. Some plan. And since you're fucking mister Class I here? That makes you as dangerous as your mom."

Kristina's face turned crimson. "You'd better take that back."

"I ain't taking nothing back. My head's clear. I don't think with my pussy like you do."

With a shriek Kristina sprang from her chair and hurled herself at Toni, who had no time to counter before their struggle slammed them both against the wall. They pummeled each other in a shower of purple curses until they raised bruises and cuts. It took four hackers to pry them apart and force them into their chairs, where they puffed and glared at each other.

"You're not fit to lead the curseil circle," Kristina attacked.

"I hate his lilly-white Class I ass! And I say we take his ass out now, so those gunships can't find us."

"Touch him, and I'll take you out!" Kristina shouted.

Toni's retort was nearly out of her mouth when Blaise cut in.

"Toni's right. I stalled too long. I'm responsible for everything that's gone wrong." He rose and faced Toni. "I deserve your contempt. But I swear, give me another shot, and I'll hack back in and take down The Cloud."

Toni looked at him askance. "Then you better do it fast."

"Do they know about the seawalls?" Blaise asked Kristina.

"Yeah, chief, we know all about that," Toni shot back. "So how long you think they'll hold after you bring down The Cloud?"

"No more than a day. Possibly two unless we get very lucky."

Toni glanced from face to face in the conference room. She had the look of someone peering in a mirror at a startling image.

"We were hoping for more time," she said in a more tentative tone. "So let me put it to our all-wise advisory committee. How fast can we organize an evac?"

Two hackers at the end of the table opposite Toni whispered to one another. One, an angular, bird-like woman with a tuft of gray hair, replied. "We can keep the bullet trains running to stations near Reseda. And we've done military hover-truck operational simulations. But there's no way to test our military guidance software on the real thing till The Cloud network goes down. And we've got to finish re-lasering the hyperloop tunnel."

Toni took a deep breath before speaking. "Assuming the trains run and the simulations work, how long to evac six million Slags?"

"Six weeks, if we run the bullet trains and the hyperloop 24/7."

Stillness descended in the room as if it had filled with molten glass.

"OK, it is what it is," Toni sighed after a long pause. "We made a little miscalculation about the death toll we're gonna cause when we liberate the world. So we put it to a vote. Show of hands in favor of letting the chief here re-upload Polyphemus now. Or do we take him out with curseil?"

Discussion followed. Some whispered among themselves. Others debated raucously. One southeast Asian woman with a thatch of lustrous black hair rose and leaned toward Toni, fingertips pressed to the tabletop.

"We can't let millions of people drown. We've got to do what we can to save them. And we can't murder the man who risked everything to upload Polyphemus."

"So what are you saying?" Toni retorted. "Let this Class I asshole go on living? So those hover-gunships can telemeter in on him and blow the shit out of us?"

"We proceed with our original plan. We let Blaise re-upload Polyphemus. But first we should run more hover-truck simulations," the Asian woman said. "We have to analyze seawall composition. Figure out how long those seawalls will hold. Make sure we have time to get people out safely after The Cloud servers fail."

"You just heard the chief here say those seawalls got two days max," Toni scoffed. "Plus, every hour we delay costs our curseil circle one helluva lotta psychic energy. Be a miracle if we can hold up another day before those gunships find us."

"We can't try to re-upload before we run more tests," the Asian woman insisted. "It would make us no better than Minsheng."

"Who you think you're kidding?" Toni bellowed. "You knew the risks! We all knew the risks! We want to take down The Cloud? You want to give this Class I fucker another shot? Well, this is the price we pay for it."

Kristina stood and greeted each face with unyielding gravity. "I agree with Toni. No one wants mass drownings. But we have to re-upload now, or everything we've labored and suffered for, including this city, will be washed down the sewers of history."

Silence descended again. A conference room full of hackers looked as shamefaced as a classroom full of schoolkids.

Suddenly a pale-faced woman burst into the room. "They've found the missile silo! They're up there now."

"Show of hands," Toni intoned. "All in favor of re-uploading now."

Hands shot up. Twenty-eight in favor. Two abstentions, including the Asian woman.

"Motion carried."

Toni turned to Blaise. "How long to hack through those firewalls?"

"I won't know till I try," Blaise answered. "How long can the curseil circle block my neurofeed?"

Toni glared at him. "Guess we'll find out, chief."

Blaise's rage burst out of him like a flare. "Don't call me chief, god dammit!"

27

BLAISE AND KRISTINA HAD A CRAMPED OFFICE WITH CHAIRS AND cots with bedding and pillows. They coded in tandem, pinging off one another as Blaise once had with Mitsuko. He was amazed by Kristina's skill; Amelia had taught her well. The hacking itself, on the other hand, was a borderless swamp of despair. The new level seven firewalls defeated all his attempts to hack through. He ran through his repertoire of coding tricks and dictated till his voice died like the breath at the end of a scream. He resorted to an ancient ergonomic keyboard but got nowhere. Eventually, the muscles in his hands cramped so badly he had to let Kristina rub salve into them, and she coded alone until he found his voice again.

Dr. Aaliyah prescribed a syrup to restore his vocal cords. It allowed him and Kristina to hack in tandem again. But after eighteen hours nonstop, eaten by anxiety that Minsheng would reactivate his neurofeed, he reached the abyss of despair.

Toni dropped by, looking exhausted herself.

"How close are you?" she demanded. "Our curseil circle can't hold out much longer."

"I'm doing everything I can to hack through."

"You'd fucking better."

She stormed out of the tiny office. Kristina rubbed his temples to relieve his pile-driving headache. His shoulders were tight as pistons, and his heart felt crushed between two tectonic plates. He pushed harder and tormented himself to find quirkier and more eccentric hacking approaches. Nothing worked. Finally, broken, exhausted, unable to go on, he slumped over the holodeck with tears in his eyes. Kristina helped him stumble to a cot, where he passed out.

———◆———

He woke to find himself in bed at Mitsuko's L.A. condo. From the kitchen came humming appliances and coffee aroma. Mitsuko appeared in her pink silk kimono with a steaming cup. She had never looked more exquisite.

"What have you been dreaming?" she laughed as she settled into bed, wafting him her fragrance. "You were talking in your sleep."

He sprang up and backed away from the bed. "How are you here? How am I here?"

Mitsuko wrinkled her nose at him and pursed her lips in a kiss. "Are you out of sorts? Maybe we shouldn't make love so late on work nights."

She gave her hair a playful toss. He snatched his robe from the chair and slipped it on. Everything looked, sounded, and smelled the same as it always had. But this had to be VR. What else could it be?

"You'd better shower, or we'll be late."

He mustered a smile, hung his robe in the bathroom, and stepped into the shower. As he soaped himself, his mind scrolled through scenarios. If Minsheng had broken through the curseil shield and reactivated his neurofeed, why was he still alive? Why hadn't the Mantis terminated him? Why bother creating this projection? Then it struck him. Perhaps Minsheng needed him alive. But why? *Gilgamesh V* had launched. Anima was irresistible. He had programmed it for lethal effectiveness. Then another thought crept into his mind, a long-familiar suspicion. What if Kristina and the hackers were the projection? He replayed moments with Kristina: their first night of love; their first visit together to Sagrada Familia; their ordeal in the desert. How could these be implanted memories? But on the other hand, his coding career argued that VR made anything possible. Gripped by anguish and uncertainty, between a desire for escape and a hunger to stay, he steadied himself against the shower wall and decided he'd better play along until he knew which reality to trust.

Mitsuko dressed in her sky blue jacket and red and blue kimono skirt and blouse. The colors accented her pale skin and the shapeliness of her forearms and fingers. He relished the way she pursed her lips while she applied lipstick. Her scent lingered like a lark's song—secret, exquisite. On their way out, he watched her hips sway under her skirt. Intoxicating. He took the bullet train with her to Mythoplex tower, just as they had so many times before. Belt-beamed next to him in a car crowded with Class Is and IIs, she whispered about work.

"If we push through those remaining glitches, we'll launch on time," she promised.

He nodded, pursed his lips, and repeated his mantra to hide his panic.

Launch what?

Concern touched her eyes as she studied him.

"Not quite awake yet," he yawned. "What's that launch date again?"

"*Gilgamesh V*. Or do you mean one of the other projects?"

"Mitsuko, I haven't been sleeping well. Just gimmie a refresh, OK?"

"*Gilgamesh V* launches in three weeks, silly. If that's what you're talking about."

He nodded and smiled. *How did I get in this time warp? The hackers said Gilgamesh has already launched.*

Minsheng must have restored his neurofeed, but without, he noticed, the braying voiceover with its endless fake news and VR promotional spots. He retraced his morning. Yes, he had been in the new city with Kristina trying to hack the firewalls that prevented him from re-uploading. But everything here and now felt so real, more real than VR: the train's velocity; the Santa Monica coastline with the sea wall holding back the Pacific; the Mythoplex logo shimmering against the hills; the garnet and amethyst skyline rushing to greet them. *But I could be wrong. This could be some new VR spin I haven't run into, something Minsheng's games planning team dreamed up, a nuance on my own advanced coding.* Suspicious of what he saw, smelled, touched, and felt, he followed Mitsuko from the station onto the greensward. They joined other Class Is and IIs heading up the hill inside the air-conditioned plexiglass tunnel, along with UCLA coeds sporting see-through blouses and self-mutilation scars on their forearms. The magnolias had bloomed, despite the blistering heat. As he and Mitsuko emerged frm the tunnel, he caught their perfume as he and Mitsuko approached the Mythoplex Tower in the morning swelter. They passed under the Vessel, with its intricate bronze-colored stairs climbing and descending to nowhere and no purpose. Inside the tower, beyond the mural showing the handshake between Chairman Mao II and President Brent Cadwallader III, they crammed into the lift. The morning ritual argued strongly for this reality, and he tried to put his suspicions about it out of his mind. They cleared SWAT security on the next highest floor and took Blaise's private lift to his office. They folded their silk jackets across their cockpit chairs and settled in at the holodeck. Blaise discovered labyrinthine firewalls protecting the *Gilgamesh V* secure server. He couldn't remember the passwords, and Mitsuko had to remind him. Scanning the neural network, he noticed other things, links and algorithms spiraling off in diverse and intricate arabesques through the Cloudscape, linking cities and their infrastructures across the world.

"Let's attack that glitch first," she suggested. "It's slowing up our coding."

He ran through debugging protocols and identified the glitch's source: a sequence buried in half a million lines of code that only Blaise, as the original coder, could detect. It took time to correct, but he managed. Soon their Gilgamesh coding hummed along, and they collaborated at the highest level of creativity a games planner could hope to achieve. And after all, why shouldn't he enjoy working with her? Didn't they plan to spend eternity together in conjugal bliss, coding like this?

Minsheng dropped by to check on his star games planners. Blaise and Mitsuko stood and gave curt bows.

"I'm very pleased," Minsheng announced. "If you two keep up this pace, you're sure to meet your deadline, possibly this week."

Blaise's head spun. "Excuse me, sir, but you're chairman of the board now," he blundered. "What are you doing in L.A.? I heard *Gilgamesh V* and Anima have already launched."

Then, as Mitsuko shook Minsheng's hand, her arm brushed Blaise's, and he detected a faint sponginess of flesh that gave her away as a VR projection. So Minsheng had coded this fantasy to lure Blaise back to debug the Gilgamesh glitch and complete the coding. How easily he had faked the Gilgamesh launch to fool the curseil hackers! A lifetime spent hiding his emotions kept Blaise's expression calm as he tried to suss out how to escape this lie.

Kristina, Kristina.

No answer.

"You look troubled, Blaise," Minsheng observed. "Are you feeling well?"

A pinhole of light pierced the fog in Blaise mind. From across the void came a reverberation as faint as a gnat's wingbeats. He urged himself toward it until he heard words forming: *We're bringing you back.*

"Is something wrong, Blaise? You seem to be confused about the launch. And your pulse rate. Your EEG. Very disturbing."

"Blaise, what's happening?" Mitsuko fretted.

"Kristina, hurry," Blaise whispered.

"I've seen this before," Minsheng told Mitsuko. "Remember? He amused himself with that Slag girl, Kristina, and somehow, as a stress response, he's become obsessed with her. It's in his psych report."

Mitsuko looked puzzled. "Didn't SWAT kill her in Reseda?"

"Yes. But she reminds him of his departed wife. He's constructed an elaborate fantasy about this girl. Blaise, I want you to see my psychiatrist again. I insist."

Blaise felt that he had never really looked Minsheng full in the face before. At first, it was like peering up a sheer granite cliff, a loftiness Blaise could never hope to scale. But then he noticed Minsheng's bullock-heavy cheeks were interlaced with striated blood vessels and pocked with tiny maculae as if he had lain underwater for ages. Despite the prosthetics, organ replacements, and disease reversals, his one good eye glowed with the fever of countless infirmities. This was the face of *Homo Deus*, the eternally rotting flesh magnetized by the glue of narcissism. Behind Minsheng's façade, Blaise sensed the presence of the carnivorous egos frozen in their lotus sarcophagi in the Hall of Heroes.

"You're dead inside," he whispered. "You're not real. Only the power you serve is real. And this, all of this, is a VR projection."

"Reality is a relative term," Minsheng philosophized. "But one thing I can assure you: what you're experiencing here is very real. Kristina is the delusion."

"No. She's waiting for me."

"You don't need that fantasy anymore."

Mitsuko approached Blaise. Her eyes brimmed with tears. "We're going to have a child. A girl. I'll make up for all the cruel things I've done to you. I'll give you back your happiness."

"There's a higher reality, Minsheng, an eternal one you can't touch," Blaise mocked. "I've seen it. So you may as well deactivate this holographic bitch. I'm not buying her. Or you."

Minsheng shook his head. "He's raving, Mitsuko,"

"I'm going to destroy all of this, you fucking psychopath!" Blaise shouted.

"Blaise, not our love," Mitsuko pleaded. "Not our future. Please don't destroy that."

Blaise rounded on her. "He killed you a long time before Kristina lasered that hole through your belly."

"This is worse than I thought," Minsheng lamented. "A full-blown psychotic break."

Minsheng's voice, freighted with the gravitas of abolute power, dismissed the reality Blaise struggled with all the strength of his soul to cling to.

"You're the psychotic!" Blaise screamed. "You've raped her since she was a girl."

Minsheng pursed his lips, but his depthless eye revealed nothing. "How could a brilliant mind like yours let such a delusion gain a foothold?"

Blaise swept his hand around in a dismissive gesture. "This is the delusion."

"Please calm yourself. Let's try to put this in perspective."

"My perspective's fine, motherfucker."

Minsheng gave Mitsuko a sympathetic glance. "I've seen this before. A brilliant games planner, a first class mythologizer, pushes himself beyond rational limits. What happens? The reptilian brain strikes back. The flight or fight response runs amok."

Please, Kristina, get me out of here.

Minsheng stepped closer to Blaise. "When did you first notice these delusional thoughts? Perhaps during a panic attack? Your psych report mentioned—"

"There's no psych report!" Blaise bellowed. "Nothing but you and your kind, slugs trailing slime through our minds!"

Minsheng patted the air with a deeply concerned expression. "Deep breaths. In, out. You have a mantra, correct? Now would be a good time to chant it."

Kristina, help me.

A smile touched Minsheng's lips. "What's needed is calm. A path back to sanity. Let's refresh the basics."

Blaise struggled to escape from Minsheng's malevolent spirit as it spread over him like an ooze of tar.

"I'm going to reconnect you with reality."

"Don't try to play the voice of reason!"

"Not the *voice* of reason. I *am* reason."

"You raped your own daughter! Raped whole populations with mind control."

Minsheng rolled his eyes. "One delusion at a time, please. First of all, where do you get this notion Mitsuko is my daughter?"

"She told me everything, asshole."

Minsheng glanced at Mitsuko. "Have you been telling lies about me?"

"Absolutely not," she gasped.

"Come off it, Mitsuko," Blaise scoffed. "I saw the look in your eyes when you told me about him. You couldn't possibly make that up."

"But you could," Minsheng interjected. "My most brilliant games planner? You could generate a storyline like that as a reaction formation."

Kristina, please.

"There couldn't be childhood rapes, Blaise, because I was never her father."

Kristina, help me.

"On to delusion two. This notion that I, that my kind, enslaved people like you."

Minsheng circled Blaise counter-clockwise, taking his time, head thrown back. Mitsuko marked him with the eyes of a startled bird as his hands described angles, arcs, like a symphony conductor.

"We enslaved no one, Blaise. We gave you everything. Brought you into the world, nurtured and educated you. Gave you a share of all the good things we had. Provided you with a sound education. Excellent healthcare. Protection from enemies foreign and domestic. And the chance to spread your wings. A full scholarship to UCLA."

Kristina, please get me out of here.

"We let you travel anywhere you had resources to visit. North Am, China, Japan, Asia, Europe. All open to you. And had you turned down your job at Mythoplex; had you chosen not to rise through the games planning ranks, why, we would've let you go and wished you good luck."

He paused to consider Blaise face to face. "But you didn't go. You stayed, knowing what kind of world you were helping us build. By doing so, you entered into an implied contract to do as we ordered."

Blaise pressed his hands to his ears. "Stop it. I won't listen."

Minsheng brought his face close enough for Blaise to catch his fetid breath. "You will listen, because you're one of us, Blaise."

"You're mass murderers!"

Minsheng's eyes glowed with lambent fire. "And so are you. You proved that during your military service, and again, when you terminated that Slag at my estate; oh, and let's not forget the SWATs you slaughtered with the Mantis in Reseda. We're just pushing what comes naturally to the next level."

"I'm not like you!"

"Humanity is a race of killers, Blaise. You know in the marrow of your bones you deserve to live, to prosper. Others, the inferior races, deserve death."

He shoved Minsheng against a cockpit chair to break the chairman's suffocating hold on his soul. Minsheng caught himself as he lost balance and dignity. His face colored red.

"I've done my best to restore your reason. If you won't listen to me or to this woman who worships you, perhaps this will make an impression."

Mitsuko froze in mid-breath. Her body went translucent. Her face fractured into sheets of crackling holographic tinfoil as her body flickered out of existence. Minsheng pointed to the holoscreen, where a scenario emerged: a room with a door that opened on red scrubland with stubby plants. Hills of striated red, gold, and white loomed in the distance. A girl of around eleven or twelve with sad eyes sat on a squalid bed.

"It's Mei. We found her in a sting operation against human traffickers. This is their safe house outside Sydney. SWAT sent in a surveillance wasp, a tiny camera for remote areas with no neurofeed. A SWAT team's in position, now, ready to take down the animals who kidnapped her."

Blaise's heart melted. "My Mei?"

"She's safe, Blaise. And I'll bring her home. If you come to your senses."

Blaise tore his eyes from the screen. "Come to my senses?"

"I'll bring the real Mei back, Blaise, not a VR image. Your flesh-and-blood girl. Your precious daughter. Just face the truth, your truth. And seize your destiny."

A door creaked on the holoscreen. Two men, one a grizzled cretin, the other a yellow-toothed ox, slouched in. The fat one slammed the door behind him. The other approached Mei, licking his chops.

"You can stop this, Blaise," Minsheng declared. "SWAT will terminate those animals right now and end three years of rape and trauma. Your precious girl will be back in your arms tomorrow. Just tell me you'll complete *Gilgamesh V* and *Anima*. You're so close to immortality. Don't throw it away."

On the screen the tall man shoved Mei down on the bed. If there was the tiniest chance she was actually alive, how could he turn away from her?

"I'll do what you want," Blaise blurted.

A sly smile touched Minsheng's lips, and on the screen, the door to the shabby room exploded. SWATs swarmed in and lasered the thugs in an organ-splattering slaughter while another SWAT carried Mei out into the sun.

"You've made the right decision," Minsheng affirmed. "She'll be at LAX tomorrow on the shuttle. You'll be there to greet her."

Minsheng had nearly taken back his soul. But then he heard Kristina's voice, *We're here,* reverberate from the abyss like a tuning fork. Blaise reached with all his inner strength to close that internal circuit. At last, his soul merged with the curseil circle; even Toni was there, fighting with the others to bring him back.

The VR projection released its hold on Blaise's mind, and the false hope that Mei was alive vanished with it.

Blaise woke drenched in sweat on a sweat-stained cot in the new city clinic.

28

Seeing the life in his eyes revive itself, Kristina embraced him, weeping.

"We thought we had lost you!"

Blaise glanced about to reassure himself he was really back in the new city. "How long did they have me?"

She covered his face in kisses. "Only a few hours." She brought a bottle to his lips. "Vitamin water. Drink. You're dehydrated."

He sipped until he had slaked this thirst and then wiped his mouth with the back of his hand.

"Minsheng faked the *Gilgamesh V* launch."

"The whole curseil circle knows now. Toni came to visit you as soon as she knew the truth."

"Tell her I'm sorry for the suffering I caused her."

Kristina nodded toward the door with a tender smile. "Tell her yourself."

Toni came in and pulled up a chair beside Blaise. Her voice trembled with the hard-won humility of a proud and fierce woman.

"I owe you an apology. I lost Zenobia back in Reseda and blamed you for it."

"There's nothing to forgive," Blaise smiled. You have the burden of leadership. That's a heavy load to bear."

Toni's face showed considerable strain. "We worked our asses off to re-block your neurofeed. Now you gotta haul ass. Those gunships have just about burned through the missile silo shield. They brought in laser cannons." She took a deep breath. "They're gonna swarm down on our asses like a plague."

Blaise heaved up on an elbow. "Well, maybe it was worth VR trip over there. I found out how to re-upload Polyphemus."

Toni's face brightened. "Yeah? How?"

"I coded in some nuances that make it next to impossible for anyone but me to finish *Gilgamesh V*. Didn't realize it till Minsheng sucked me back in today. He's desperate, and desperate people make mistakes. He let Mitsuko, I should say her VR projection, show me the new level seven firewall passcodes."

"Fan-fucking-tastic!" Toni whooped.

"But here's the thing. I've gotta move before he changes those passcodes. Help me up, here."

"We'd better send for Dr. Aaliyah first," Kristina cautioned.

"No time for that. Please."

Soon he was back before the holoscreen he and Kristina had shared. He felt giddy and disoriented, but his body gradually adjusted to being back in reality.

"The new board will terminate Minsheng if he can't deliver *Gilgamesh V*," he told Kristina and Toni. "So depend on it, he'll keep trying to reactivate my neurofeed. How long can we block him?"

"Our energy's drained," Toni fretted. "Few hours, tops. I'll let you get to it. Our programmers are running evac simulations for those military hover-trucks we want. And our Reseda tent city's up and running."

"Good thinking."

Toni rushed out while Blaise pulled up a holoscreen menu and spoke the access codes for the *Gilgamesh V* server.

He glanced at Kristina. "I'm pretty sure I can hack into level seven security clearance with what Mitsuko showed me."

"What about the new AI firewalls?"

He flashed a smile. "Back in the day I was on a coding team for quantum servers. When Minsheng dragged me back there today, I saw some of the AI source code. Think I can hack around it."

The holodeck asked for the level seven clearance code. Blaise issued it in a quavering voice, his stomach twisted into knots of uncertainty. Delight followed when the passwords worked. He inserted the upgraded Polyphemus chip and ordered the upload.

"Initiating," the holodeck announced. "Twenty minutes to full upload."

They watched module after module soar into cyberspace through varicolored arteries interlaced like lymphatic vessels in a vast cyber-organism. Burnt-orange worm trails attacked servers, and The Cloud launched defenses. Blaise's counter-commands hacked past them. Kristina sat beside him, her arm on his shoulder. Their hearts pounded with hope and despair while the worm surged across The Cloud with lethal effectiveness. New firewalls loomed, and Polyphemus circumvented them only to be thwarted by fresh defenses. Polyphemus had tenacity, but so did The Cloud.

"Fifteen minutes to full upload."

AI defenses spread across Polyphemus's path like deep ocean tides. But Blaise was in his element now and hacked past firewall after firewall with speed and finesse, his voice going strong as he issued commands. Time vanished as he deployed a lifetime of hacking skills to the challenge.

"Ten minutes to full upload," the holoscreen announced.

"This is as far as I got the first time I tried to upload Polyphemus," Blaise warned Kristina.

"We'll make it," she encouraged him. "Visualize it. Believe it."

More firewalls loomed, more serpentine than the others. Blaise hacked past them, but they danced around his efforts like elusive ballerinas, vast blocks of code that attacked Polyphemus.

"Gotta get creative," he murmured and redoubled his efforts.

He wracked his brain for arcane hacking tricks he hadn't tried before. But he knew that quantum-computer-based AI programs ran many orders of magnitude faster than he could think. He was locking swords with a super-being programmed for self-preservation and armed with the cybernetic prowess of The Cloud's best computer engineers. Before he could finish his command sequences, the firewalls reconfigured to block the spreading Polyphemus worm. He sweated through dozens of hacking routines until his voice grew hoarse, and his head pounded as if a herd of buffalos galloped through it. Nothing worked. He was losing the battle against a far more cunning and efficient opponent. Hopelessness descended like black rain from a ruined sky. He had exhausted his mind's resources. A horrible conviction gripped him. Minsheng and the other psychopaths on the board would rule the earth forever. He recalled how Minsheng had described scale, unlimited power, and eternal life at his desert estate when he forced Blaise to terminate his first Slag. Minsheng and The Cloud had scale. Blaise's hacking skill was impotent against them. Everything was lost. Any minute now, the gunships would burn through the old missile silo shield and use lasers and MOAB bombs to reduce hacker city to a smoking crater.

Despair pushed his mind into unexplored regions, and he uttered a prayer. *If you're there, God, please help me,* and it was as if, having fled a thunderstorm through soot-blackened Slag Zone streets, he turned an inner corner and found himself in fertile meadowland. His despair dissipated, and a thought struck him.

For all its deftness and lightning speed, AI had no defense against irrationality. So he coded with the energy of despair and launched preposterous code configurations against the firewalls, guided by urges and insights dredged up from somewhere deeper than his reptilian brain. Finally, he stumbled on a coding sequence that allowed the Polyphemus worm to burst through firewall fissures. The breach grew exponentially, frying server after server like a brushfire ravaging a prairie.

"Five minutes to full upload," the holoscreen announced.

"It's working!" Kristina sang out.

"Nothing can stop it now, not even Minsheng," Blaise reassured her. He threw up defenses against servers as distant as Antarctica while The Cloud launched new firewalls at stupendous speed in a final effort to outmaneuver Polyphemus.

"Two minutes to full upload."

Blaise's head pounded, and his eyes itched and burned. He pressed his palms against them to wipe away tears of weariness.

"Blaise, there! Another firewall!"

He glanced up and saw a new stain sweep across the cyberscape.

"It's alright. Watch and see."

"One minute to full upload."

Polyphemus accelerated as it destroyed more servers. It had spread so far and grown so vast that the new AI firewalls were swept aside like dandelions in a gale-force wind.

"Upload complete," the holoscreen announced.

Kristina whooped and hugged him, and he buried his face in her hair and wept tears of gratitude.

"You did it, you did it," she gasped between sobs of joy.

"Let's not get ahead of ourselves," he laughed. "It took thirty years to program The Cloud network. May take days, possibly weeks, for servers to shut down globally. Maybe there'll be enough time for our evacuation plan to work."

"Better see what's up with those gunships," Kristina concluded. "You strong enough to come with me to the command center?"

Blaise got to his feet, woozy and exhausted but stronger now. "Yes. Absolutely."

She led him to a room the hackers had converted into a command center. Holoscreens glittered above makeshift workstations. On a back wall stood a slender server bank. Kristina explained that it was the hackers' own quantum computer built from stolen Cloud components over several years.

One holoscreen monitored the gunships beached near the old missile silo. Cloud airmen had set up laser cannons that fired at the silo's protective seal.

Toni caught Blaise's eye. "If the virus worked, how can those bastards burn through our seal? Why aren't their lasers deactivated?"

"Backup servers," he revealed. "In their base at Camp Pendleton. Those will crash, too. But it could take hours."

"They're gonna burn through that silo shield in minutes, jerkoff."

"Aren't some of our hovercars laser-mounted?" Kristina asked.

"Yeah, four," Toni affirmed. "But they can't outshoot gunships. Besides, we got only three pilots."

"Four," Kristina corrected her. "I flew to L.A. and back, remember?"

"These are air force pilots. They'll slice and dice you like lettuce."

"Have to risk that. We'll keep 'em occupied till Polyphemus kicks in."

Terror flooded Blaise's heart at the thought of losing Kristina so soon after surviving their brush with death in the desert. They had been through so much together; his life made no sense without her.

He took her arm as she turned to go. "Kristina, the other pilots can handle this."

She kissed him then held him at arm's length. "I have to do this. We have to buy time."

He saw fierce determination in her eye. "That source of yours, the one I saw in Sagrada Familia, it's gonna look out for you?"

"It answered your prayer, didn't it?" She grinned and was gone.

Exhausted by his ordeal, his worry about her, and the cumulative angst that throbbed in his heart, Blaise sank into a chair and studied the holoscreens as if they might solve the dilemmas he and the others faced.

"How long till those lasers break into that silo?" he asked.

Toni gave him an anxious look. "Twenty minutes, if we're lucky."

"How fast can Kristina get airborne?"

"Pretty fucking fast. There's a tunnel to a camouflaged surface shaft with a hovercraft hanger at the base. Air force built it back in the day, in case the Russians put a nuke down the silo. Look."

A screen showed Kristina and thee male pilots bolt into a hanger, board hovercars, belt-beam in, and lift off.

"Can you shield their takeoff?"

"With enough curseil juice, barely. How long before the Cloud servers crash?"

"Can't say. What about coastal cities? Slag evacuations?"

"Bullet train's running. Refugees are pouring into Reseda. We've stocked supplies and tents till we can commandeer army hover-trucks."

Blaise cut his eyes to a screen, where a surface camera showed a disk of desert-colored polycarbonate glide back from a black gap. A hovercar rose through the gap, followed by three more, and then they streaked out of camera range. Another screen showed Cloud laser cannons burning through the missile silo shield. The hacker hovercars streaked overhead and strafed the desert, driving the airmen below to cover. The laser cannons blasting the silo shield shifted their barrels skyward and raked the sky. The hovercars veered away, but one was hit. It spun out and smashed into the desert, where it gouged a trench.

"Kristina!" Blaise sputtered.

His thoughts were drowned out by a saccharine female voice as it brayed statistics about Cloud quarterly agricultural production and military victories.

———— • ————

Before Blaise could alert Toni and the others that Minsheng had reactivated his neurofeed, he found himself inside yet another VR projection, with the chairman in his office high up in the Mythoplex building. Blaise's head reeled from the disorientation of being thrust back again into an alternative reality.

The Minsheng who greeted him had lost much of his bearing. He wiped sweat from his face and neck with a handkerchief and flashed a malignant smile.

"How did you pull me back in?" Blaise demanded. "The Cloud's servers . . ."

"You're the director now, Blaise. Have you forgotten your emergency server?"

Blaise had forgotten: the backup server could run for weeks on its storage charge after The Cloud servers crashed. It had limited range, enough to keep Mythoplex headquarters operational; but that was enough to keep him enslaved in this VR projection. He figured his only hope of escape lay with the hackers using curseil to wrench him free. To buy time, he reasoned with Minsheng, a strategy with little chance of success.

"I've resigned as director. Please kill my neurofeed."

"No one appointed by the board resigns."

"I'm setting a precedent, Minsheng."

"You're going to find your way back to sanity. And you will address me as chairman."

"We've been down this road, and recently," Blaise reminded him. "There's no way back to what you call sanity. This is VR."

"Even so, it's reality. I'm reality. L.A. is reality. The millions who live here are reality. If you cooperate, you'll be reality again, too." He gestured toward the glittering towers stretching to the Pacific. "The seawall, it's going to collapse. You must deactivate that worm."

"Can't be done. It's spread too far."

Minsheng glanced at the towers outside, as if he expected something. What did he imagine was coming? Salvation? Deliverance? A stay of execution? Sweat ran in rivulets down his cheeks. Panic glittered in his eyes like a constellation of accidental stars.

"I made you *Homo Deus,* immortal," he croaked. "I, I gave you my own daughter for your fuck toy. I made you one of us. I created you! I OWN you!"

"Sorry. Not for sale."

"Disable that virus, Blaise. Otherwise, you'll drown all the Slags you're trying to save." He barked at the holodeck. "Screen on!"

A bullet platform appeared on the holoscreen. Hundreds of Slags jostled, elbowed, and clawed each other in desperation to board a car. Fights broke out. Shouts and curses pierced the air. Many more men, women, and bedraggled children crowded in from escalator stairwells until the platform was an ocean of panic-stricken animals. The passenger car doors slid shut, and the train streaked away. The crowd surged forward, plunging many onto the tracks.

"The same thing is happening all over the Slag Zone," Minsheng underscored. "Thousands scrambling to get out to what, Reseda? That ghost town? How many will make it? A fraction of the six million scrambling to flee. And if the train servers crash with these lucky ones en route? They'll drown when the Pacific reaches them."

Blaise's rage erupted. "Suddenly you care about the Slags? The ones you want to drive into oblivion like lemmings?"

Minsheng dismissed this with his customary aplomb, though his confidence was a shadow of itself. "Those hackers of yours claimed you'd liberate billions? Nonsense. You'll send the world into a new dark age. And I understand you called on some god for help? A so-called useful fiction. Well, in the name of that fabricated deity, come back to us. And you will save lives. Yours and mine. The natural leaders."

Minsheng's jibe struck home. "We'll pay a terrible price to pay if those people drown," Blaise grimaced. "But maybe we won't have to."

"You'll have nothing to regret if you deactivate that virus."

"Polyphemus is eating through The Cloud like a plague."

Minsheng's face paled. Then his cheeks flushed with rage. "You idiot!" he shrieked. "Did you think destroying The Cloud will make you a god? It makes you NOTHING!"

The maculae marring Minsheng's skin stood out like birdshot scars. Sweat beaded his upper lip. His good eye burned with manic intensity. But he drew himself up to his full military bearing.

"We are the gods of this world! Not you!"

"You were never anything but a megalomaniac like those psychopaths in the Hall of Heroes. Their chillers will fail. Their brains, squirming to regain power, they'll putrefy. So will you. Your eternity is infinite black. Nothingness."

"I'll show you NOTHINGNESS!"

The rasp of a million crickets reverberated through the office as a spiky green horror coalesced from a swirl of fireflies. Its eyes glittered like jewels as it spider-crawled toward Blaise. From its mandibles came a mangled roar of protest, precipitating a vision of lotus-shaped sarcophagi in Hong Kong, where five malignant spirits hissed "Die!"

As the Mantis claw stretched toward Blaise, he willed a second Mantis into existence, one as horrifying as Minsheng's and just as lethal, thanks to Blaise's own coding refinements. The two Mantises circled each other, mandibles working, claws opening and retracting like two enormous pairs of greenish scythes. Minsheng sweated freely from the effort of wielding his own Mantis. Blaise focused his whole will on directing his chirruping nightmare against the other one. Minsheng's Mantis lunged at Blaise's defender, and Blaise countered, willing his Mantis to rise on its spiny legs and plunge into the other. Soon the two creatures were locked in a lethal embrace, turning crazily on spiny legs, smashing furniture in their struggle to shake loose from each other. Minsheng's Mantis grasped the other's claw and cleaved it off, but Blaise's Mantis countered by lopping off its opponent's claw. The battle became more desperate as Blaise and Minsheng tried to maneuver their wounded Mantises into a position where they could deliver the coup de grâce. The creatures hacked at each other with their remaining good claws, but it was no good. They were equally matched and operated by two determined opponents. In the end, the Mantises hacked each other to pieces, splattering gooey green entrails and leaving Blaise and Minsheng sweating and drained from the effort.

His face flushed with the strain of wielding his Mantis, Minsheng pivoted and rushed to the massive desk, wrenched open a drawer and grasped a laser burner. Blaise ducked and rolled clear as Minsheng raked the room, the beam passing close enough to singe Blaise's arm as it gouged a furrow in the wall.

Desperate for something to defend himself with, Blaise grabbed the smallest of the seven onyx sculptures near him on the floor. He spun round twice and hurled the thing at Minsheng. It struck the chairman in the chest and knocked him back with enough force to make him drop his burner. Blaise lunged for the floor and scooped up the burner, but Minsheng had recovered enough to rush in and choke him with his elephant-leg arms. The office broke up into splintered fragments against a backdrop of infinite black as Minsheng strangled him. In the clarity of his panic and despair, Blaise thrust forward enough to make a savage short-arm jab to Minsheng's belly. It loosened the chairman's grip. Blaise wrenched himself free, whirled round, and delivered a roundhouse kick aimed at Minsheng's throat, but Minsheng dodged and delivered a counter-kick to Blaise's chest powerful enough to slam him against the wall. The impact stunned Blaise, but he had kept his grip on the laser burner and fired at Minsheng's chest. Inexplicably, the beam passed through Minsheng with no effect.

Minsheng wiped sweat from his glistening forehead and guffawed at Blaise's shocked expression. "Imagine that. In your rush to terminate me, you forgot."

Blaise fired the burner again, but the beam penetrated Minsheng's body like an arrow through a cloudbank.

"What the fuck?" Blaise gasped.

Minsheng flashed a rueful smile. "Blaise, really, I'm shocked. I told you months ago: we've weaponized Mantises for the Caliphate wars to slaughter Hadjis through their K-spots. Laser burners, on the other hand, are still just good, solid CGI. Impressive to watch but harmless in VR."

Blaise's mind raced to find his way out of a reality so convoluted that not even his coding brilliance could disentangle him from the webs it had spun.

"What about our little wrestling match?" he sputtered. "That felt pretty real."

"Blaise, please," Minsheng guffawed. "Can your memory be that flawed? You're the one who made VR more immersive, remember? So viewers can fuck each other in their favorite VR series."

Minsheng picked up the onyx sculpture and hurled it at Blaise, who veered away, but the sculpture caught him in the ribs. "That felt real," he gasped, clutching his side in pain.

"Blaise, please, stop playing the fool. That sculpture's an extension of my body, real as a dildo in VR entertainment mode." The chairman chuckled. "I think that hacker whore of yours, Kristina, is making you lose your edge."

"Leave her out of this!"

"Oh, couldn't leave her out. No, no. Our gunships are penetrating hacker city as we speak. Lasering down every hacker and every turd of a Slag your hackers managed to rescue. Of course, we'll take Kristina alive. Her pathetic air attack from a jerry-rigged hovercraft failed. The air force boys shot her down.

They're gang-raping her, but that's just the start. I've ordered a slow, agonizing death for her."

Blood filled Blaise's eyes, and he trembled with rage. These taunts were meant to throw him off balance just when everything depended on clarity. So he repeated his mantra silently, with the energy of despair, knowing nothing could silence his panic. Then he saw his chance in the chairman's flushed and bloated face. Minsheng had a vulnerability. Blaise could sense it, perhaps his own nascent curseil skill picked it up from Kristina's instruction: a vibration of fear quavering like an off-key tuning fork behind the chairman's imperial arrogance. Mitsuko had revealed Minsheng's secret weakness: hypertension, the one medical condition that *Homo Deus* couldn't reverse, despite all its genomic sophistication. You could live forever, but the blood pulsing through your brain could still betray you if you didn't keep your EKG within safe ranges.

"Ordering slaughter just rolls off your tongue," Blaise laughed.

Minsheng knitted his brow; he obviously hadn't expected such a retort. But he kept creeping closer, looking for the best angle of attack, and he was slowly backing Blaise into a corner of the ruined office where he could spring on him, and Blaise had no room to veer away. Blaise saw it coming and edged himself away from the corner.

"Human lives mean nothing to a god, isn't that what you told me?"

"Absolutely correct," Minsheng retorted. He made a feint that Blaise easily dodged.

"What about Mitsuko?"

Minsheng's good eye was hardened into its customary impenetrability, but it was no use. Blaise sensed this was a sore subject for the Chairman, and pressed his advantage.

"Mitsuko. The only human part of you left after a lifetime of murder. Did you feel anything for her when you found out Kristina lasered her through the belly? What, she meant nothing to you? I don't buy it. Know why? 'Cause you were still fucking her, right up to the second we killed her."

Minsheng's face turned purple, and the bellows of his breathing came in gasps of rage. He advanced like a winded buffalo, arms open like a scissor to close in on Blaise. Blaise evaded him nimbly, edging away from corners as he stumbled through green gore oozing from the dead Mantises.

"What's the matter? Missing Mitsuko, fruit of your loins? Your darling daughter, the one you've raped since she was a girl?"

"You know nothing," Minsheng hissed and lunged at Blaise again, but Blaise avoided his grasp yet again. Blaise knew he had struck a nerve, and he had to rip it wide open and douse it with the acid of his words if he was going to survive.

"I know plenty," Blaise spat. "You call yourself a god, Mr. *Homo Deus*? You bray to the world that you're immortal. You think you have absolute power, Director Minsheng?"

"I AM CHAIRMAN OF THE BOARD!" Minsheng intoned as he made another lunge.

Blaise danced out of Minsheng's grasp yet again. He could feel Minsheng's moves coming now. "Chairman of what? What's left after the servers crash? What kind of empire will you have after the floods wash over the sea walls and bury L.A., Hong Kong, all the Cloud cities? I'll tell you. You'll have nothing. Nothing but a pathetic old man who has no power without his Mantises, SWATs, server banks, and his fuck toy daughter, Mitsuko, the one Kristina and I slaughtered."

Minsheng charged again, more winded than the last try. Blaise sensed that he was weakening.

"You're a god, remember?" Blaise pressed. "You've replaced your defective organs, had your skin-grafts, reversed every known disease, except one. The one in your heart. Did you know Mitsuko loved you? She told me that with tears in her eyes. She hated you and wanted you dead, but she loved you with clenched teeth, filled with rage for what you'd done to her, but clinging to her love for you because you're her father! Despite the humiliations, the rapes, despite all her hatred and eagerness for revenge against you, she still loved you."

"Shutup!" Minsheng screamed as he made another lunge, but by this point, he was so winded, so soaked in sweat, that he lumbered like an elephant barely able to drag its trunk along.

"How did you feel when you fucked her? Did you feel powerful? Godlike? Or maybe you secretly despised what you did. Did each rape send you into a tailspin of self-loathing? Did it plunge you into an abyss so bottomless the only way you could bear yourself was to fuck her again? Was she your Anima, your drug? What about it, Mr. Chairman? Was she your flesh morsel? Your salvific little snatch, to help you forget how in your heart of hearts, you despise yourself for what you did to your own child?"

Before he could react, Minsheng charged him and slammed him into the wall, knocking the breath out of him. Face distorted with blood and rage, he choked Blaise with the full fury of his fleshy hands. But then a strange expression overcame him. He winced like a man blinded by a bolt of lightning. His hands slipped from Blaise's throat like two fleshy seals sliding down a rock. He stumbled backward, clawing at his head as if it were filled with stinging wasps. Then he collapsed in a heap on the floor, convulsed, and lay still. A trickle of drool escaped his lips.

There came a roar of rushing waters. Blaise saw a black mass with a frothy, prodigious crest, a viscous mass that surged up like lava in the distance outside the picture window. The tidal wave toppled rank upon rank of glittering towers, obliterating a century of vainglorious labor before it smashed into the Mythoplex tower in a thundering rain of shattered glass. The force swept Blaise against the back wall with all the submerged tonnage of the City of Angels. As his mind winked out, a last thought flared: *It is finished.*

29

A FRAGRANT BREEZE MURMURED THROUGH THE FIR FOREST. High above, the cavern spread across a firmament illuminated by sunlight refracted from fissures hidden among clustered stalactites. Kristina led him along a verdant bank leading to a stream fed by a spring that wound through kilometers of copses.

They spread a blanket and laid out a basket of sandwiches, fruit, and wine. After they ate and drank, Blaise rested his head in her lap. He relished the way the tree scent mixed with the perfume of Kristina's body, a natural, wholesome mix of odors that spoke of ancient rhythms and a fertile future. In the woods across the stream, a fawn showed itself before darting away.

She studied his face "Are you feeling sad today, my love?"

He caressed her cheek. "No, not sad, really. Resigned, maybe. We lost so many."

"We got thousands here on the bullet trains. And the hyperloop."

"But millions all over the world drowned."

"It would have happened without us. Those seawalls couldn't possibly have held."

"It all sounds very reasonable, what we did. We were like Shiva, that Indian god you told me about, destroying a world to create a new one. But I feel the loss of the old one." Mitsuko sprang to mind as she often did in his dreams, more often even than he dreamt of Cherry and Mei.

He pressed deeper into Kristina's lap. "Will the world we create be a better one? Can we keep ourselves from creating another Cloud?"

"That's not for us to know," she soothed. "We've done what we could. It's up to others to use what we've given them and build something better."

"I can't help but worry. Like when I thought those laser cannons blasted your hover-car out of the sky."

She smirked. "The military servers crashed and silenced those lasers. Left those warship crews wandering in the desert like babies. They joined us when we sent up a team to the surface for them." Kristina brushed his hair with her lips. "Please rest your mind now. Forget the purgatory you've been through."

"How can I forget? It's made me crazy my whole life."

"I can't tell you in words how you'll forget," she answered. "But remember the light in Sagrada Familia? The heart of light. The light before the beginning and after the end. The Omega Point."

She slipped a paper from inside her blouse and showed it to him:

What might have been and what has been point to one end, which is always present.

"It's beautiful. What is it?"

"From *Four Quartets*. By T.S. Eliot."

"My mother used to read from him."

"I know. Thomas gave that couplet to me before he died. It meant a lot to him."

"So are you," he laughed. "But tell me, what about the Caliphate? What happens now there's no Cloud empire?"

"We deactivated the nanobots we sold them. Of course, they'll come after us to get them back if they can find us. Or they'll devour themselves. Through infighting. They'll have to work out their own destiny."

He sat up and tenderly took her face in his hands. "Do we have a destiny, Kristina?"

"Yes," she whispered. "We're creating it, heartbeat by heartbeat."

They kissed long and deeply while the stream plashed, and a breeze stirred in the firs, and it was like the first kiss between man and woman, living without fear for the first time.

THE END